AN AMERICAN IN PARIS

AN AMERICAN IN PARIS

A Novel

Margaret Vandenburg

CLEIS
PRESS

Published in the United States by Cleis Press Inc.,
P.O. Box 14684, San Francisco, California 94114.

Printed in the United States.
Cover design: Scott Idleman
Cover photo inspired by Manassé Studios
Text design: Karen Quigg
Cleis Press logo art: Juana Alicia
First Edition
10 9 8 7 6 5 4 3 2 1

Library of Congress Cataloging-in-Publication Data

Vandenburg, Margaret.
    An American in Paris : a novel / Margaret
    Vandenburg.—1st ed.
        p. cm.
        ISBN 1-57344-107-4 (alk. paper)
    1. Americans—France—Fiction. 2. Paris (France)—
    Fiction. 3. Young women—Fiction.
    4. Lesbians—Fiction. I. Title.
    PS3572.A647 A8 2000
    813'.6—dc21
    00-063903

CHAPTER ONE

The Making of an Expatriate

Sapphists had no doubt lived in Bliss, Utah, before. Our town certainly had more than its fair share of spinsters and maiden aunts. Their suspiciously private lives fascinated me. As a child, I used to spy on them between the perfectly regular slats of their picket fences. But it was a big fat waste of time.

At the dawn of the twentieth century, Sappho's daughters were painfully aware that theirs was the love that dared not speak its name. Even the most worldly women's magazines, like *Vanity Fair* and *Harper's Monthly*, balked at any mention of female sexuality, let alone sapphism. Their most daring features were corset ads.

Local housewives censored these ads, snipping them out with razor-sharp sewing scissors before letting their daughters read suitable articles devoted to etiquette and pioneering discoveries in domestic science. My mother was more fashionable, though no less upright. So she left our magazines intact, corsets and all. She was, in a word, straitlaced.

I got the message. Women were expected to confine their sexual desires within rib-cracking whalebone corsets. These instruments of torture were hidden, of course, under voluminous skirts that made bondage look proper, even dainty.

On some profound and inarticulate level, I think my poor dear mother suspected there was something different and more than a little dangerous about me from the start. I could tell, because she was even stricter with me than with my sisters, squelching every impulse except to grin and bear children. Intuitively, she knew that the sooner I started cinching in my errant tendencies, the better.

Show me a corset laced dangerously tight, and I'll show you a sapphist turning blue in the face, struggling to contain her bulging desires. With the clairvoyance of a child, I knew I had to escape. The alternative was to spend my life in a perpetual swoon, sniffing enough smelling salts to fill the Great Salt Lake.

Young girls in America's vast deserts were trained to aspire to the three P's, our most sacred Protestant virtues: propagation, propriety, and patent leather. As I look back, I realize the only real change in Bliss during the first quarter of the century was to add Prohibition to this hierarchy of Middle-American virtues. Outside of the realm of home appliances, true-blue westerners hate progress.

And we weren't even Protestant, just a family of stranded Catholics trying to hold on to a few decent bloody rituals in a town whose spirituality consisted of an endless round of pancake feeds. If there was one religious concept I really grasped while growing up, it was the notion of spending an eternity in hell. By the age of eighteen, when I finally left permanently to attend college at Radcliffe, I was a damned expert on the subject. The whole town mourned my defection to East Coast liberalism.

They thought I was rebelling. Really, I was just trying to survive. Growing up with all that well-intentioned hick morality was like being forcibly fed through the nose like the passivist suffragettes of the Great War. By the time I escaped to Radcliffe in 1918, I was starving for contact with what the dictionary at school called *inverts*. I was very shy in those days, so it took months for me to actually engage in a conversation with the real article. I shouldn't imply that there were no sapphists at Radcliffe. Of course there were. It was, after all, Gertrude Stein's alma mater. I used to watch them as they traipsed across campus as if they owned the place. In Bliss I reckon we would have tried to stuff the whole lot of them into one giant collective corset.

During the War, most of the sapphists still wore their hair long, tamed into prim buns that barely camouflaged the indecorous, swaggering way they held their heads. But though they masqueraded as genteel young ladies, they looked more like freight trains in dresses. Quite frankly, they scared the hell out of me.

Let's face it. The term *mannish woman* wasn't just a pejorative coined by sexologists. The inverts at Radcliffe were, in fact, mannish women. I was hopelessly confused, alternately titillated and repelled. It took me a while to understand that the masculine facade of inversion was just a clever disguise for female desire.

Despite my sexual ambivalence (so typical, it turns out, among virgins), I did finally manage to lose my hymen (which I didn't know I had until I lost it). But my heart wasn't in it. I simply chose the least mannish invert on campus and pretended to be in love with her.

In my heart of hearts I was dreaming of the sapphists I had become obsessed with in *Variety*, the highbrow magazine version of the syndicated newspaper gossip columns we all read at Radcliffe. We hung onto each delectable detail like survivors reading messages in bottles on distant deserted islands. Of course *Variety* never came right out and said Gertrude Stein and Alice B. Toklas were homosexuals. But we could read between the lines. Basking in every minute description of Natalie Barney's soirées, even I knew that the word *salon* was just a euphemism for sapphic orgies.

In the glamorous scenarios that unfolded in my mind's eye, none of the Parisian sapphists were mannish, with the obvious exception of Gertrude Stein. But her genius, I told myself, excused her masculine proclivities. In the Paris of my dreams, all the femmes were both frilly and fatale.

Imagine my excitement when my parents finally agreed to fund a summer trip to France. European tours were actually standard at Radcliffe. Rich daddies were wont to give this one last lavish gift to fond daughters before they tied the knot with some blue-blooded bachelor upon graduation. Needless to say, I didn't really fit this profile, if only because my father was a cattle-rancher rather than a gentleman, a graduate of the potato famine rather than Harvard. But the price of beef must have skyrocketed that year, or someone discovered a cure for hoof-and-mouth disease, because my envelope on the tree that Christmas contained a promissory note announcing my parents' intention to foot the bill for my passage across the Atlantic to join the annual Radcliffe Art History pilgrimage to the Louvre.

Of course my family couldn't really afford it. My sister must have gone months without Saturday afternoon matinees at the brand-new movie palace. And I had visions of my Mom selling her pet pig to pay for second class rather than steerage. There was my family in Utah deprived and maybe even embarrassed, already the only household in a fifty-mile radius without an electric Victrola, because of my East Coast pretensions. And here I was gallivanting around Europe like some nouveau-riche heiress in a Henry James novel. Who was I kidding?

Imagine how guilty I felt, especially since I was misrepresenting my motives. First of all, I was much more interested in the Montmartre of Picasso, Matisse, and Braque than in the Rembrandts and Caravaggios in the Louvre. But more to the point, my real reason for traveling to France was not to witness Cubism and Fauvism first-hand but to see if it were really true that sapphists had colonized

Paris. Unbeknownst to them, my poor parents were eating cube steaks instead of T-bones in order to fund my research into avant-garde sexuality.

Don't get me wrong. I loved the Louvre as much as all the other Radcliffe girls, with the possible exception of Martha Howell, who actually fainted in front of the Mona Lisa. But I also snuck off to renegade gallery exhibitions on the Left Bank and auctions on Montmartre. Parisian sapphists were decidedly artsy-fartsy, and there was no telling who might show up at even the most obscure atelier in the Faubourg Saint-Germain. Maybe even the dashing painter Romaine Brooks herself. I had studied her photographs assiduously and assumed I could identify her by her hat alone—a bowler, a derby, or maybe even a top hat at more formal affairs.

Once, at a private showing I snuck into on Montparnasse, I could have sworn I spotted Lily de Gramont, the Duchess de Clermont-Tonnerre, across the gallery, perusing *Head of a Young Girl with Upswept Hair.* Her leopard pillbox gave her away, or so I thought. But by the time I wove my way through the throngs of gawkers to the Matisse in question, she had vanished.

It got to the point where my obsession proved embarrassing. When I was sure that my Radcliffe buddies were going somewhere particularly unpromising (what sapphist in her right mind would be caught dead shopping for seam stockings at Les Halles, for example?), I would feign a headache or feminine indisposition. My friends looked at me queerly. I had never been particularly given to illness. Like most westerners I had the constitution of a span of oxen. But finally they just gave up, regretting my inclination to rot in my hotel room. Or so they thought.

Almost before their tracks cooled, I was off stalking my prey. While the others went to La Comédie Française, I prowled the streets and gardens where I had read, in *Variety* and other chichi gossip columns, that the likes of Gertrude Stein and Natalie Barney took their daily constitutionals.

The Bois de Boulogne was my most frequent destination. There, it was rumored, one could catch a glimpse of a lone equestrienne on the horizon, her magnificent blond mane blowing in the wake of her galloping steed. It was none other than the Amazon, Natalie Barney herself. The image of the Amazon reining in her stallion with one hand as she whipped him over hedge after hedge with the other, was indelibly printed on my imagination. And I had yet to even lay eyes on her.

I had heard that Stein and Barney were rivals, vying publicly for the title of Paris's most influential salonnière. But I cast them as clandestine friends, maybe even lovers. In my mind's eye, they took long walks together, engaging in endless tête-à-têtes that determined the aesthetic future of the avant-garde.

For those two weeks in Paris, I was an habituée of the soft, romantic recesses of secret gardens. And though the Bois failed to produce real live sapphists, I saw any number of them like mirages in the distance, walking arm-in-arm and even beckoning to me as dusk fell and my fantasies took wing.

When it became too dark to make out even the figures in my own dreams, I proceeded to Café des Deux-Magots or le Dôme where I had heard tell that the writer Djuna Barnes sat on countless gray days, drowning her sorrows with Côtes du Rhône in the wake of yet another betrayal by her infamous lover, Thelma Wood. Rumor had it that Thelma had almost as many notches on her belt as Natalie Barney, who held the uncontested record for romancing more women than any other living soul in all of Europe, male or female, French courtesans not excluded.

I would have done anything to meet just one of their cast-off lovers, let alone gain access to Natalie Barney's salon. There, women purportedly took turns playing sexual musical chairs in her renowned

Temple of Love. But on that, my first visit to Paris, I was left high and dry, with nothing more substantial than my fantasies to take back as souvenirs to Cambridge.

Disappointed, but not defeated, I vowed that I would return. Dreams of expatriation made me impatient to finish my degree. It wasn't that I didn't like Radcliffe. It was just that Paris had made me unfit for ordinary college fare. Boston seemed little better than Bliss in comparison with the city of love.

I took a girlfriend to pass the time—a woman named May whose claim to fame was that her uncle, a prominent American art dealer, had once attended Gertrude Stein's salon with his niece in tow. In fact, May's most appealing quality was that she indulged me by reminiscing about that one fateful night at 27 rue de Fleurus. To this day I still feel a little guilty about my relationship with May. I was so intent on finishing my degree and launching into my fantasy life as an expatriate, I was grotesquely inattentive. The last I heard, May was married with four kids. I've always felt vaguely responsible for her defection to heterosexuality, as if I could have had such a profound effect on a woman I treated like a hobby.

No matter where I went, or what I did, the memory of Paris tugged relentlessly at my imagination. Even in Bliss, when I went home to visit my family for the holidays, my mind wandered off, crossing the Rockies, the plains, the watery expanses of the high seas to Paris, the sapphic oasis beyond the desert that surrounded me.

Once, I made the mistake of mentioning moving to Paris to my mother. She crossed herself precipitously, as if to ward off temptation. Thereafter, I kept my dreams of expatriation to myself.

I desperately wanted to leave everything American behind me. I lived for the day when I could move to Paris, realizing only much later that I was cultivating the terrible habit of squandering the present, dreaming of elusive and seductive futures in typical Romantic fashion.

Truth be told, it took me a few years to finally get back to Europe. Unlike the Gertrude Steins and Natalie Barneys of the world, I didn't have the legacy that usually goes along with expatriation. After the War, the franc outdistanced the dollar by a long shot, and living in Paris was actually more economical for them. My dream was their expediency. But then expatriation isn't just about saving money, especially since homosexuality is grounds for confinement, and not just in those corsets I was talking about. In the salons of Paris, we were told, sapphists roamed free, unmolested except by each other.

After graduating from Radcliffe with a degree in Art History, I entered the field of journalism like Janet Flanner and Djuna Barnes before me, convinced by their example that the only way for a poor woman to travel was to make it her profession. I don't mean to sound conceited by including myself in their prodigious company; all we really had in common in this case was our poverty. After fighting in the trenches of New York City as a cub reporter, I finally established myself sufficiently as an art critic to land a job as a foreign correspondent. In 1925, I embarked on my real life as an expatriate.

Miss Henrietta Adams
69 Hudson Street
New York, N.Y.

February 28, 1925

Dear Miss Adams:

We are pleased to announce that after painstaking
deliberation our Board of Editors has approved your
proposal for a column covering the American involvement in
the avant-garde art movement in Paris, France. You are
authorized to book your passage immediately with a view to
preparing your first submission to be included in the June
issue of En Vogue. We suggest the S. S. Victorian leaving
New York on March 18. Needless to say, this and all
arrangements essential to your travel and lodging will be
reimbursed by the magazine immediately upon receipt of
your expense account. Congratulations! We are thrilled to
have you on board and trust that your timely submissions
will add tremendous breadth to our already unparalleled
coverage of the American arts.

Sincerely,

Irving P. Dickey
Senior Editor

cc: Board of Editors
En Vogue

CHAPTER TWO

Montmartre

O n the long journey across the Atlantic I devised a plan. The wide expanses of the high seas inspired me to think big. If I could just get an interview with Gertrude Stein, I could set my vainglorious plot into motion, gaining access to artists for business and sapphists for pleasure. I would use my credentials as a journalist to get my foot in the door of her salon.

I wrote Gertrude Stein an elaborate letter requesting an interview so that I could feature her in my very first *En Vogue* column. I shamelessly exaggerated the magazine's circulation and stature. Highlighting the privilege of inaugurating a whole new editorial series devoted to the avant-garde, I unwittingly fell into Gertrude Stein's obsession with being the first of everything—the first genius from Allegheny, Pennsylvania; the first American collector to buy Picasso; the first salonnière to serve cucumber sandwiches; the first truly modern writer. I told her Radcliffe was our mutual alma mater, playing what I hoped would be an Ivy League trump card. I even dropped the name of May's uncle, pretending we were great chums, though I'd only met him once five years before, and only then for tea in Harvard Square.

I rewrote the letter at least five times before we finally docked at Calais. It wasn't perfect, and it certainly wasn't true, but even I had to admit I looked pretty good on paper.

Once in Paris, I booked a room at the Pierre Étoile, a hotel centrally located so that I could conveniently scout out more permanent lodgings. Then, even before I ventured out for my first café crème, I posted my letter in the lobby, kissing it surreptitiously before slipping it in the slot.

Imagine my surprise when I received a note by return post from Alice B. Toklas! Gertrude Stein needed English-speaking readers, and Alice could smell an audience a mile away. Toklas, it turned out, was so much more than companion, social secretary, publisher, and excellent five-minute cook. She was the consummate publicist.

Her note, written in a meticulous yet flamboyant hand, struck me as a polite command. It read, "If you would be so kind as to drop by Kahnweiler's gallery on Saturday, Gertrude Stein will entertain questions about her work." The signature read "A. B. Toklas."

Actually, I had said next to nothing about Gertrude Stein's work in my letter. The subject of my proposed interview had been her role as patron of the arts in general, Cubism in particular. But I would have talked to her about flea circuses, if that had struck her fancy. I responded immediately, telling Alice I'd be delighted, and I was.

Saturday finally arrived. I was too nervous to eat breakfast. I changed clothes at least five times, realizing that I was ill-prepared to play the part of the chic expatriate. Then, to top it off, I got lost. Where Manhattan is geometric and predictable, Paris is circuitous and astonishing—a mysterious maze with dreams around every corner. Such romantic travels take time.

Montmartre is the most magical *quartier* of all. It is as if its steep hills are traversed by a single narrow cobblestoned street no wider than a hansom cab—a rue that neither begins nor ends, curving infinitely like a snake eating its tail. If there really are more streets than one, they loop in impossible arabesque patterns that go nowhere at all. Yet no one cares. Montmartre is too beautiful for destinations, with all its chandelier shops, galleries, and cafés open to that one endless street.

Having gotten lost repeatedly on the labyrinthine streets of Montmartre, I showed up late to Kahnweiler's dingy gallery at 24 rue de l'Abreuvoir. The rest is history.

I was disappointed. Although there were a number of goatees and turbans scattered here and there in the gallery, the crowd was not nearly bohemian enough to suit my tastes. The place was crawling with lorgnettes and furs and lap dogs, and neither Picasso nor Gris seemed to be present. In my naïveté, I thought artists attended their own exhibitions. Juan Gris apparently disdained the idea that his art had commercial value, preferring to adopt the starving-artist pose, except at dinnertime when he insisted on ordering foie gras and Châteauneuf-du-Pape. The exquisite taste of his palate was at perpetual war with his aesthetic idealism. As a result, his dealer Kahnweiler and patron Gertrude Stein had to schedule periodic auctions to appease his restaurant creditors, let alone his concierge.

Although Pablo Picasso was far less queasy about money, Kahnweiler usually arranged for him to be otherwise engaged during his exhibitions. Picasso's fiery temper, and his chronic impatience with the airs of the French haute bourgeoisie, had blown more than one lucrative sale.

I learned later that Gertrude Stein, on that particular night, had convinced Kahnweiler to entice buyers by selling a handful of Picasso's paintings with a bunch of Gris's. Apparently Juan's girlfriend had a toothache and Gertrude Stein was a little short on cash that month, having just bought Picasso's *Sleeping Peasants*. Somebody had to pay for the dentist.

I therefore owe my initial success as an expatriate art critic to Juan Gris's girlfriend and the peppercorn that cracked her tooth eating *le petit déjeuner* on Tuesday, March 31, 1925.

For if her molar hadn't precipitated this financial crisis, Stein would have taken off, as scheduled, for her country house in Bilignin. And while being the subject of my first column in *En Vogue* appealed to her pioneer egotism, she informed me later that subsequent issues would have interested her far less. She used the analogy of Charles Lindbergh to illustrate her point. Would he be risking his life to complete a solo transatlantic flight if it weren't the first? Who would care?

She wouldn't. Being first was everything to Gertrude Stein. She simply had to be first, always and everywhere. It was the crux of her genius.

I scanned the gallery, but she was nowhere to be found. Despite my impatience to meet my first Parisian sapphist, my attention was repeatedly diverted by the cacophony of art surrounding me. There were more modern masterpieces crowding the walls than I had seen since my last visit to Paris some five years before. Already, I noticed a change. They were less angular, less angry, as if the hostility of the War years was finally starting to wear off. They were more random, more dizzying, and maybe even insane.

There was no sign of Prohibition in Parisian art. It looked drunk.

I tried to tear myself away from the paintings to search for Gertrude Stein among the furs and top hats. With each perusal of the gallery, I was struck by the way the art clashed with its audience. To illustrate the conservatism of the crowd, I need only say that the ratio between women and lap dogs was about two to one. With patrons like these, no wonder artists starved. Just as I began to lament the demise of the avant-garde, the patron saint of Cubism arrived to save the day.

I knew immediately that it was Gertrude Stein, because of her legendary size. Yet though she was massive, a veritable mountain, she seemed to glide rather than walk, as if propelled by some rarefied form of genius that hung in the weighty folds of the bizarre burlap dress she wore like a toga. She had the stature and brow of a Roman senator.

I know it sounds crazy. But the minute Gertrude Stein's eyes met mine a bell rang in my head. My whole soul reverberated with the pure, unadulterated force of her character. Where other people have mere personalities, Gertrude Stein was more like a portable salon, even without the accoutrements of 27 rue de Fleurus.

I'm not the only one who experienced this. I found out later that Alice B. Toklas said the same thing, attributing what we call the chime phenomenon to the stroke of Gertrude Stein's genius. I had never seen a brow as lofty as hers. She was a phrenologist's model of intelligence. When she addressed me it felt like I was like talking to Big Ben.

"Henri Adams, I presume?" she asked, extending her hand. Her voice, resonant as a pipe organ, matched her stature.

Having been Henrietta since birth, I was rendered speechless by my new identity. Gertrude Stein's first act was to rename me, instigating no less than a re-creation of my entire character in Paris. What's in a name?

"Gertrude Stein," I finally managed to blurt out by way of greeting. My voice sounded like a piccolo. It even warbled a little.

"With a name like that you should run for president," she decreed.

I smiled mutely, even weakly, I'm afraid.

She seemed amused. "Judging from your letter, I was expecting someone older."

Panic gripped me. I thought I'd been found out, masquerading as an established journalist but feeling more like a cub reporter than I had since my first assignment in Manhattan so many years before.

"You look a little wet…" Gertrude Stein fired a provocative look right between my eyes "…behind the ears." I couldn't make out what she meant by investing this cliché with such a pregnant pause. I assumed that since this was gay Paris, and she was Gertrude Stein, there was a risqué subtext. So I blushed.

Looking back, I doubt very much if Gertrude Stein had intended anything suggestive at all. She wasn't exactly prudish. But of all the expatriate sapphists I have known, Gertrude Stein was the most loyal and discreet, saving her every erotic innuendo for the ears and various and sundry other orifices of Alice B. Toklas.

I was scared to death until she smiled. Her smile was as friendly and inviting as an ear of corn at a county fair. Despite her formidable demeanor and later her public renown, Gertrude Stein was one of the most down-to-earth people I'd ever met. Even when she'd become a household word, or what she called a publicity saint, she treated me like her best Girl Scout buddy. And always and forever, Alice B. Toklas acted the part of the zealous Scout leader, fond but firm.

"I am," I stammered. "I mean I just got here."

"*La nouvelle bohème,*" she said. Although she rarely spoke French, she couldn't resist clichés, admiring their simple clarity almost as much as I do. But somehow they were always endowed with new meaning on her lips. I felt as if she were knighting me, gracing my shoulders with an invisible sword the size of Excalibur. In an instant, I was transformed into a real, albeit apprentice, expatriate. I attempted a clever sally.

"Two weeks ago I was interviewing broken-down Ashcan painters in Greenwich Village. Now here I am in Montmartre hobnobbing with the likes of you."

Gertrude Stein guffawed. The magnitude of her laugh startled me, and I jumped noticeably as her hilarity reverberated throughout the gallery. At least a dozen people turned to sneak a peak at us. Gertrude Stein was already that famous. People watched her surreptitiously, especially when she perused the canvases that lined the gallery walls. I think they thought that by watching her responses to the paintings they could determine which ones to buy.

I was certainly prepared to hang on her every word. A budding art critic, I also desperately wanted to be educated by Gertrude Stein, one of the most clairvoyant collectors in all of Europe. I wanted more than anything to find out how she had known before anyone else that Picasso was the Prometheus of modern art. Even her brother Leo had scoffed at her, preferring Matisse and Cézanne all through the decade of the Great War until Gertrude and Pablo emerged victorious, the undisputed champions of the avant-garde. As it turned out, she had another agenda entirely. Although she readily acknowledged Picasso's genius, she was infinitely more interested in her own.

"And what, pray tell, do you mean by the likes of me?" Gertrude Stein demanded.

"I mean you're so…"

"Famous?"

"Yeah, famous. Ever since I can remember, you've been a legend. Especially in college. You're Radcliffe's most famous…"

"Go ahead and say it," she said with a flourish. "I'm Radcliffe's most famous…genius."

At first the magnitude of Gertrude Stein's ego shocked me. But very quickly, her charisma mesmerized me, and I began to take her genius for granted. This must have been a common conversion experience among her admirers, and even in the world at large. There is no other way to explain the fact that when Gertrude Stein composes what would be called inexplicable nonsense if written by anyone else, she is lauded for her genius.

The author of "a rose is a rose is a rose" is either a brilliant con artist or the most avant-garde of the avant-garde. And her ego leaves no room for the former interpretation.

"So you've come all the way from America to interview the likes of me," she said with evident satisfaction. "Fire away."

As I started to formulate my first question, Gertrude Stein grabbed my elbow and maneuvered us into a discreet corner, as far away as possible from the throngs of gawking spectators. Just as I was about to ask her what, if anything, had replaced the War as the avant-garde's principal site of fascination, she addressed me in a conspiratorial tone.

"It's a good thing you've flown the coop, you know. No one in their right mind lives in the States these days—no one, that is, with half a brain in their head."

Given Gertrude Stein's reputation as America's most patriotic expatriate, I was surprised by this comment.

"Why not?" I asked, a little defensively, despite my own exasperation with American puritanism.

"The States are great for cars and skyscrapers," she conceded. "But if you prefer trains and art, which I assume you do, Europe is the obvious choice. We were all destined to move to Paris. It's our home away from home."

"What do you mean?"

"There's no there there."

"There?"

"In the States. Aesthetically speaking, there's simply nothing there. It's like a great geographical void—great if you're a mapmaker, but if not, not."

"Yet you almost always write about the States. I thought you loved us. Them." Already, expatriation was confusing my sense of nationality. "Whomever," I concluded, trying desperately to muster up some kind of journalistic authority.

"Of course," she replied. "America is my subject, but not my home. As a writer in English, Paris is my home. I love writing English sentences surrounded by French sounds. It makes English all mine, to do with what I please."

I nodded. For the first time in my life, I measured the fluidity of French phrases against the stark boundaries of English diction. Gertrude Stein was right. She and I were utterly alone, queens of our very own linguistic empire.

"You'll see," she continued. "Even you, a journalist, will discover this. American critics wage war on great English prose. Poetry is scrutinized to death in one after another of our stuffy old universities. Paris, on the other hand, is oblivious to a well-turned English phrase. Sentences and even paragraphs roam the streets. And no one even gives them a second glance. It's gloriously liberating."

Although fascinated, I started to wonder who was actually conducting this interview. Thus far, I had not managed to get a question in edgewise, and I did, after all, need material for my column. I tried to maneuver a discreet segue from prose to painting.

"And Cubism? What does Cubism do on Parisian streets?"

"It multiplies like rabbits, one geometric pattern after another," Stein said without skipping a beat. I detected a note of condescension in her tone, as if everyone knew the habits of Cubist rabbits on Parisian streets.

"And how, exactly, do you define *Cubism?*"

"Cubism is realism," she said, evidently a bit bored, now that the subject had drifted away from the English sentences that originated at 27 rue de Fleurus. But she continued, obligingly enough. "It's what we really see when we aren't looking through the lens of aesthetic constructions. Like Classicism and Impressionism. Who, after all, really sees Michelangelo's *David* on the streets of Florence, or Monet's water lilies, even in the quaintest of Givernine ponds?"

Having asked this question quite indignantly, Gertrude Stein glared at me. I responded with an incredulous, slightly disgusted shrug. "Who indeed?"

"We see shapes and colors," she declared.

"Just shapes and colors?"

"Shapes and colors. Plain and simple. Take my *Three Lives,* for example. It's Cubism in prose. Natural, repetitive, and unmediated, the way we really think and see. Complex in its simplicity."

"Yet some people find *Three Lives* disturbing. Maybe even a little frightening," I said, trying to couch my confusion in critical qualifications. Far from simple, I had found the three novellas almost incomprehensible.

"Considering how dangerous everything is, nothing is really very frightening," she said, nodding her head knowingly as if she had finally clarified everything once and for all.

"But what has all this got to do with Cubism?" I asked helplessly. The interview seemed wildly out of control, hopelessly unprofessional.

"Cubism is simply simple in its complexity. It's anything but disturbing or abnormal. If I've said it once, I've said it a million times. The normal is so much more simply complicated and interesting."

Given Gertrude Stein's penchant for repetition, she probably really *had* said it a million times. Yet I still didn't get it.

"Give me an example of what you mean by complex simplicity," I said, thinking she would choose a painting to illustrate her point. There we were, surrounded by the angular shapes and discordant colors of outrageous canvases painted by the most famous Cubists of all time, but Gertrude Stein was completely indifferent to them.

"A rose is a rose is a rose is a rose is a rose," she said instead, referring to her signature tautology.

"That's Cubism?"

"Precisely."

"But what does it mean?"

"It means a rose is a rose, not a prig or a cow jumping over the moon."

"But do people really think a rose is a prig?"

"They would if I didn't set them straight. Far too many people would."

"Is that your role as an artist?" I asked, desperately trying to return to some semblance of a topic I could comprehend. "To tell people the truth?"

"My role as an artist is to be who I am."

"And who is that?"

She looked me straight in the eye again, and then spoke slowly and very distinctly. Judging from the triumphant expression on her face, I am quite sure she felt she had finally discovered a fundamental concept even I could understand.

"I am I because my little dog knows me," she said conclusively.

Although I became increasingly confused, Stein remained admirably patient, painstakingly trying to play Socrates to my pathetic approximation of Plato. It wasn't for lack of effort. I certainly sat at her feet attentively enough. But the meaning of her words eluded me.

At first I thought her cryptic remarks were designed to shut me up—to stop my incessant questioning about Cubism so that she could pursue the topic of her own writing. But then I realized she was genuinely trying to express everything as simply as possible. And though she readily understood my obsession with Cubism, she assumed—correctly, it turned out—that I would never truly understand modern art until I could wrap my mind around such self-evident truths as "I am I" and "a rose is a rose is a rose."

So finally, she gave up on my professional ineptitude and took matters into her own hands.

"Follow me," she demanded. And I obeyed.

Patrons and prospective buyers parted like the Red Sea as Gertrude Stein led me out to one of the little round café tables that were scattered on the patio of Kahnweiler's gallery. Suddenly very conscious of my escort's masculine audacity as we sat down together, I felt I was broadcasting my sexual tendencies to the entire gallery. She threw a short stack of papers on the table.

"Read this," she said emphatically. "Pretend I'm not here so that you can concentrate." The title read "Melon Mustaches."

"But my interview…" I protested feebly.

"Later," she insisted. "First things first." She patted the pile of papers with her fingertips. "Besides, you might learn something."

Sometime around noon, just minutes before departing for Kahnweiler's gallery, she had finished composing a poem. Her inspiration, it seemed, relied on being read hot off the press.

Ordinarily, Alice B. Toklas did the honors, reading Gertrude Stein's work almost as quickly as she wrote it, typing up each early afternoon what the master had written in the wee hours of the morning. But Alice was indisposed that day. As always, she was in charge of domestic arrangements, and that evening after the auction a soirée was planned at 27 rue de Fleurus. Alice was at home overseeing the creation of soufflés and tarts. Meanwhile, Gertrude Stein's poem couldn't wait until after the auction, after the soirée, and maybe even after a good night's sleep. She needed a reader, a portable fan club, a literary cheerleading squad, and she needed them now. Apparently I was sufficiently educated, adoring, and available to pinch hit for Alice B. Toklas.

For the first few minutes I couldn't focus because my heart was beating in my ears. I kept trying to say something instead, but Gertrude Stein waved away my feeble attempts at conversation as if they were hopelessly trivial in comparison with the poem she had presented to me. The moment I had been dreaming of had arrived— I was sitting at a table with one of *Variety*'s most celebrated Parisian sapphists. But she wouldn't talk to me.

Finally it dawned on me that the only way I would ever be able to continue communicating with this particular celebrity was to finish her manuscript, so I settled into reading. Exactly what I read about, I shall never know.

The words on the page repeated themselves over and over, something about "automatic mornings make melons even after cannons sound mustaches" repeated in endless configurations until I felt hypnotized by the rhythm and oblivious to the meaning. Every once in a while there would be a significant variation so that "mustache mornings silence automatically while melons sleep deep." But for the most part, "even after cannons sound mustaches automatic mornings make melons."

I found myself agreeing, though I couldn't for the life of me figure out why. Surely automatic mornings *do* make melons. Perhaps I was so intimidated by my first real contact with an expatriate icon— for there was Gertrude Stein facing me with the stature and impassibility of a Buddha—that I was being brainwashed. In my confusion, I felt increasingly trapped by the words, a helpless fly in her linguistic web. Then the sensuality of the poetry itself began to seduce me. And I felt, on a subliminal level, the kind of nagging itch that you can just never scratch. Or that I was being watched, not by a voyeur but by a phrase full of disembodied connotations that would ravage me at the turn of the next page. I couldn't wait.

As I look back, I understand now what was happening to me. I had never read homosexual, let alone sapphic, words before. But at the time I was just overwhelmed, almost unconscious like a ripe virgin losing her hymen to her first lingual lover. Yet in my daze I managed to finish reading. I sensed vaguely that I would be expected to speak.

"It reminds me of a song my mother used to sing to me," I finally said. Then I felt stupid and tried to say something more befitting a Radcliffe scholar. "It's like a nursery rhyme for philosophers. Or an orgy for linguists."

Gertrude Stein said nothing, as if silently encouraging me to go on and on and on about the poem, which I did. Fortunately, I am hyperbolic by nature, and I really outdid myself. Alice B. Toklas herself could not have paid more rapturous tribute to "Melon Mustaches." Judging from the ecstasy writ large on Gertrude Stein's face, I had succeeded in satisfying her every authorial desire.

"You're a genius," she said, after she had savored every last word of praise. I suspect she was talking about us both as a unit, as author and reader engaged in the mutual seduction of writing. The entire exchange was erotic, in the strictly platonic sense of the word. We had shared a simultaneous intellectual orgasm.

In this first encounter, we established the dynamics of our future relationship. For Gertrude Stein, the first condition of friendship is unconditional admiration, even homage—the only thing she cannot provide for herself. And since my favorite childhood game was follow-the-leader, I flatter myself we fit together like hand in glove.

I was prepared to attach myself to Gertrude Stein with the permanency of a barnacle. But our platonic interlude was cut short when she suddenly remembered the time. Alice B. Toklas, she claimed, would be wondering what had become of her, especially since it was her job to act as royal taster, making sure that each and every dish was delectable enough to be served to their guests.

"If you must know," she concluded, gathering her colossal person together in preparation for departure, "that poem *is* modern art. The very latest thing." She began to glide away but then imparted one last word of wisdom over her shoulder. "If you want to really wow your readers, tell them about melon mustaches."

And with that, she disappeared back through the crowd en route to 27 rue de Fleurus to taste the tarts.

I must say I felt high and dry, for a number of reasons. For one thing, I experienced a terrible case of what felt like postcoital depression. The dream of a lifetime had come true—I had hobnobbed with Gertrude Stein. Now that I had expended my one legitimate excuse for rubbing elbows with bohemian royalty, I feared I might never see her again.

Worse yet, at least from a professional point of view, I wondered how on earth I could ever extract an article about avant-garde painting out of what had turned out to be a private poetry reading. It was one thing for Gertrude Stein to claim that *The Portrait of Madame Cézanne* had somehow inspired the Cubistic prose of *Three Lives*. She was, after all, Gertrude Stein the creative genius. And I was Henri (née Henrietta) Adams the hack journalist. As far as I knew, Henrietta Adams didn't have a creative bone in her body.

But then it occurred to me that perhaps Henri Adams did. Perhaps I too could make something from nothing, fabricating a full-blown interview out of the few stray comments I had managed to pry out of Gertrude Stein before she had transformed me into a captive audience.

I had little time to take in the Picassos and Grises. Yet I knew the paintings weren't going anywhere. But Gertrude Stein's words were somewhat less permanent, and infinitely more nebulous. I rushed back to my hotel while they were still fresh and vivid in my auditory memory banks.

Never before had I felt so inspired. I worked all night and into the next morning, staggering into a cafe around eleven o'clock to put the finishing touches on the first piece of creative journalism I had ever written. Its resemblance to the actual interview was minimal.

I had written an expatriate manifesto. What better way to inaugurate my column than to explain how the phenomenon of expatriation itself had animated avant-garde art in Paris? It was a free-wheeling creation account of the genesis of modern art. And Gertrude Stein, as both patron and literary Cubist, was the prime mover.

In my portrait of Gertrude Stein, she was American individualism personified, the only artist I had ever met whose power was not masked or muted. The irony, of course, was that this quintessential American could only survive abroad.

I dug deep into the most mythic regions of my imagination to present expatriates as noble outlaws. True Americans like Huck Finn used to light out for the Territories, I claimed. But when the last bison was conscripted into Buffalo Bill's Wild West Show, and the last beaver pond dam was discovered by fly fishermen—maybe even Ernest Hemingway himself—Paris became the new frontier. We all lit out to Paris in search of the aesthetic and sexual freedom that would replace the once vast expanses of our own continent. Little wonder F. Scott Fitzgerald insisted that Gertrude Stein's broad, sturdy frame reminded him of an old covered wagon, especially with her rough burlap attire.

The same was true of the expatriates from other nations. Just as only the French Gauguin could render the spirit of Tahiti, so only the Spaniard Juan Gris could re-create France as it really was, uncluttered by the domestic ideologies that perverted the real essence of the place itself.

In Paris, Picasso could paint Madrid. *Olga in a Mantilla,* I argued, could never have been painted in Spain. Freed from the confines of time and geographic space, it was more Spanish than Spain itself.

I confessed that I had always suspected that, historical factors notwithstanding, Michelangelo and Leonardo da Vinci had single-handedly carved the original Renaissance out of the cold, hard headstone of a medieval past. Gertrude Stein and Pablo Picasso were equally intent on entombing nineteenth-century propriety and aesthetics. Although I pretended to be wary of the theory that geniuses shape history, which my professors at Radcliffe had condemned as undemocratic, I had to admit that I *did* think Stein and Picasso had almost singlehandedly ushered in the heroic age of Cubism.

I laid it on as thick as I could. By the time I finished my article, I believed every last word I had written.

Before sending my column off to the editors of *En Vogue* in New York, I made a copy for Gertrude Stein. Needless to say, she loved the article, so much so that I received yet another return post letter from the ever-efficient Alice B. Toklas, inviting me to tea at 27 rue de Fleurus.

Readers and certainly my editors might have suspected that my portrait of Gertrude Stein was a little over the top. But to her it was as baldly realistic as a Picasso print. Far from exaggerating her epic stature, I had merely presented the facts of her genius. Someone had simply finally acknowledged her role as the oracle of modern art.

Our tea party was scheduled for the following Friday. I carried the invitation around with me wherever I went, pulling it out to read over and over whenever I had a spare minute. When it started to get dog-eared, I decided it was time to get it framed.

When the big day finally dawned, I left so early that I had an hour to kill even after getting lost repeatedly in the winding streets of the *quartier latin*. I thought I'd sip a *pastis* to calm my nerves or, more accurately, to still my pounding heart. I shall never forget that afternoon. I felt as if I were teetering as close to the brink of greatness as I had ever been, before or since.

On that magical day, when spring had swung wide the glass panels of the cafés on the boulevard Raspail, I pinched myself. It's a long way from Bliss to Paris, but there I was drinking *pastis* at the Café des Deux-Magots. I still couldn't believe I had finally embarked on my career as an expatriate.

Fleetingly, I thought about what I might be missing back in the States—the sheer power and velocity of greenbacks and progress, accelerating with the indiscriminate momentum of blind idealism. But already I felt, as the French would say, *chez moi*. Home.

Gertrude Stein was right. The word *expatriate* is a misnomer. Far from leaving our homeland, we've come home at last to Paris. Whenever I am nostalgic, I reminisce not about Bliss but about my coming of age as an American in Paris.

Miss Henrietta Adams
Hôtel Résidence les Cèdres
12 rue des Dames
17th Arrondissement
Paris, France

April 15, 1925

Dear Miss Adams:

We are extremely pleased with the timely submission of your first editorial which, with very few incidental changes, will be included in the June issue of En Vogue. I must say the scope of your editorial is somewhat more ambitious than we expected for a first submission. But to the extent that your analysis of the complex relationship between expatriation and the avant-garde sets the scene for all future columns, it is invaluable. With such a panoramic backdrop in place, you should now be ready to focus more directly on individual artists and shows--in a word, on more bite-sized chunks of the avant-garde movement.

I don't mean to underestimate the intellectual stature of our readership, but this first submission is almost too theoretical, not to say sophisticated. You don't want to scare off potential readers by intimidating them! To use the analogy of illumination, perhaps we should proceed with a view to enlightening them incrementally one insight at a time rather than blinding them with too much light all at once.

A word, too, about your tone in the column. At its best, it is lively and engaging--something of a romp. But

at times it seems hyperbolic, even grandiose. Although I
do share your epic assessment of the almost heroic
aesthetic achievements of the avant-garde in Paris, such
hyperbole is more suited to fiction than to fact.

But, lest you misunderstand me, let me return to
the many accolades the Board has already showered on your
first submission. We are, as I said, very pleased with
your work thus far. Inevitably, new contributors
experience a kind of initiation period where they search
for just the right voice to fit into the chorus of En
Vogue's overall editorial style. We've no doubt you will
discover yours very soon.

Mr. Fliegel has written a very engaging
introduction for your new column, and we have added you--
very ceremoniously, I assure you--to the magazine's Table
of Contents. And let me reiterate that the Board was
unanimous and enthusiastic in its acceptance of your first
submission. This all bodes very well for the success of
your column which, at your suggestion, we have called "An
American in Paris: Notes on the Avant-Garde." You've
gotten off to a great start, and we look forward to next
month's editorial.

Sincerely,

Irving P. Dickey

Irving P. Dickey
Senior Editor

cc: Board of Editors
En Vogue

CHAPTER THREE

27 rue de Fleurus

27 rue de Fleurus was just off the boulevard Raspail in a seedy but bohemian quarter on the Left Bank of Paris. The neighborhood reminded me of Greenwich Village except that there were cats and old ladies everywhere—perched in windows, lounging on stoops, and pontificating on street corners with lungs like auctioneers. The frailty of elderly French women is matched only by the ferocity of their voices. They are the most emphatic people on the planet, making even itinerant salesmen seem tentative in comparison.

I learned quickly that I'd rather get permanently lost and starve to death than ask a French *vieille dame* for assistance of any kind. But on that day, I was still innocent and once again, I was lost.

I had located the rue de Fleurus before stopping in at the Deux-Magots, but number 27 was nowhere to be found. Apparently, Parisians disdain street addresses, because there were no numbers anywhere. Where in America we boldly display addresses above doors and even pay high school students to paint them on curbs to raise money for worthy causes, the French are far less civic-minded.

I cannot help but elevate all such incidental customs to the level of emblems. And I have become convinced that Americans, utterly lost on a profound cultural level, must therefore map out their geography with obsessive exactitude. There are more signs on the streets and byways of the United States than in any other country in the world, insistent reminders that Americans, at least, know where they are going. In fact, this proliferation of signs is an index as to how lost we really are.

In France, there are virtually no road signs, and no one is ever lost. The French have an innate sense of knowing that everything is where it should be.

Rather than city streets littered with signs, there are old ladies everywhere. And I made the mistake of asking a knot of them if they knew where Gertrude Stein lived.

"You mean that woman who wears circus tents?" demanded one, scowling as if angry.

I figured she was referring to Gertrude Stein's size, but I ignored this veiled insult. "You mean the loud American and her friend with the mustache?" accused another.

"Well, I don't know," I answered, nervously. "She lives with her friend Alice Toklas."

"With the mustache!" the woman repeated triumphantly.

They had me at their mercy. I was bewildered by their reference to the mustache, yet quite sure they knew exactly whom I was talking about. Then it dawned on me that perhaps they were senile and thought Gertrude still lived with her brother Leo. Little did I know that French *vieilles dames* never suffer from senility. They just get more and more obtuse as they figure out increasingly creative ways to vent their spleen.

I felt they were trying to trap me into saying Gertrude Stein was fat and Alice hairy. I was desperate. I knew from our conversation at Kahnweiler's how much Gertrude Stein hated it when people were late.

"Yes, that's right," I finally admitted. "She's rather large and you've probably seen her brother. Does she live near here?"

"Who knows?"

"Couldn't tell you."

"Don't know her," they all said simultaneously, and turned their backs on me.

I was so stunned by their magnificent rudeness that I stood transfixed as if recovering from a blow. Finally, a little kid tripped out of a doorway, and I almost grabbed him.

"Hey. Do you know where Gertrude Stein lives?"

"Right there," he pointed, and giggled as he raced down the street.

The stairs up to Gertrude Stein's apartment were so narrow and precarious that only a true expatriate could possibly have safely maneuvered them. Clinging to the banister with mounting vertigo, I was reminded once again that I was still a hopelessly American immigrant.

When I finally arrived at the doorstep, I was winded from exertion and excitement. This was it. The salon of Gertrude Stein!

I raised the heavy brass knocker, which vaguely resembled an artichoke (later I found out it had been sculpted by Juan Gris for Gertrude's cook, Hélène), and with a loud bang I announced my arrival at the most famous salon in Paris.

No one answered.

When I banged again, the door opened instantly, and I was greeted by a face whose exasperation could only be compared to that of the crones on the street. Everyone was at their wits' end, and somehow I was to blame.

"De la part de qui venez-vous?" the woman snapped, holding a finger up to her nose as if the question was so crucial that the balance of our lives lay in the quality of my response.

I learned later that this was the standard question posed to all visitors, a kind of code to determine whether they were friend or foe with regard to homosexuality.

If one said "Hemingway," that meant that Ernest had acted as the liaison or was responsible for the introduction. And Hemingway, at least during those early years, was sympathetic to the daughters of Sappho.

But if one said "Clovis Sagot," for example—an important art dealer but well known for his aversion to homosexuals—then the whole household would sweep everything under the carpet for a few hours. It wasn't that Gertrude Stein's sapphism was a secret—a ridiculous notion anyway, given her aggressive masculinity. It was just that she liked everything to be clean and simple. Nothing bored her more than unnecessary drama.

"It's all right," I said, oblivious. "Gertrude Stein is expecting me."

"De la part de qui venez-vous?" the woman repeated in exactly the same querulous tone.

"Don't worry, Alice Toklas invited me to tea. Just tell her Henri is here."

The guard at the door was unimpressed. She blinked, but otherwise remained utterly impassive, pretending she hadn't heard a word. There was a code and there was a password, and she was a woman whose respect for rules and regulations bordered on the neurotic.

I learned later that she wouldn't even consider cooking an omelette unless the eggs had been mollycoddled at room temperature to exactly twenty-five degrees centigrade. In cold weather, guests sometimes waited hours to eat while the eggs were courted by the gentle heat of candlelight. It was Hélène, famous throughout Paris for her omelettes.

"De la part … "

I felt like I was stuck in a whirling ferris wheel and she was the sinister carny refusing to let me off, torturing me at the bottom of every revolution with the same inane incantation.

"De la part de qui… de la part de qui … "

Just as I was about to give up and leave my calling card, another woman suddenly appeared at the door. She called Hélène off, as if she were a guard dog. I stifled a gasp.

This new woman had a very impressive auburn mustache.

"It's all right, Hélène. Hemingway sent her," she said in French, but with a decidedly American accent.

Of course this was not true. But Alice clearly knew better than to try to convince Hélène to make an exception. The mustachioed Toklas had simply dismissed her by using the formula. As I would learn, this was vintage Alice B. Like Hélène, she did everything by the book.

I found myself wondering who really wore the pants in the family. Then I noticed that from the ground up to the mustache, Alice was dressed in an exotic yet refined silk dress, complete with pearls. In fact, she was always impeccably and fashionably dressed, a great contrast to Gertrude Stein's slovenly attire. Alice's femininity was as elaborate and studied as Gertrude's masculinity was haphazard and abrupt.

As I saw it, Alice's mustache was one of the great ironies of their relationship. On Gertrude Stein, it would have been redundant, blending in with the pervasive machismo of her persona. Yet on Alice it was bizarre, like a bulging bicep on a ballerina, or, to coin a metaphor she herself might have used, a big ol' meatball in a delicate lobster bisque.

With time, I came to view it as yet another testament to the intimacy of their marriage—as if it were really Gertrude Stein's mustache, but she had given it to Alice B. Toklas to wear like a ring, as a token of her undying love.

As Alice ushered me into the apartment, I found my tongue. "Hi, I'm…"

"I know who you are. You're Gertrude's new westerner." Although Alice meant this as a compliment, I can't say I was flattered. I had always been somewhat embarrassed by my homespun roots. Where I wanted to breathe in Paris's urbane culture, Gertrude Stein was nostalgic for the scent of pines and lonesome trails dusty with disuse. She was attracted to westerners like a big old horsefly to a pile of good, clean prairie manure.

"Alice Toklas?" I asked politely. "I'm Henri Adams."

"Not a very western name, I might add," she remarked. "But then neither is mine."

"I didn't know you were from the West," I said, surprised that such a sophisticate could have been raised in western soil. There was hope for me, I thought.

"Sure. California," she announced proudly. "Gertrude prefers westerners. We're more expansive, and she needs the room."

As Alice hung my coat in the closet, I surveyed their apartment. I am a firm believer that interior design and decor can be read the way psychics read palms: as maps of the personalities of the inhabitants. Gertrude and Alice's furniture was predominantly Tuscan Renaissance—ornate and massive. Yet the effect was surprisingly homey, even cozy, with pillows and overstuffed cushions everywhere. Somehow, the decor struck a precarious balance between domestic comfort and almost sacerdotal grandiosity, as if the room itself were a shrine to the sanctity of their love.

Then, of course, there were the paintings on the walls—Picasso, Matisse, Braque, Gris, Cézanne, Vallotton, Bonnard, and a few I didn't recognize—crowded on every wall, all the way up to the fourteen-foot ceilings. Absolute aesthetic chaos and sacrilege. The contrast between the furniture and the pictures was shocking, like displaying a Pompeii orgy frieze in a shrine to the Virgin Mary.

I have never been as bowled over by art as I was at that moment, teetering between revulsion and fascination, and then just plain *bouleversée*, as the French would say. Of course I had been exposed to Cubism, Expressionism, and the Fauvists on my first trip to Paris. But five years had passed. With the exception of my brief encounter with the Picassos and Grises at Kahnweiler's exhibition the previous week, I had only seen one or two truly modern pictures in private collections in the States, and a few photographs. The cumulative effect of so many paintings at close range was overwhelming. Holding a photograph of a baby rhinoceros in a zoo is far different than being chased by its rampaging mother in the bush. The paintings were that vivid, that primitive, and that modern.

Each canvas was more insane than the next. Soon enough, I would be able to decipher the method in their madness. But on that first encounter, I couldn't distinguish aesthetic hysteria from art.

The initial impact of this visual assault was so literally staggering, I found I was tightly gripping the sturdy back of a huge Tuscan chair when Alice returned from the closet. Dazed, I only recovered my powers of reason and speech when I wrenched my eyes off the pictures.

"I hope I'm not barging in."

"Not really." Somehow Toklas seemed unconvinced. "Gertrude told me you were coming. She's just not finished writing yet. She got a late start. We had a little crisis."

Gertrude Stein's priorities were certainly consistent. As Alice prepared a tea table with exquisite exactitude and economy of motion, it became apparent at a glance what Gertrude Stein saw in her, besides the allure of the mustache. Alice was clearly Gertrude's tidy domestic counterpart, the perfect complement to the professional aesthete.

Already I was beginning to revise my preconceived image of 27 rue de Fleurus. In my fantasies, Gertrude and Alice lived in a salon, not an apartment. They never really ate eggs, took naps, or tended to mundane chores the way mere mortals do. They were too busy entertaining artists and celebrities. As it turns out, I couldn't have been more wrong. They elevated domesticity to a fine art, or at least Alice B. Toklas did.

I settled back into a chair fit for a bishop, flattered that Gertrude hadn't broken her routine for me—it showed she already thought of us as intimate enough to slight each other without fear of petty repercussions. Our rendez-vous was typical of Gertrude Stein's double standards. As much as she hated people being late, she was habitually late herself, usually detained by a word, a phrase, and sometimes even a paragraph. Thank God she had dispensed with punctuation in her writing, or she would have been later still.

Alice seemed preoccupied with her almost ritualistic preparation of tea, so I was free to admire the accoutrements of their domestic haven. Although I had courted a number of women in the States, none of these liaisons had ever actually progressed to the stage of setting up housekeeping. The Stein/Toklas ménage seemed like a utopia.

"You seem to have made a cozy life for yourselves, Alice."

She looked at me as if trying to discover a hidden motive behind my trite statement. In fact, she continued to eye me so suspiciously I began to wonder if I had inadvertently offended her. During the uncomfortable silence that ensued, I remembered some of the less-than-charitable gossip I had heard about her back in the States.

Alice B. Toklas seemed to be particularly prone to vicious rumors—that she was bossy; that she guarded Gertrude Stein like a jealous watchdog; that she had a mustache. I had always attributed these character assassinations to jealousy and friends scapegoating Alice for the fact that Gertrude herself had simply lost interest in the offended parties. But since even the most far-fetched rumor about the mustache was true, then perhaps there was some truth to them all. I figured I'd better ingratiate myself with Alice B. Toklas or I might never get to see Gertrude Stein again.

The silence continued to torture me. "What I mean is, I don't think I've ever seen two women with such a lovely home." I invested the phrase "two women" with romantic overtones, trying desperately to compliment Gertrude and Alice as a couple.

"Frankly, I'm a little jealous."

Alice nearly dumped her tea on the sofa. Of course I realized my mistake immediately, but it was too late.

"I don't mean jealous of you and Gertrude per se," I tried to explain, digging myself in deeper. "I mean I'm jealous of your domesticity in general." As if domesticity could ever be general. "I guess what I'm saying is that I'd also like to be married, with a lovely china tea set and Picassos and Matisses on the wall. But not to Gertrude, of course. To someone else."

A new expression of dismay swept across Alice's face, and then I realized what I had just said. Obviously she had construed my comment to mean that I'd rather be married to anyone but Gertrude Stein. I thought I'd better try a new tactic, and I shut my trap.

Once again the silence assailed me, though Toklas seemed perfectly content to just sit and twirl her tea with a spoon. I noticed she drank it without anything at all in it, though you'd have thought she was stirring in an entire bowl-full of sugar, given the vehemence of the circles she traced with her spoon.

Finally Alice said something. But the way she said it—with deadpan deliberation—and the way she looked at me so suggestively made me think it was some kind of parable. And I was damned if I could understand it.

"You have no idea how domestic Gertrude Stein is. Even geniuses can be housebroken," she concluded enigmatically.

I didn't know whether to laugh or say amen. This was, after all, Gertrude Stein's wife. She must have a sense of humor somewhere buried beneath all her paranoia. So I treated her strange comment as a joke. Fortunately, we were both rescued from the apparent perils of taking tea with a total stranger by the entrance of Gertrude Stein.

"Henri!" Gertrude Stein exclaimed energetically, gusting into the room like a strong warm summer breeze. Her charisma was so palpable the whole room seemed to flutter once, before settling in to rapt attention.

Out of deference to Alice's territorialism, I tried to contain my excitement at seeing Gertrude Stein again. The trick, I thought, was to relentlessly acknowledge their status as a couple.

"How kind of you two to invite me into your home," I said, looking first at Gertrude and then at Alice.

"You're quite welcome," Gertrude Stein replied, spreading her arms wide as if to embrace the entire drawing room. "Feel free to make yourself at home."

Alice looked alarmed at this instantaneous intimacy, and I tried once again to acknowledge the sanctity of her union with Gertrude.

"Don't worry, Alice. I'm not moving in," I joked. Gertrude and I laughed, but Alice looked skeptical.

"I'm sorry I was late in coming out, Henri," Gertrude said. "Alice may have told you we had a crisis."

"Yes. But she was very mysterious about it."

"Nothing mysterious about it," Gertrude said. "The plumber came by last week to fix some pipes in the kitchen, and they burst on us again, ruining a tart Hélène had been making for dessert, let alone the floor boards. You'd have thought the kitchen had burned down."

"It might as well have," said Toklas.

I smiled before I saw that she was serious, and still angry about the tart.

"It was a beautiful frangipani tart with a light puff-paste crust and a full four eggs and eight yolks, not to mention almonds and Jamaican rum—very hard to come by these days," Alice lamented with remarkable attention to the details of the tragedy.

"When the plumber came back by this morning, Alice let him have it," Gertrude Stein said proudly. "He won't make that mistake again. When Alice gets riled up, she's a force of nature. But then again he's lucky we didn't unleash Hélène on him. We purposely sent her out shopping. Of course she felt robbed of righteous retribution for her tart, but a dead plumber can't fix pipes."

"He purposely does a shabby job so that he can come back and charge double," Alice insisted.

"As if you care about the money," Gertrude Stein said affectionately. "Don't worry, Alice. I'll find you some more Jamaican rum the next time we're in Marseilles. Surely some grisly old pirate will donate a bottle from his stash, once he hears it's for one of your famous tarts."

This culinary compliment seemed to quell Alice's indignation. For the first time since my arrival, her face relaxed as she looked fondly into Gertrude's eyes. And I noticed a shade of shyness in Gertrude Stein's demeanor as she returned her gaze. The intimacy of their exchange embarrassed me, and I looked away.

After we finished our tea, Gertrude Stein proposed a tour of the rest of the apartment, including the atelier where the majority of the famous paintings were hung. Alice accompanied us, but her presence was more like a gargoyle than an actual human being. She seemed to want to oversee our exchanges but with absolutely no intention of joining in. Where only moments before they had been engaged on such an intimate level, as soon as we broke up the tea table, Gertrude Stein pretended Alice wasn't even there. They both acted as if this were perfectly natural.

I knew that I was missing something. The worst part of it was that I couldn't tell whether I should follow Gertrude's cue and also ignore Alice. I felt that I had offended her enough for one day. Nevertheless, though I tried to disregard her, I couldn't help noticing Alice's animated expressions as Gertrude and I spoke. She had one of those plastic faces that can't hide a thing, and she didn't even try. I often caught her blatantly staring at me, but she was apparently operating on the premise that if Gertrude Stein chose not to see her, then neither would I.

As I said, the apartment was brimming with antique furniture of unspeakable grandiosity and weight. But on that first visit, I could see nothing but the paintings. There were dozens of them, crammed willy-nilly on walls, almost on top of each other, they were so numerous. The nudes alone included Matisse's *Music*, Manguin's *Standing Nude*, Vallotton's *Reclining Nude*, and Picasso's *Young Girl with a Basket of Flowers*, *Seated Nude*, and *Standing Female Nude*. Most breathtaking of all was Bonnard's *Siesta*, the model prone on her stomach with legs slightly agape on the silken folds of her disheveled bedsheets, revealing the most softly seductive cave in western art.

The landscapes looked more like hallucinations than scenes from the natural world. Fragmented fields and streams. Swirling meadows. Forests on drugs.

Gertrude Stein, who watched my face attentively, seemed to delight in gauging my reactions to the paintings. The more extreme my responses, the more tickled she was, even chuckling outloud when I looked scandalized by particularly bizarre Cubist Braques and Picassos.

Alice B. Toklas watched both our faces with equal attention. One minute she looked pleased, the next dismayed, but I couldn't decipher the motivation for either extreme. For a long time, we must have made a queer picture, each of us a link in a voyeuristic chain, with me assessing the paintings, Gertrude appraising my assessments, and Alice doing God knows what calculations in her head.

The most shocking painting of all was Picasso's *Nude with Drapery*, because of its beautiful barbarism. His nude had breasts like ballistic melons; they would explode if touched. Her left hand was a boxer's glove poised to bludgeon, her right the blade of a guillotine. Her legs consisted of what looked like intricately joined axe, sword, and saw blades balanced on the clawed paw of a ghastly saber-toothed tiger. If she were seductive, it was an invitation to dismemberment and burial rather than to pleasure. Yet her violence was exquisite. And that is what scared me. Where I had once been a spectator, Picasso had turned me into the pleading masochist.

Gertrude Stein followed my long stare and smiled at my discomfiture. "Beautiful, isn't it?" she said.

Alice's face sharpened, her eyes focusing like an opera glass on my response to this comment. So carefully scrutinized, I was starting to suffer from a kind of stage fright. But I attempted to speak nonchalantly.

"If I tried to live with this in the house, I would never sleep for the nightmares. What is it, do you think, that makes Picasso *see* the way he sees?"

"What do you mean?" Gertrude asked.

"I mean her face. It looks like an African voodoo mask."

"Actually, she has always reminded me of Meryle, the young Lyonnaise who works in the pâtisserie on the rue du Petit-Musc."

I thought Gertrude Stein was joking, so I grinned. But she looked back with a touch of impatience.

Alice's face relaxed. Her relief was obvious enough, but I still couldn't pinpoint the source of her mood swings.

"Pablo agrees with me that Cubism is true realism," Gertrude Stein continued. "He says what other people call realism is just a romantic form of wish-fulfillment. Artists paint complete and cohesive pictures to mask their discomfort with ambiguity, ambivalence, and all those other 'bi' words, including bisexuality, I suppose. Although as far as I'm concerned, bisexuals make lousy artists. They're too wishy-washy."

"I'm not so sure," I said tentatively. The idea of questioning the aesthetic manifestoes of Gertrude Stein and Pablo Picasso seemed presumptuous, and I still couldn't fathom the notion that realism is relative. "If you will pardon my contradicting the master, Cubism is anything but realistic. It's more like an intellectual and aesthetic treatise on perception."

"Exactly. And perception constitutes reality."

"You've got me there."

"You know, I really understood what he meant when we saw our first tanks. We were all walking innocently enough down the boulevard Raspail when they came rolling up the street. It was 1916, or '17. When Pablo saw the camouflage patterns painted on the cannons, he said *'C'est nous qui avons fait ça'*—'We made that'—and he's right. More than any snapshot of trenches or painting of widows sobbing in vineyards, camouflage captures the essence of Europe during the Great War. And modern art doesn't just represent it. It *is* it."

"Give me an American counterpart. Maybe then I'll get it."

"There isn't one. America may be the oldest modern country in the world, but for some reason we're afraid of modern aesthetics. I guess we're hopelessly romantic after all, deep down in the corny marrow of our bones."

"What do you mean the oldest modern country?" I asked. "It seems to me America is childish compared to Europe. Even infantile."

"Romantic, but not childish. Besides, when it comes to that, the child is the father of the man."

Only ten minutes into our conversation, and Gertrude Stein was on a roll. I think one reason she and I had hit it off from the start was that we both reveled in philosophical conundrums. I had come prepared for a wild intellectual ride. I raised my eyebrows quizzically.

"What I mean is, America was born modern. In fact, our technology invented modernity itself. And since American culture moves so quickly, we age more quickly than other countries. We'll be old before our time."

"So it took an American to transplant modernity into European aesthetics?" I suggested, implicitly referring back to my *En Vogue* article.

Gertrude Stein nodded once, with convincing finality. Alice nodded at exactly the same moment, as if they had rehearsed. Cued by this uncanny simultaneity, I began surreptitiously comparing their gestures, which, even when they were not looking at one another, often coincided.

"I couldn't have done it without Pablo, of course," Gertrude Stein admitted. "Americans and Spaniards understand abstraction. And modern art is nothing more than abstraction."

"I thought it was realistic," I said, getting lost once again in the maze of Gertrude Stein's superior, albeit convoluted, logic. But I was making progress, because I suddenly anticipated the analogy that clarified her whole aesthetic system. Eager student that I was, I rushed to say it before she had to spell it out.

"Which means that abstraction is realistic," I concluded.

Gertrude Stein and Alice nodded once again, the former with apparent pride in the progress of her pupil.

"But how is it that Spaniards and Americans understand abstraction better than, say, the English?" I asked, somewhat wary of her nationalistic typecasting.

"Unlike the English and the French," Gertrude Stein explained with characteristic patience, "we have no real ties with the earth. With nothing to actually ground us, we wander off into cultural abstractions. Americans love their machines, and the Spanish love their rituals. We are culturally disembodied and constitutionally abstract, the prerequisites of modern art. And of course Pablo took to modernity like a fish to water. He says Americans in Europe are really Spanish. And I often accuse him of being American. He's joking, but I'm not."

I knew better than to smile. I knew she meant it. She and Picasso had already convinced half the world, and all of Paris, that they had created modern art. And wasn't my *En Vogue* article designed to convince the other half?

"What is it that you and Picasso have that others don't have?" I asked. "Besides genius?"

"We're not depressed. It's as simple as that. It's the same damned thing that ultimately set my brother Leo and me apart. You see I don't believe in depression. Leo, on the other hand, thrives on it. And of course Freud came along and gave him license to really revel in it. I mean, Freud preaches that you're either depressed or stupid. Whereas I think *if* you're depressed you're stupid."

"Isn't that a little inhumane, let alone simplistic? I mean, some people really have a lot to be depressed about, don't they?"

Alice made a little clucking sound, as if I'd disturbed her eggs. "It's never worth it," Gertrude Stein insisted. "Besides, depression is never connected to real things. It's just romanticized adversity."

With Gertrude Stein, I could already tell it was pointless to argue. Yet things like this always cropped up—ridiculous, unequivocal declarations that discounted whole legions of human beings. "But what if depression is constitutional? What if it's a disease like cholera?"

Gertrude Stein waved her hand, dismissing my argument like a fly. "I say stay away from the carriers. Now you know why I made the break with Leo."

"But where did *he* catch it?"

Once again Alice seemed faintly amused by our intellectual sparring, and her proprietary shield lowered another inch.

"From Dr. Freud," Gertrude explained. "Where else? Leo's not the first perfectly normal human being that damned pervert has seduced with all his erotic talk about pathology."

Leo's defection to Freud was obviously a painful loss.

"So much for all those foolish American art critics who claim that Cubism is Freudian," I said scornfully.

"Exactly. Now I'm beginning to remember why I like you so much, Henri."

"But how do you explain the fact that Cubism is also fragmented, like the psychoanalytic model of the psyche?" I asked. "Coincidence?"

"Look, Henri. Freud didn't invent modern fragmentation. The Great War blew the psyche to smithereens, along with the rest of Europe. Cubism has a hell of a lot more to do with the war than it does with a Viennese cocaine addict with delusions of phallic grandeur."

Of course I laughed. "Can I quote you? I see an article in this, and I've got a deadline just around the corner."

"Quote the master himself," Gertrude Stein said. "I'll set you up with an interview with Pablo right away. We all know your success at *En Vogue* depends on your befriending 'the likes of us,' as you put it so indelicately at Kahnweiler's." Stein pretended to be teasing me by flexing her enormous ego.

"You're a peach, Gertrude. But you know it's not just because I'm a journalist. It's all one big dream come true. I know I've only been in Paris a few weeks. But it feels like home—like I've finally come home to a place where I can really be me." I paused, a little embarrassed by my almost maudlin naîveté. Nevertheless I completed my thought, blushing ever so slightly. "Whoever that is. I mean, whoever I am."

Gertrude Stein grinned. Nothing pleased her more than the ingenuous authenticity of Americans, a quality that had long since vanished in Europe's more cultivated soil.

"And people wonder why we expatriate," Alice B. Toklas suddenly said out of the blue. "Welcome to the salon."

I was startled. Apparently, I had passed muster, successfully measuring up to whatever checklist of qualities Alice had been itemizing during my conversation with Gertrude. From that moment on, Alice became progressively hospitable, even generous, and I grew very fond of her.

"Would you like to stay for supper?" Alice asked with unprecedented enthusiasm.

"I can think of nothing I would like better," I said.

"Fine. Then I'll go see to things myself." Alice turned to Gertrude. When their eyes met, I lowered my own. Once again, I felt almost embarrassed to witness such an eloquent, albeit silent, expression of love. "You know how Hélène hates last-minute guests," Alice continued very gently, much more gently than the content of her words warranted. "I believe I'll do the cooking myself tonight to celebrate your appearance in your friend's *En Vogue* article."

She left Gertrude Stein and me alone among the paintings in the atelier to create her own culinary masterpieces in the kitchen.

"She likes you," Gertrude Stein announced.

"How do you know?"

"She invited you to dinner, didn't she? And she's cooking. I think this is the first time she's ever invited anyone on the first day."

"So I passed the test?"

"Yes. You didn't flirt with me. Not even once. Or you'd have been out on your ass. She went so far as to try to ban Hemingway from the salon, even though she knows his gender completely disqualifies him. She's very strict."

"Hemingway flirts with you?" I asked, more than a little surprised that such an apparently macho man would flirt with an almost equally macho woman. I was, if possible, even more naive about avant-garde sexuality than I was about art.

"Everyone flirts with me, Henri. Except you." Gertrude gave me a knowing look.

I wondered if this were true. I wondered what it said about me.

Miss Henrietta Adams
Hôtel Résidence les Cèdres
12 rue des Dames
17th Arrondissement
Paris, France

May 18, 1925

Dear Miss Adams:

Congratulations on the superlative quality of your second
submission, which arrived promptly (as per our agreement)
on the 10th of the month. I don't mind telling you that
the Board practically applauded when they heard you had
managed to obtain an interview with Pablo Picasso. To our
knowledge, a more candid interview of Picasso has never
appeared in the American press, and it is eminently
apparent that you did not exaggerate the value of your
connections in Paris (not that we doubted you for an
instant!). In addition, your original analysis of
Picasso's career and his impact on the avant-garde is
everything we hoped it would be.

One word of caution: though we're hardly a prudish
magazine, we do have to bear in mind that a fair number of
our readers lack your cosmopolitan savoir faire. Here at
En Vogue, of course, we're all perfectly aware that
artists have their saltier and sometimes even seamier
sides. But we'd like to present them in the best possible
light--as aesthetes rather than bohemians. Picasso's
history of mistresses and marriages is certainly colorful,
but hardly relevant to the artistic vision that generated
Les Demoiselles d'Avignon.

I'm not advocating lying or even whitewashing the truth. Far be it from me to question the value of journalistic veracity. It's more a question of selection-- in a word, all the news that's fit to print. Having worked for the Times, you of all people surely know exactly what I mean. This is a suggestion, not a reprimand. Exercising a little discretion on your end will simplify the editorial process on ours.

Concerning the photographs you enclosed, try for a darker print quality in the future. Only two of the ten were usable, and they were not necessarily the best of the lot. Given the great success of your column thus far, we are adding a new credit line to your expense account to defray the cost of a professional photographer. We are counting on you to use your judgment, erring (if at all) on the conservative side; but when you are convinced the article warrants photographs, you may dip into this new fund.

Your work thus far has been outstanding, and we're thrilled to have you on board. Vive l'avant-garde!

Sincerely,

Irving P. Dickey
Senior Editor

cc: Board of Editors
En Vogue

CHAPTER FOUR

La Nouvelle Bohème

By the end of my first month in Paris, I was happily ensconced at the Hôtel Résidence les Cèdres at the foot of Montmartre, which was generally considered the most bohemian section of the city. Only those living in the Quartier Latin disagreed, claiming this dubious distinction for themselves. True to its name, the hôtel was surrounded by ancient cedars dating back to prerevolutionary Paris when it had been the winter residence of the Baron de Polignac. A guillotine had cut short his proprietorship, and les Cèdres had been seized temporarily by the libertarians before becoming first an inn and then a residence hôtel. In exile from American democratic mediocrity, its aristocratic architecture and history appealed to me.

But the main reason I chose the Hôtel Résidence les Cèdres was that its clientele consisted primarily of displaced northern Europeans. I had always fancied that despite my hopelessly Anglo-Saxon name I looked Danish, with my broad cheeks, blue eyes, and blond complexion and hair. And then there was my height, which could only be explained by northern European ancestors hidden somewhere in the gnarled roots of my family tree. I was a full five feet eight inches tall, though I was rather dainty in build, so I always pretended to myself that I straddled a fine line between feminine elegance and masculine stature.

Well aware of my phobia of masculine women, my friends in Cambridge and Manhattan used to tease me, pretending I was mannish. Of course one cannot be teased about something that is not at least partially true. But wanting little or nothing to do with men, I hated the term and was more than a little afraid of the look itself. I thought that at the Hôtel les Cèdres I would melt right in with all the tall, statuesque northern Europeans and could pretend I wasn't an American as long and lanky as a cowboy's drawl. I still have an almost preternatural horror of Americans abroad, as if they were a horde of latter-day barbarians let loose upon the civilized world just to terrorize me. In fact, that's one reason I liked Alice Toklas so much. She was uncharacteristically genteel for an American, especially one from California. Gertrude Stein can say what she wants about loving America and writing about things American. I don't see her living there.

The only American thing I did deign to do in Paris was to go to the famous bookstore Shakespeare & Company. I figured the elevated aesthetic sensibilities of the literary icons who frequented the bookshop would somehow ennoble even the barbarism of the American tourists I feared I might encounter there.

As part of my quest to become bohemian, I almost bought a beret en route to Shakespeare & Company. But I realized just in time that it would have been too queer. Americans in berets always remind me of those little dogs with crocheted sweaters. It would have been like corn chowder posing as bouillabaisse, so I ditched the idea.

Given our native provincialism, Americans in particular must be very careful not to treat European sophistication as if it were a garment that could simply be donned at will. Ezra Pound was the most embarrassing example of this kind of American *poseur*, though T. S. Eliot, who had become more British than the British, was giving him a run for his money. For all Pound's pontifical pretense, posturing as the reigning dean of modernist letters, I knew damned good and well that he was really an incurable rustic from Idaho. Once a potato, always a tuber, and I don't mean a truffle. If I were ever going to evolve into a bohemian, the transformation would have to emerge gradually from within. For the time being, when I looked at berets, I kept picturing a dusty old spud with a pancake on its head.

Reminded in this bizarre stream-of-consciousness fashion of Ezra Pound, I almost took it as a sign to forego my pilgrimage to Shakespeare & Company. I really began to actively detest him a couple years earlier when he wrote the postscript to Rémy de Gourmont's *Natural Philosophy of Love* in which he described the avant-garde as a legion of "spermatozoid charging the great vulva of London," as if urban aesthetics were the provenance of male rapists. Little did he know that the vulva of sapphists would mow him down like a wilted hayseed as the velocity of the avant-garde art movement accelerated.

The idea of meeting H.D., Mina Loy, or better yet Janet Flanner outweighed even the threat of Pound's provincial misogyny. And if Djuna Barnes flapped through the poetry section in her gothic black cape, I'd simply ascend to the heaven reserved for aspiring bohemians.

Of course none of them were there. Even Sylvia Beach, the proprietor of the shop, was in the back room, presumably brushing the rich weave of her impeccable tweed suit. I had already heard from Gertrude Stein that one of the big debates among Parisian sapphists was whether or not Sylvia Beach and Adrienne Monnier would ever publicly proclaim their love. Adrienne was the proprietress of La Maison des Amis des Livres, the most avant-garde French bookshop in Paris, which was across the street. People like Paul Verlaine and Léon-Paul Fargue frequented her shop. Sylvia and Adrienne had lived together for years, since way back in the early days when Natalie Barney made sapphism one of the mainstays of the bohemian diet.

Shakespeare & Company was a cozy and picturesque enough shop with its well-worn antique furniture, black-and-white Serbian rugs, and portraits of Poe, Whitman, and Wilde scattered about discreetly papered walls. But I hadn't hiked halfway across Paris to the rue de l'Odéon for the sake of ambiance alone. Disappointed that there weren't any literary geniuses there for me to gawk at, I was on the verge of leaving before some ordinary American assailed me with that exaggerated, desperate kind of camaraderie tourists wear like armor against anything foreign.

But then I stopped dead in my tracks. Someone extraordinary was in the poetry section, squeezed into a skirt so tight I knew she had to be French. An American in a skirt like that would have been agitated by puritanical fears of a possibly exposed buttock. Instead, this woman accentuated the dangers of the skirt by leaning over to finger volumes of contemporary verse. From the waist down she looked like an exotic antelope. Never before had I seen a gazelle reading poetry.

I was paralyzed by the ivory expanses of her bare legs, covered only by the silky down of unshaven sensuality. When she turned to me, the feline browns and hazels of her eyelashes and eyes captured me with the lazy ferocity of a prowling tiger in heat. Too frozen with fear to flee, I was rescued by her smile. Wild animals do not smile. I had mistaken her for a mythic beast in the jungle, but she was really only an exquisite French woman, thumbing through the selected poetry of William Blake.

I smiled back, trying to be rakish or at least debonair. But suddenly the discrepancy between her discreet flirtations and my bungling desire shamed me back into paralyzed embarrassment. Before I could recover my self-esteem, she had disappeared forever into the tangled streets of the Quartier Latin.

I would have to travel a long way down the road of expatriation to ever be able to flirt with, let alone seduce, a woman like that. Since when did aardvarks woo gazelles?

As I walked through the glamour of Paris, I looked down at my clunky shoes and shapeless, dowdy gray skirt, which had been my professional uniform in the States. I didn't have to become chic overnight, but it was high time to stop looking like a Yankee frump. I spent the afternoon shopping for tailored black suits, preferably silk, and a pair of the pearl button-down shoes I had noticed on the more refined women. As the afternoon wore on, I saw my new image as a bohemian rake take shape before my eyes.

Inspired, I even got up the courage to buy a couple of pair of trousers, though I pretended they were for an imaginary boyfriend I called Alec. The haberdashers were very helpful, sure that Alec would have a delightful birthday with such exquisite gifts.

My new alter-ego was born. Somehow, wearing gentlemanly attire in Paris seemed potentially elegant and sexy where it had been just plain masculine and embarrassing in the United States.

The fact is, the concept of mannish women was a contradiction in terms, an oxymoron perpetuating the myth that we had anything at all to do with men. Of course the opposite was true. By definition we were women who loved women. And despite all the propaganda, we were zesty and gay, not maladjusted and depressed the way the sexologists portrayed us. Having survived the perilous journey between the Scylla and Charybdis of their pathological labels, the Parisian sapphists defied gender typecasting. The longer I lived in the City of Love, the more I realized that the powerful Gertrude Stein and the dashing Duchesse de Clermont-Tonnerre were not mannish at all. Not to mention the gorgeous Djuna Barnes, who straddled the fluid line between masculinity and femininity like the latest fashions of the day.

I felt all the more at liberty to transform my image because I didn't have to answer to the bosses and protocol of my profession now that I was working freelance. *En Vogue* had never had an International Arts editorial, so I was pioneering new territory. I had a lot to prove.

But I could prove it on my own time and on my own turf without having to dress the part. Free to dress stylishly in Paris, I realized that professional American women are forced to wear unflattering suits and sensible pumps to stigmatize themselves as females who have deviated from their sacred domestic duties. My reaction to this epiphany was so profound that I actually gave away my shapeless old skirts to the *Petites Soeurs des Pauvres.* I had finally exorcised the last of my mother's three P's. Having shed the shackles of propagation and patent leather when I left Utah, it took Paris to finally inspire me to tear off the garments of propriety and all that they stood for.

Changing my clothes certainly hadn't changed my essence, or so I thought. Yet I found that my journalistic voice actually gained considerable authority. The whole process of writing my *En Vogue* articles was more exhilarating than any professional work I had ever done before. Not only had I gained access to so many famous painters, collectors, and art dealers through Gertrude Stein, I was also coming of age as a reporter. The education of Henri Adams had truly begun. And, as usual, knowledge would prove to be a very dangerous thing.

The editors at *En Vogue* were particularly impressed by my article covering the controversial history of the Kahnweiler Gallery on the rue de l'Abreuvoir. I knew from Gertrude Stein that long before Cubism was accepted, let alone valorized by the Parisian art world, Daniel Kahnweiler had devoted almost the entire stock of his gallery to Picasso, Braque, Derain, and later Gris, though he still showed a few Matisse and other non-Cubist members of the avant-garde. Kahnweiler's commercial investments were almost as instrumental as Gertrude Stein's patronage in launching the original Cubist movement.

With the persistence of a nagging Basque grandmother, Picasso had warned Kahnweiler, a German, that he ought to adopt French citizenship in case of war, but the prospect of military service deterred him until it was too late. The Great War caught Kahnweiler with his pants down. Forced to seek asylum in Switzerland, he watched helplessly as the entire contents of his gallery were sequestered during the first full year of the war, leaving the Cubists without their commercial champion.

The opponents of Cubism, especially the older dealers who had lost considerable business to the upstart Cubists, tried to destroy the movement by attaching it to Kahnweiler, as if its aesthetics were tainted by his nationality. Of course the Cubists themselves were Spanish and French, and Braque had even won the *croix de guerre* and *légion d'honneur* for his valor in battle against Germany. But during this brief and ultimately unsuccessful smear campaign, Kahnweiler's name was coupled with Cubism, and the painters themselves faced financial ruin. Eventually, the whole fiasco blew over. Kahnweiler was exonerated, and his gallery reopened in 1915. Once again, the Cubists knew where their next meal was coming from.

I had originally planned on slanting the article toward the problematic relationship between politics and art, focusing on Kahnweiler's controversial recovery of both his reputation and his gallery after the rumor of his German sympathies. But then life happened, and the article took on a whole new dimension much more suited to the high-speed-chase mentality of my editors and audience. I couldn't have chosen a more auspicious day to visit the Kahnweiler Gallery and interview its owner.

Daniel Kahnweiler was not exactly known for his graciousness, but he went out of his way to make me feel welcome at his gallery, even offering me a shot of schnapps before our tour commenced. For one thing, he knew that an article in a prominent American art magazine had the potential to bring him additional tourist business.

Despite his German past, Kahnweiler was the picture of French middle-class propriety. Dapper in a well-tailored though slightly smudged black suit, he showed me painting after painting that blew the lid off modern art.

I have never seen such a clash of beauty and filth. Not beauty, really. More like exotic prehistoric protea poking out of a dung heap. Nothing in art would ever be languid again.

The paintings were monstrously beautiful. My favorite was Picasso's *The Acrobat's Family with a Monkey* in which the representation of mother and child is disrupted by the gaze of an ape whose expression is far more tender and refined than that of any of the humans depicted. The elegant, sympathetic expression on the monkey's face made my skin crawl.

Later, when I told Gertrude how much I liked it, she agreed, saying it was breezy enough to lift the skirts of a whole pew full of Bostonian spinsters. What I thought was shocking, she thought was just rambunctious and oblivious to genteel conventions.

Kahnweiler seemed preoccupied throughout the tour, but I attributed his distraction to a survival mechanism—a way to deflect some of the power of the paintings. About halfway through our tour of the main gallery, a French policeman arrived and motioned to him.

"You will excuse me for a moment," Kahnweiler said, bowing.

The policeman followed him, and they disappeared into his office.

Shortly after Kahnweiler disappeared, a woman with an enormous hat entered the room. It almost looked like she had modeled her appearance after Matisse's *La Femme au Chapeau,* the painting that people had tried to vandalize at the Vernissage des Indépendents, scratching the paint off in their outrage. They were simply not ready for Matisse's vision of the world as aggressive splotches of crazy color. I had the same feeling about this woman, quite sure that I would never be ready for her.

I could tell immediately that she was American. Her movements were three times larger than they needed to be, and she was carrying a rat doing an imitation of a lap dog.

The woman smiled at me with that aggressive grin Americans think is friendly and Europeans think is rude. *"Bon jour,"* she said. *"Je m'appelle Myrtle."* French out of her mouth resembled a tooth extraction. Given her dubious charms, I was flattered that she thought I was French. *"Vous travaillez ici?"* she asked in a Texan drawl. Typically, she opened the conversation with an insult, assuming I was there to wait on her.

I hid behind her prejudice, feigning incomprehension.

"Comment?"

"Hell." She fumbled through her purse with sausage fingers, disrupting Fifi so that she yapped once. "Where is my French phrase book? Oh, never mind. I'll just wait for Fred. Fred!" she yelled over a humongous shoulder pad.

A spindly man swaggered in, sporting a brand new, bright-red beret that he wore tipped back like a cowboy hat. Taking advantage of the commotion of this reunion of husband and wife, I slipped up the back staircase Kahnweiler had shown me, to the attic portion of the gallery.

At the top of the stairs I almost staggered in amazement. I felt as if I had stumbled into the largest fun house in the world, where trick mirrors of every shape and size had distorted the bodies and especially the faces of a host of hapless bystanders. If humanity was really the subject of these paintings (and I had my doubts), the artists were the side-show carnies and we the gallery of hunched and gaping freaks.

My first impression of Kahnweiler's attic was that it was brutal and ugly—an open mass grave in which traditional art lay dismembered and disgraced, lacking only the final outrage of the burning lime. While individual paintings conjured up the frenzy of the single shell-shocked trench, the spectacle as a whole captured the modern massacre of Romanticism.

But as my eyes adjusted to the mêlée, beauty crawled out from beneath the mutilated bodies.

I began to see the humor of it all, the breezy quality Gertrude Stein delighted in. The real aesthetic pleasure was in this nakedness, so refreshing after the long years of repression and the tedious belief in progress that had made the nineteenth century take itself so seriously.

Of course that was the difference between Picasso and Freud. The great doctor smoked his pipe and pontificated, where Picasso's *Student with a Pipe* was a spoof of everything academic. Where Freud cultivated his status as the Professor, Picasso ridiculed all authority, beginning with this student's carnivalesque pipe and ridiculous doctoral hat.

I had my first avant-garde epiphany. The battleground of paintings was transformed into a three-ringed circus.

Just when I was really starting to enjoy myself, the Americans suddenly appeared out of nowhere. I was so startled I forgot my French disguise and returned Myrtle's greeting in English. She chose to ignore my annoyance and focused instead on my sudden and convenient lapse into her native language.

"I thought you were French. But you said that without a trace of an accent."

"I'm Belgian. You know how we are with languages. Such a little country with nothing to sell but our translating skills." I thought this explanation would appeal to her ethnocentric, capitalist sensibilities. It worked. Now she could fill her travel diary with news of the Belgian friend they had met that day, instead of the duplicitous American sapphist.

"Great." The bargain-hunter in her pounced. "Perhaps you can help us cut a deal with Kahnweiler. I'm afraid he doesn't speak one word of English."

Apparently, the pattern I saw emerging was lost on Myrtle. I wondered if even in Texas she found it difficult to find people who spoke her language.

"Our accountant told us if we invested in a few of these paintings we'd never regret it. Do you have any suggestions?"

"About?"

"About which paintings to buy. Believe it or not, I'm really out of my league here."

"Noooooo," I crooned, as if incredulous. "Really?" I was torn between the desire to promote the work of starving artists—especially Juan Gris, who I knew was living hand to mouth—and the horrific vision of one of their paintings hanging in a Dallas living room sandwiched between a framed photograph of the Spindletop oil field and an embroidered rendition of "Home on the Range."

Then I remembered that Gertrude Stein insisted that art was democratic—that it was equally accessible to connoisseurs and plebeians alike. So I decided to conduct an experiment on these Texan bipeds.

"Well, do you want a landscape or a portrait?"

Wife looked at husband and seemed to find an answer in his vacant stare. Periodically he popped a peppermint into his mouth or checked the angle of his beret. He was absolutely mute. Yet the way his wife referred every question to him made me wonder if he were telepathically in control, using his wife as a mere mouthpiece.

"Landscapes," she said adamantly. "They have a more stable market value." Monsieur le Peppermint slipped a candy between his lips as if to validate her remark.

"Why?"

"Our accountant told us that some portraits—like the one of Gertrude Stein by Picasso—are worth more simply because of the subject. But who wants an obese woman hanging in your living room?"

I almost choked at her derogatory reference to my new friend. But Myrtle continued with characteristic oblivion.

"We'd rather have pretty little European landscapes or cute little Parisian café scenes." She shook her head regretfully. "Not that any of this modern stuff is actually pretty. Frankly, I'd rather stick to the Impressionists. But our accountant insists we've got to buy Picasso. Says he's the biggest thing out since Michelangelo."

I had traveled all the way across the Atlantic to escape the travesty of capitalist aesthetics, but Myrtle had found me. As if determined to elicit a response, she edged excruciatingly close to me, lowering her voice to the kind of deafening whisper gossips use to make sure everyone hears them.

"I've also heard these avant-garde artists are frightfully immoral," she hissed. "Or what they call bohemian, which amounts to the same thing."

Increasingly afraid I might lose my temper, I fled from her side, making a beeline for the largest nude in the attic. But both she and Fred followed me.

"If you ask me, these bohemians are an index of the lax morality that will ruin Europe. And I'd just as soon keep them out of Texas. But there's no accounting for taste, and money is money."

This last fact seemed to pain her beyond measure, as if money itself had betrayed her delicate moral fiber. I had never heard a clearer, more concise statement of capitalist ethics. I was tempted to tell her that Michelangelo had been a sissy, but I was temporarily too impressed with her carefully constructed edifice of prejudice to topple it with superfluous facts.

"We're also interested in still lifes," she added, still intent on taking advantage of my aesthetic advice.

"Yes. I guess one doesn't have to worry about the morality of fruits," I said, still thinking of Michelangelo.

"Exactly. How to choose from all these pictures..." she broke off suggestively.

Let the experiment begin. I led Fred and Myrtle over to a group of particularly obtuse Picassos to test their interpretive prowess. I felt as if I were unveiling Cubism to Huckleberry Finn, except that he was much more ethically advanced.

"How about this one?" I pointed to *Still Life with Fruit, Glass, Knife, and Newspaper.* "Or this one?" I indicated *Houses on the Hill.*

Of course the paintings were almost all unmarked, so Myrtle didn't have access to their titles, which so often clarify the content of Cubist paintings. When I first saw these two pictures, they looked like a jumble of random shapes, until I carefully deciphered their oblique references to real objects.

"Well, I must say I'm not wild about the colors in that first one," Myrtle said without skipping a beat. "But I like the shape of that pear—cute, like a cartoon—and I *love* the way he's made that knife with what looks like the handle of a baseball bat. It's really very funny—a happy painting; if only he'd included a few flowers to brighten up the color scheme."

I nodded my head, biting my tongue so as not to influence this aesthetic critique by the great unwashed. I couldn't believe my ears. I also found the cartoon quality of *Still Life with Fruit* to be its most appealing feature. When later I told Picasso what Myrtle had said, he, too, nodded—he who usually all but sticks his fingers in his ears in the vicinity of critics.

"But I prefer this other one," Myrtle continued, nodding at *Houses on the Hill.* Fred popped another peppermint into his mouth.

"This painting reminds me of Texas. The way the houses are growing out of the hills. That's the thing about Texas. The land is in our blood. I like that one there, too." She pointed at *The Reservoir.* "If that's not Texas, I don't know what it is."

"It's Spain," I said.

But she was right. It might as well have been Texas. The way the water and the little hilltop village and the reservoir all fit together like a jigsaw puzzle of vivid earth-tone cubes suggested that the people, though they were not pictured, would also have consisted of pleasantly angular shapes that would just as easily snap into place without disrupting the restful yet dynamic symmetry of the whole.

"It sure looks like the Lone Star state," Myrtle insisted. Every single one of her observations corroborated Gertrude Stein's theory that Americans and Spaniards have the same expansive and kinetic bottom natures. And Myrtle had actually articulated the origin of this transatlantic kinship. It's their abstract relationship with the land, the wide open spaces of deserts and mountain ranges.

"But, you know, that one over there—the round one with all the squares and cones piled on top of each other ..." She pointed to *The Architect's Table,* my favorite by far in the entire gallery. I hadn't pointed it out because I wanted to show it to Gertrude Stein to see if she'd be willing to add it to her collection. The idea of this master-piece being lost forever, like a drop in the ten-gallon hat of an unannointed Texan barbarian, nearly killed me. But then I remem-bered the point of my experiment.

"Why do you like that one? It doesn't look like Texas."

"No, but it reminds me of my father's desk when I was growing up. I know it's a little busy—a little too cluttered with shapes—but I'm nostalgic. He died when I was only fourteen."

I was afraid to ask the next question. "What was his profession?"

"He was an architect."

Far from casting pearls to swine, Myrtle consistently responded with uncanny insight. Perhaps modern art *is* democratic. And we just cloud our vision with presumptuous and extraneous erudition. Perhaps Gertrude Stein was right again.

Just then Myrtle saw the words "Miss Gertrude Stein" painted in the corner of *The Architect's Table* and her appreciation froze. "Damn," she said. "What architect in his right mind would have a letter from Stein lying on his table? Forget it, we'll stick with—"

Suddenly Kahnweiler burst into the attic gallery, his face creased with anguish.

"You must all leave," he panted. "I am very sorry. Something terrible has happened."

The police officer who had retired with Kahnweiler into his office strode into the room. I noticed now that he was a French sergeant, or *brigadier*.

"Something has been stolen," he said.

"What?"

"I am not at liberty to tell you."

Kahnweiler looked at me with unspeakable distress. He turned his head away from Myrtle and Fred and mouthed the words "Juan Gris."

"Clear the atelier," the *brigadier* barked. "You must all come with me to the station for questioning."

Needless to say I was shocked. To this day I can't believe they actually hauled us all into the police station. Talk about innocent bystanders! I think Kahnweiler must have said something to implicate us. It wasn't the first time false leads were dangled in front of eager noses to distract the law from the scent of real criminals. Although the civilian in me was a bit nervous, I must admit that as a journalist I was titillated.

What followed will always remind me of a particularly bad Keystone Kops movie. The bungling incompetence of the French police was so exaggerated, it seemed orchestrated to catch us off guard. I know it tests the limits of credibility to report that they all had scraggly little mustaches, but that's the way I remember it. A ring of cops brandishing the French equivalent of billy clubs loaded us all into a giant paddy wagon and then almost forgot to bolt the door. We four prisoners practically tumbled into one big heap on the floor as we lurched into motion. How we all ever arrived at police headquarters in one piece I shall never know. By the time they finally escorted us into the station, poor Myrtle had turned a shade of green that matched her husband's garish tie.

Throughout the ordeal, Kahnweiler was wearing a classic Charlie Chaplin expression, a crazy mixed-up confusion of surprise and mischievous excitement. He seemed to be playing a caricature of himself. I suspected he was hiding something beneath his hyperbolic protestations of innocence. As we all waited together under the hot bright lights of a cramped interrogation cell, he kept reminding the police that he, Daniel Kahnweiler, had originally reported the stolen painting, and he resented being treated like a common criminal. As one, the guards nodded their heads, smiling with the oblivious detachment of a battalion of Cheshire cats.

I gathered from his scandalized monologue that this was not the first time the cops had been called in to investigate art theft. The Kahnweiler Gallery had been robbed no fewer than five times and he, Daniel Kahnweiler, was beginning to believe the robberies weren't just isolated incidents. He began to spin an elaborate story about an intricate Turkish crime ring complete with a sinister mastermind intent on dragging high art into the depths of the black market. Never mind that his gallery seemed to be their sole target. This was simply an indication that these particular criminals had exquisite taste.

God knows, Kahnweiler had cooperated with the authorities. But they had not been able to track down the thieves, leaving him with no choice but to cash in on the insurance policy he had taken out, just prior (thankfully) to the first theft some three years before. Previously, the *brigadier* had shown up at the gallery, just as he had done today, as part of an ongoing routine investigation. But the police had never questioned Kahnweiler himself, let alone hauled him into the station. The whole thing was preposterous.

Throughout his monologue, when he wasn't ranting and raving about Turks, Kahnweiler kept glancing suspiciously at the Texans, and even at me. I just sat there, looking as innocent as you please, taking mental notes of the proceedings for my next *En Vogue* article. But then good old Myrtle started getting on my nerves again.

The poor woman was beyond agitated, too involved in her own hysterics to attend to Kahnweiler's. She had obviously read one too many accounts of the indiscriminate brutality of foreign police. She entertained visions of being locked up and tortured (or worse), all of which she shared with Fred and me until I couldn't stand it anymore. If I heard the phrase "Chinese water torture" one more time, I thought I'd explode.

"We're not in China, for Godsake," I finally barked at her. "Let alone in trouble."

But then I felt guilty. Robbed of her histrionics, she crumpled into a hopeless little heap onto a chair that was nailed to the floor.

Fred, on the other hand, was as oblivious as he had been at the gallery, popping an occasional peppermint into his mouth, but otherwise utterly impassive.

They left us cooped up in that holding tank for what seemed like hours. Finally, the *brigadier* who had first sequestered Kahnweiler at the gallery returned and escorted him into an adjoining room for further questioning. And then they came for me.

A plainclothesman led me down a long, damp corridor lit with bare bulbs hanging from frayed electrical wires. Everything in the interrogation room itself was gray—the walls, the floor, the detective's face as he took my name, address, and other vital statistics. When he found out I was American he disappeared and a lieutenant returned to take his place. The lieutenant, whose nameplate read "Dupin," was much more polite, almost deferential. For the first time since I had arrived in Paris I was grateful for being a Yankee.

As we proceeded, his deference made me more and more nervous. He was handling me with kid gloves because he couldn't believe what a valuable witness I was. An American art critic securely ensconced in the salon of Gertrude Stein (Dupin noted with mounting relish in his little black book), I had burgeoning personal relationships with virtually all of the key players in the case, most notably Picasso, Gris, and Braque, whose paintings had so mysteriously disappeared and been so handsomely compensated for by the firm insuring Kahnweiler's collection. The lieutenant saw the words "Stool Pigeon" written all over my face.

I'd stumbled on a potential gold mine, the inner workings of a scandal the likes of which would blow the socks off my readers. If Kahnweiler was right, this crime ring infiltrated the domain of the most famous of the famous—the founders of Cubism who, since 1908, had captured the American imagination more vividly than any other group since Lautrec and the Impressionists. This was the melodramatic stuff that American journalists' reputations were made of, yet I sensed immediately that my good fortune might generate dangerously divided loyalties. Needless to say, my own expatriate patron, Gertrude Stein, was implicated somewhere in the wings of this case, if only by proximity. She was, after all, Kahnweiler's most loyal buyer, and friendly with all the painters in question.

The minute Dupin showed me the list and descriptions of the five stolen paintings, I knew I was in way over my head. I felt like a scientist on the verge of a revolutionary discovery that could destroy the world. I had a sneaking suspicion I had seen at least three of the paintings already—two at Picasso's own atelier and maybe even one in Gertrude Stein's private studio.

I wondered if the lieutenant also saw the words "Insurance Fraud" written all over my face. If Kahnweiler had just shut his mouth and submitted himself to questioning, I never would have doubted his integrity. But talk about protesting too much!

It seemed clear that Kahnweiler had made a pretty penny collecting insurance compensation for paintings he had actually just given back to the artists themselves. What I couldn't figure out was what the artists got out of the deal. There was, of course, always the possibility of the paintings' resale value. But if my memory served me correctly, a number of the works still hung in the ateliers of their respective painters. Of course they were, after all, hot. It wouldn't do to call attention to a stolen painting by selling it too soon.

My imagination went wild, fabricating ingenious plots to smuggle the paintings to the United States, maybe even to Texas! For who would suspect Myrtle and Fred of contraband? In no time, I had Picasso hiding the stolen canvases under two-bit decoy paintings, disguised in seemingly ordinary, custom-made frames with secret compartments that fooled even the most canny customs officers. While the amateur sleuth Henri Holmes hatched these harebrained schemes, the mild-mannered art critic Henri Adams feigned innocent incomprehension as Lieutenant Dupin described the stolen paintings.

Even in college at Radcliffe, I had a photographic memory that just got sharper and sharper with practice as an art critic. I could see a painting once at a museum and critique it from memory in minute detail. So I was damned sure I'd seen Picasso's *Man with a Guitar* before, right in the master's own atelier when I had interviewed him for my second *En Vogue* editorial. I would have recognized that canvas blindfolded with my hands tied behind my back.

The police records were laughably inaccurate, almost indecipherable. They used adjectives like "bright," "jumbled," and "confusing" where an art critic might have said "bold," "geometric," and "abstract." But the color scheme alone gave the painting away.

Worse yet, the word "bass" was emblazoned in the right-hand rose-colored panel. If I were a crime consultant, I might have suggested to Kahnweiler that he choose a less easily identifiable painting to disappear from his gallery. I suspected that Picasso wasn't overly fond of *Man with a Guitar* anyway and had selected it the way an agnostic shepherd might choose a mangy ram to sacrifice to a God he suspects isn't really there.

The other four missing paintings were Picasso's *Calligraphic Still Life,* another relatively inferior painting I thought I had noticed at his atelier, and his *Still Life with Calling Card,* which I had definitely never seen. Braque's *Nature Morte à la Pipe* had disappeared only a few months before. And that particular day, Juan Gris's *Dish of Pears* had supposedly been stolen from Kahnweiler's gallery. It was this last painting I was almost sure I had seen at Gertrude Stein's atelier. Of the five, *Dish of Pears* was by far the most wonderful, a carnivalesque study of fruits the shape of gumdrops hugging each other in an Art Deco bowl—soft, gooey, friendly pears. If my suspicions were justified, Gertrude Stein was "storing" the most valuable of the stolen paintings for Kahnweiler or Gris or whomever was behind this racket.

It was also possible, and infinitely more reassuring, that Gertrude Stein was oblivious to the whole scam, in which case Kahnweiler had already cashed in twice—first for the insurance money and then again selling the painting to the unwitting Gertrude and Alice. Desperate, I clung to the idea that Gertrude Stein had simply been duped, though she wasn't exactly the gullible type.

"Do you recognize any of these paintings?" the lieutenant kept asking me as we painstakingly reviewed their descriptions.

My imagination was so cluttered with the twists and turns of fantastic plots, I was finding it difficult to concentrate on Dupin's constant stream of questions. But thank God I had the wherewithal to stick with vague, noncommittal answers. I knew myself well enough to realize I was perfectly capable of making a mountain out of a molehill or, in this case, of fabricating an international crime ring out of a few misplaced canvases.

Who says the whole screwball scenario wasn't just the wild imaginings of a bored journalist? It wouldn't have been the first time I'd spun a perfectly feasible story out of thin air. Perhaps it was all just one big mistake that Gertrude Stein would clear up with a simple explanation.

Ordinarily I'm a typically earnest American, honest almost to a fault. But right then and there I discovered it's very easy to lie in a foreign language, even to a police officer. It's funny. A part of me always felt like someone else—my bohemian alter-ego Alec, for example—when I spoke French. So I just let my other half do the talking.

"Non," I said regretfully. "And I've got a very good eye for art, so I'm pretty sure I'd remember them if I'd ever seen them."

"You'll be sure to contact us if you do remember anything?" Dupin said at last. "Or if you see them in your travels—in the salons, or in someone's atelier—wherever."

I remember wondering if there was any middle ground between being an accomplice and a stool pigeon. *"Mais bien sûr,"* I said, relieved to finally be free to blow the joint. "I'll keep my eyes open."

And my trap shut.

Miss Henrietta Adams
Hôtel Résidence les Cèdres
12 rue des Dames
17th Arrondissement
Paris, France

July 19, 1925

Dear Miss Adams:

You will be very happy to know that the mail in response
to your first few editorials has been very enthusiastic.
We sincerely hope that you are well on your way to
becoming an institution here at En Vogue.

I am also pleased to report that the Board has
approved your extremely provocative editorial on the
phenomenon of art theft in Paris. There is a kind of
detective quality in your prose style that complements the
subject matter very effectively, and we encourage you to
continue to experiment with this clever wedding of style
and content. The balance between dramatic content and
aesthetic critique also works very well. This is another
technique worth utilizing in future editorials.
Specifically, your suspenseful account of undercover
sleuthing and the black market allows you to insert your
characteristically trenchant analysis of the paintings at
the Kahnweiler Gallery without lapsing into the
potentially dry intellectual analysis we try to avoid in
En Vogue. If anything, you could add an even more in-depth
account of your experiences at the police station and your
follow-up of their investigations. Therefore, we would
welcome any such additions to the enclosed, slightly

revised version of your manuscript, providing you send off the final copy by Monday, August 1. If not, we can print it as it stands now and will still have a fine column for the month of September.

There is one aspect of this article I must warn you to avoid in the future. The critique of the American tourists was entirely too harsh--almost a caricature. But we're going to edit it out entirely, so don't bother revising that part of your original manuscript. In the future, bear in mind that since your audience is primarily American, you might want to be more sympathetic to their foibles.

Once again, you have more than lived up to our expectations, and we are especially pleased with the great contrast between this submission and, for example, your piece on Picasso. Although you have only written three articles to date, you have already demonstrated the kind of breadth that is so vital to the longevity of a monthly column. As always, we look forward to next month's installment.

Sincerely,

Irving P. Dickey
Senior Editor

cc: Board of Editors
En Vogue

CHAPTER FIVE

The Salon

Picasso's high-pitched, whinnying laughter and Stein's contralto guffaw burst through the door as Hélène opened it. They sounded like two animals in a zoo, a Spanish horse and an American donkey heehawing uncontrollably. Something was very amusing. It was Hemingway.

I maneuvered my way through Gertrude Stein and Alice B. Toklas's studio toward the sound of their laughter, quivering with the anticipation of attending the celebrated salon for the first time. My excitement had temporarily eclipsed all thoughts of Lieutenant Dupin and his infamous crime ring. I wasn't about to let the lieutenant's suspicions ruin my debut as a salonnière.

Ernest Hemingway looked especially sullen against the backdrop of Stein's and Picasso's merriment. The more hangdog his expression, the harder they laughed. The two men were standing, and Gertrude was on her favorite ornate Florentine throne, so high her feet dangled as she held court.

By way of introduction, Gertrude Stein drew me immediately into the conversation. "Henri. You know Picasso, and this is Hemingway. They just met, and already they're in an argument."

"It's not an argument," Hemingway said. I could hardly believe my ears. I had imagined him with such a deep, dominant voice, and he was whining. "I just resist the way Picasso stereotypes people. Gertrude does it, too. I find it offensive."

"Let Henri be the judge, then," said Gertrude.

"Fine," said Picasso, finessing us all with his colossal charm. "It's very plain. I simply told our Mr. Hemingway here that Americans have a virginal quality. Unrelated to their actual experience, of course. I don't notice so much that you are men or women but that you all seem like virgins. You, too, Henri, seem very virginal."

"Thank you, Pablo," I said, feeling immediately comfortable with him this evening, as I had when I interviewed him for *En Vogue*. The possibility that he might have stolen paintings stashed in his atelier did flash through my mind, but I was determined to assume he was innocent until proven guilty.

"You see?" Gertrude gloated. "Henri agrees. And she's not offended."

"Henri is a woman," Hemingway said dryly.

"And a virgin," I added.

Hemingway gave me a horrified look, and then realized I was kidding and pretended to be amused.

"What's your point, Hemingway?" Gertrude Stein asked.

"Virginity in women is considered a virtue," he explained. "In men it is considered a lack of some kind. A defect rather than an ideal."

Gertrude started laughing hysterically, great roars of pure joy, drowning out Hemingway's very serious gender distinctions.

"A virtue? By whom?" Gertrude Stein asked. Then she turned and shouted across the room. "Hey Alice, is virginity a virtue?"

"Only in Protestant fairy tales, and then only among the dwarves," Alice responded instantaneously. To this day I have never met anyone who could deliver nasty witticisms as quickly as Alice. She was the Calamity Jane of dry humor. Without skipping a beat, she resumed her conversation with the group of wives she was entertaining on the side of the studio nearest the kitchen.

"Don't mistake impotence for virginity," cautioned Picasso.

"You're treading on thin ice, Pablo. Impotence is Hemingway's favorite subject," Stein said.

Hemingway, who had roused himself momentarily to clarify the difference between male and female virginity, plunged back into humorless annoyance. I could see that he shared my horror of being made fun of, so I attempted to alleviate his distress. "He's got a point," I said, quickly trying to think of one.

"Don't be so literal, you two," said Gertrude Stein. "Pablo just means Americans approach everything fresh every time. It's because our land is virginal. I have always said that in America there is more space where no one is than where anyone is."

"Yes," said Picasso, applauding Gertrude Stein's explanation with delicate claps, vaguely rhythmic like a flamenco dancer's. He was always very dramatic, yet equally refined. "You can't push an American down. He will get up again and start somewhere else, over and over. He will never learn."

Hemingway seemed about ready to take offense, but Picasso held a finger up to shush him. "That is why you make so much progress," Pablo continued, wagging his finger. "In Europe we have learned far too much. We have prostituted ourselves to learning. The only virgins left in Europe are the statues in Catholic churches, and most of them are badly chipped. Even my own daughters were not born virgins. They knew everything about everything, including men. Their hymens were a mere formality."

"I didn't know you had daughters," I said.

"Don't be so literal," he laughed. "You see? Only the virgin believes everything she is told."

"Ah yes," I said, "the gullibility of virgins."

Hemingway made a face. I couldn't understand why the concept of virginity irked him so much.

"Don't worry," Pablo said. "No one is calling *you* a virgin, Hemingway."

"At least not *that* kind of a virgin," Gertrude Stein added. "God knows you've had your share of *women*. As for the rest of it," and Gertrude Stein looked straight at me, "your guess is as good as mine."

That did it for Hemingway. He retreated to the sideboard at the far end of the studio to pour himself another glass of eau-de-vie.

Gertrude and Pablo looked like two mischievous children. Although I readily subscribe to Alice's view that they are both geniuses, I must say I wonder that genius has such a juvenile, antic disposition.

"What makes your baby-faced protégé so defensive?" Picasso asked.

"Have you met his wife?" Gertrude Stein said ironically.

"Yes, but ..." Picasso looked quizzical.

By way of explanation, Gertrude Stein nodded across the room in the direction of the clutch of women Alice had herded into the corner. Conspicuously there, among others, was Bryher, the very wealthy and generous patron of so many women of letters, most notably H. D. I had often seen her picture in *Variety,* photographed at some benefit or other in Capri or London. Heiress to the shipping fortune of Britain's Sir John Ellerman, Bryher had married the writer and fellow homosexual Robert McAlmon to get her family out of her hair. Having secured her inheritance, she lavishly spent her millions on the arts.

Next to the heiress was a mousy but pretty young woman who wasn't exactly hanging on Bryher but clearly wouldn't leave her alone. I assumed correctly that it was Hadley, Hemingway's wife and the mother of Bumby, Gertrude and Alice's godson.

"Oh," said Picasso, shaking his head sympathetically. "Poor Hemingway. I too used to be attracted to sapphists."

"Back in your virginal days?" I asked.

Picasso laughed. "No. Back when I was afraid of women."

"Oh, so now sapphists aren't women?"

"Don't be silly, Henri," said Gertrude. "We never were. Gender is approximate. And we've slipped through the cracks."

"Gender is approximate," I repeated. "I bet Hemingway would just love that."

"He does. That's his problem."

Picasso smirked.

"But it's his night," Stein continued, "and we've got to stop torturing him. Though I admit there's no one more fun to rib than Hemingway, except maybe Fitzgerald."

"Whose gender approximates that of a debutante," observed Picasso. "Trapped in a male body, of course. His skirts tucked into his jockstrap."

"Picasso, you're incorrigible," Gertrude Stein said. "Fitz is much more the Southern courtesan type. But let's not split hairs." Standing up, or rather shimmying off her high throne, she strode across the room, adopting a much more official countenance. She splashed a little eau-de-vie into a goblet and then turned to face the assemblage.

"Now that Hemingway has filled his glass..." Gertrude announced.

"Which is not exactly a novel event," murmured Picasso.

"...I would like to propose a toast to our distinguished guest of honor."

"Hear, hear," cried the wives energetically in the corner.

"To the publication of *In Our Time,* a work of young genius..." Stein continued.

"The premature ejaculations of a budding virgin," Picasso whispered, and I realized with this fresh burst of hostility that he was jealous of Gertrude Stein's apparent affection for Hemingway.

"...may it be the first in a long line of prodigious novels!" Stein concluded with great fanfare.

Everybody raised their glasses and drank. Hemingway's stature, so slight, even treacly, moments before, swelled impressively. I saw for the first time the criminally handsome American prodigy that would rise with phallic magnificence into such an icon of masculinity. But the phallus is such a vulnerable and fickle fellow. I wondered if his art would ever survive this whimsical side of his character, filled to the bursting point one minute and limp the next.

As everyone continued clinking glasses and Hemingway poured himself yet another eau-de-vie, Bryher detached herself from Alice's peanut gallery. I noticed that Toklas warily surveyed her every move. Although Bryher was dressed in suit and tie, was a sapphist, and referred to herself in the third person as "he," she was earmarked a "wife" and was always relegated to Alice's corner at 27 rue de Fleurus.

Gossipmongers claimed that Alice had strict orders to keep all the wives preoccupied while Gertrude Stein conversed with their husbands. And it is true that she was forever whisking women off to show them some bibelot or trade recipes in the kitchen. Sylvia Beach was particularly critical of Alice's "wife-proof" technique, which she considered an insult to women. Even Alice kidded that she would one day write the book titled *Wives of Geniuses I Have Sat With.*

But I knew better. Alice never had strict orders to do anything. At all times, she was in charge of everything. The criteria of farming out people to Alice's sewing circle had relatively little to do with gender. It was a method of weeding out the bores. And since intellectual snobbery has for some reason always been considered more heinous than discrimination against women, Gertrude and Alice let the rumors run rampant, as though being a wife—a role Alice herself played with consummate virtuosity—were a less exalted position. They never let on that the opposite was true, and that Alice really wore the pants in the family.

So did Bryher. She sidled up to Gertrude Stein, put her arm around her (which made Stein squirm until the arm was removed), and raised her glass. "And I, too, would like to propose a toast," Bryher said with forced bravura. Ordinarily reserved, she was obviously embarrassed by her own audacity in proposing a toast.

I wondered at the time why she tortured herself with such public exposure, but I figured out later this was just one in an endless series of unsuccessful ploys designed to secure Gertrude Stein's friendship. "To Gertrude Stein's *The Making of Americans,*" Bryher continued, almost inaudibly. Alice eyed her like a collie watching a straying ewe. "Let us build on the momentum of Hemingway's triumph..."

Hemingway beamed.

"...the triumph of one of Gertrude Stein's most precocious protégés..."

Hemingway rolled his eyes.

"...to get this masterpiece into print."

Picasso turned to me. "All one thousand one hundred and twenty-three pages of it."

My jaw dropped. "Gertrude never told me her novel was *that* long."

"Brevity is the soul of wit," he quipped.

"Hear, hear!" everyone shouted again, and Gertrude Stein basked, enjoying the attention but not dependent on it to pump up her already buoyant ego. So unlike the inflatable Hemingway.

Like the gag hooks that pull bad performers off vaudeville stages, appearing out of nowhere, stage-left, Alice was the human hook. And Bryher was the hapless performer, whisked off center stage and back into the wings along with the Cone sisters and Hadley Hemingway.

The wonder was that although Bryher's "husband," Robert McAlmon, was publishing *The Making of Americans,* she still wasn't admitted to the inner sanctum of Gertrude Stein's court. This was all the more mystifying since everybody knew that McAlmon's press, the Contact Editions, was funded almost entirely by Bryher's estate. Yet

Hemingway, who was merely checking the novel's one thousand one hundred and twenty-three page proofs against Alice's assiduously typed original, was allowed to fraternize with Picasso and Stein, unmolested by Alice's herding instincts.

I doubted if Bryher could possibly be that much of a bore and began to suspect that Alice found her threatening rather than tedious. She was attractive in that clipped, repressed British way, and I concluded that Alice's "wives" consisted not only of bores but also of rivals.

As time went on I realized that Alice's jealousy was just part of the problem. Of all the salonnières, Bryher was the most politically minded, with the obvious exception of Janet Flanner, whose *New Yorker* columns focused increasingly on foreign policy. And Gertrude Stein was as uninterested in national politics as she was in the so-called cause of women. She purposely avoided newspapers, and habitués knew better than to talk politics at 27 rue de Fleurus. Alice took it upon herself to make sure that Bryher's incessant chatter about affairs of state didn't intrude into the ivory tower of Gertrude Stein's genius. Although their political indifference would eventually unnerve me, when I first arrived in Paris I was too awed by the aesthetic merits of the salons to worry about their cloistered oblivion to the world at large.

The *raison d'être* of the salons was art for art's sake. Gertrude Stein had improved on this motto to the extent that at 27 rue de Fleurus, all art was for *her* sake. Everyone there that evening was enlisted in the endeavor of getting Gertrude Stein's magnum opus published. Yet the evening was purportedly in honor of Hemingway.

Once again I was astonished at Alice's skill as stage manager. Much of Gertrude's true genius resided in her having found Alice B. Toklas. They were the perfect couple.

What did Alice get out of this arrangement? She presided over one of the most dazzling bohemian salons in the Western world. She had a professional status as personal secretary, agent, publisher, and publicist. And she had love.

Gertrude Stein returned with Hemingway to where Picasso and I stood. I took advantage of this changing of the guard to join Alice's wives. Alice greeted me graciously and introduced me to everyone, including Hadley Hemingway, Bryher, and the Cone sisters—Etta and Claribel. Gertrude Stein had met the latter two while attending medical school at Johns Hopkins where Dr. Claribel Cone was doing research in pathology while simultaneously holding a professorship at the Women's Medical College of Baltimore. I would eventually discover that Etta was an equally accomplished woman. I must admit, however, that their intellectual statures were not immediately apparent to me.

It was all I could do not to stare at the Cone sisters. Their appearance was as goofy as their names. In fact, they bore an uncanny resemblance to Alice the Goon, and I suddenly realized why she had been my favorite comic-strip character as a little girl back in Bliss. I must have sensed a kind of kinship with her, not because I was particularly gawky or maladroit, but because her clumsy charm and irresistible foibles somehow appealed to the nascent sapphist in me. It didn't take me long to figure out that Etta and Claribel were in the process of being conned by Alice into spending even more of their formidable fortune (they were one of the First Families of Baltimore) on yet another Picasso. Gertrude and Alice had chosen the Cone sisters as Pablo's unofficial patrons. When he got particularly hungry, it immediately became apparent that they desperately needed another of his paintings.

Thanks to Alice's badgering, the Cones' collection of Cubist masterpieces was second only to Gertrude Stein's. Yet they were still reluctant collectors, not yet fully converted by the evangelical zeal with which Gertrude Stein preached modern art.

"But we already have three from the Blue Period, Alice," Etta said.

"Four," corrected Claribel.

"But it's magnificent," Alice argued.

"But where will we put it?"

Never had I heard such a luxury question, the problem of where to put yet another Picasso. "It's an investment," Alice advised them.

"What does Gertrude think?"

"If our money wasn't so tied up now in the publication of her novel, I assure you we'd be buying it ourselves."

Both Etta and Claribel's brows furled, besieged with the worried expression that only the very rich wear when contemplating parting with money they won't even miss. Alice pulled out the last stops. "Gertrude wants you to buy it." They acquiesced immediately. The Sibyl of Montparnasse had spoken through the Oracle of Alice.

I wondered secretly if the painting in question was listed on Lieutenant Dupin's registry of stolen art, so I nonchalantly asked Alice to point it out. By way of answering, Toklas gestured towards *Prodigal Son among Pigs,* which was hung in precisely the same spot on the wall where I remembered seeing Juan Gris's *Dish of Pears.* Gris's canvas was nowhere to be found.

I breathed a sigh of relief. Perhaps I had been wrong after all. Perhaps my memory of the stolen paintings was nothing more than an elaborate fantasy born of Dupin's conspiracy theories and my own latent paranoia.

While Alice was conducting her informal auction, Hadley's coquettish assault on Bryher continued. I pretended to be engaged in Alice's investment schemes in order to observe Mrs. Hemingway on the sly.

"Bryher, I understand your marriage to Robert is merely a formality," Hadley said suggestively. She all but winked.

"Yes, of course." Bryher, knowing full well what Hadley was up to, gave her a curious look—as if she were watching the movements of a bird of prey, or a magpie raiding another bird's nest: very detached, with a sort of morbid fascination. Ordinarily, one saw this look on the faces of jaded married women watching their husbands' shameless flirtations. "One of the problems with being an heiress is that you must appease your family," she explained. "I'd have cut off relations with them long ago, but I'm rather fond of my inheritance, you know. How else could we get people like Djuna Barnes and Ezra Pound published? And your husband, of course. Even he was published on the strength of my legacy before his latest triumph."

"My husband," Hadley sighed. "Sometimes I wish I'd married for convenience. If I could just pass myself off as married, the way you do, I'd be free to do what I please for a change."

"What do you mean?" Bryher asked, pretending ignorance while clearly finding a sort of prurient pleasure in Hadley's clumsy advances.

"I'm married to a goddamned fairy, for Chrissake!" Hadley hissed.

Bryher was hooked. "Hemingway, a fairy? What on earth do you mean?"

"I mean he wants me to ravage him. You know, play the man in the bedroom. And cut my hair like his so I look more masculine. And all I really want is to be like you."

Tears flooded Hadley's eyes. Bryher looked like a civilian shoved into a priest's confessional booth, hearing what she shouldn't be hearing.

"I mean, we're just like you and Robert," Hadley sniffed, "two married homosexuals. But Ernest won't admit it! He keeps pretending there are married couples all over America and Europe and God knows where else sodomizing each other."

What had started out as a flirtation had turned into a maudlin heart-to-heart.

"I've told him time and again that *women* are supposed to use dildos. Not married couples."

I suspected Hadley shared, at least that evening, Hemingway's overfondness for Alice's homemade eau-de-vie. Although I had often heard that the Fitzgeralds aired their dirty laundry for all of Europe to see, getting the lowdown on the Hemingways' bedroom caught me unawares. The dynamics of the whole phenomenon of expatriation were quickly becoming clear to me. Imagine trying to be a sapphist in Utah, or a spinster goon in Baltimore. Imagine the repercussions of referring to yourself as "he" in Surrey. Imagine Hadley venting her marital frustrations at a party in St. Louis. And you'll be on the next steamer to gay Paris.

Expatriation was such a fabulous alternative to burning at the stake.

Bryher's British propriety did not permit her to respond this time. But as an American, I of course had no shame and could no longer remain silent.

"Hadley," I said. Her face jerked toward mine, a lone tear streaming down her cheek. "Have you told him?"

"Told him what?"

"That you're a sapphist."

"God, yes," she groaned.

"And what did he say?"

"He said that's why he married me!" she wailed.

The news was indeed shocking. I wanted to ask Hadley what had possessed her to marry him if she was so adverse to dildos, let alone the penis itself. But Alice had noticed Hadley's mounting hysteria, and she abruptly whisked her off to the kitchen to show her all the things one could do with eggs.

Etta and Claribel were taking advantage of Alice's absence to deliberate on how much a Blue Period was really worth in American dollars these days. Bryher looked vacant and a little dazed. In deference to her violated sense of decency, I decided to squelch my impulse to explore the ramifications of the Hemingways' phallic skirmishes.

"Your jailer is gone," I said as if in cahoots, nodding in the direction of the kitchen and Alice. "Want to try to crash the genius's party again?"

Bryher looked grateful and relieved.

"Maybe Gertrude will let me join them if I'm with you. I'm afraid she never forgave me for marrying Robert, even if it was 'just a formality,' as Hadley put it. I know Gertrude doesn't approve of married sapphists, but I can only take so much of the wives."

"Apparently they're dangerous," I said over my shoulder as we walked toward the husbands. Gertrude Stein was adjudicating a very heated conversation from her Tuscan throne.

"If it's not autobiographical, it smells of museums."

"That's very surprising, coming from you," Hemingway said. "Your work looks more like stylistic innovation than autobiography to me. I fail to see the autobiographical component of, say, *Tender Buttons*."

Bryher and I burst out laughing.

"You wouldn't," Stein said dryly.

"Why?" Hemingway asked.

"It's not about virginity or impotence," Picasso suggested.

"Come on," Hemingway insisted. "Why?"

"You tell him," Stein said, looking at me.

"Because it's about the clitoris. Or the plural of clitoris, which is what? Clitorises or clitori? You know, tender buttons."

Hemingway actually blushed.

"Nonsense," Gertrude Stein said. "I'm surprised at you, Henri. It's about female sexuality."

"Same difference."

"Maybe in your impoverished existence, but my sexuality is not limited to the clitoris…"

Hemingway all but ran to the bottle of eau-de-vie across the room. "And he wonders why I tell him he's ninety percent Rotarian," she said with disappointment.

"Come back, Hemingway. We promise we'll only talk about penises from now on," Picasso said. He walked over to Hemingway and whispered something apparently lewd. They both laughed with the gruff fellowship of toughs. Thus fortified, Hemingway rejoined us with a replenished glass.

"What I mean is this, Hemingway," Stein continued. "Someone like James Joyce looks modern because he puts old words on the page in a new order. But he really smells of museums because it's the same damn story all over again. Just another tedious history of the phallus. He couldn't even think of a new title. *Ulysses.* It's pathetic. We all read that in college, for pity sake. Let's move on."

"Oh, hell, Gertrude," objected Hemingway. "You're just jealous because he's causing a big splash and you're not."

"The very fact that he's being praised proves my point. You see, it's generally the people who smell of museums who are accepted. The truly new are ridiculed."

"Using obscurity as the basis of your superiority seems desperate, Gertrude. Even pathetic."

"It's true, Hemingway. Ask Picasso. Remember when they laughed at Matisse's *La Femme au Chapeau* at the Salon d'Automne des Indépendants?"

"Actually, it was worse than that," Picasso said. "They scratched at it. They tried to peel the paint off."

"Exactly. And what is the subject of that painting?"

"Well, of course, it is a painting of his wife, who is a milliner."

"I rest my case," Gertrude said, triumphantly.

"Unfortunately, I don't know what your case is," Hemingway complained.

"Precisely this: that autobiography is the crux of the avant-garde. If only you, Hemingway, would write about yourself, you could leave the museums behind forever. As it stands, your style is revolutionary.

But your subject matter is embalmed in mothballs."

"I thought you liked *In Our Time.*"

"I love it. Now write about yourself. Unless you're afraid to. Are you afraid the skeleton in your closet looks like Dorian Gray?"

"I don't have a skeleton in my closet."

"Now you sound like me saying I don't have a subconscious."

"But what about your famous iceberg technique, Hemingway?" I asked. "If the great writer submerges seven-eighths of the story, what are you hiding beneath the tip of the iceberg?"

"I'm hiding nothing. I'm just not cluttering the truth. It's there, like a clean, well-lighted place. It's stark and true and..."

"...and hard." Gertrude Stein finished his sentence.

"Yes. Very hard."

"And what is it, exactly, that separates the hard from the tender?" Gertrude Stein asked him in all seriousness. They had transcended their petty emotional defenses, and for the first time the salon ascended to the exalted aesthetic level I had always fantasized about back in the States.

"I'll tell you exactly what the difference is," Hemingway said. "I want to write one true sentence. I say things barely, not even once. You say them over and over and over again."

"Yes," Gertrude Stein agreed. "Like a dog lapping water. But that's not repetition. That's realism. Your one true sentence is make-believe. As if a photograph tells the whole story. Stop telling fairy tales, Hemingway."

"Like a dog lapping water," Hemingway repeated. "Explain."

"It all started with the rhythms of my own splashings in the bath," Gertrude said, holding her finger up for silence as if we, too, could hear the sound of the water if only we perked up our ears. "Listening to them, I discovered how to say what I needed to say. It wasn't that the newness was in the splashes themselves, but they were the medium."

Hemingway was rapt.

"Later, when we got our poodle, Basket, and I heard him drinking water, the noise of his lapping tongue showed me the difference between sentences and paragraphs. I knew then—and know it every time I listen to Basket—that paragraphs are emotional and sentences are not. It's very clear, particularly if the water is very cold."

"Why water?" Hemingway asked.

"Why tongues?" I asked simultaneously.

Gertrude Stein shot me a knowing look, but chose for the sake of Hemingway's Rotarian conventionality to answer his question instead of mine.

"Its fluidity, no doubt. You see, there is your answer, Hemingway. Your sentences are hard and static, and mine are tender and fluid."

"Is it because you're a woman and I'm a man?"

"Not at all. It's a question of museums. Museums are full of hard sentences, written in stone and canonized by professors. Fluid, tender sentences threaten their authority. They feel the need to exclude writers like me to protect the sanctity of the canon, the static quo."

"Yet they asked you to speak at Oxford and Cambridge," Hemingway reminded her.

"Yes. But that was more like a carnival, and I was the freak show."

This image must have tickled Picasso because he snickered and performed a bizarre series of pantomimes, apparently impersonating Gertrude Stein as the star of a three-ring circus. Gertrude Stein ignored him, though Bryher and I cracked a smile.

"I'm not complaining, mind you," Stein continued. "And neither did the students. So many of them are bored stiff with the cold, hard authority of academe. They desperately need to stretch their legs, if only to thwart the dons."

"You know, your pasture story says it best, Gertrude," I said, recalling an anecdote she had recounted over tea the previous week.

"Even more than dogs lapping and tubs splashing."

"Which pasture story?"

"The one where you and Alice made pilgrimages to cow pastures so that you could write."

"Of course. That's how I wrote *Before the Flowers of Friendship Faded Friendship Faded*. I used to set up my camp stool, and then Alice would maneuver a cow from one side of the field to the other. She prodded their behinds with a little stick to get them going, and then steered them with a bigger stick. Ambidextrous. Very agile. When they had traversed the entire field, I folded up my camp stool and stationed myself at the other end of the pasture and she herded the cows in a different direction. The clinking and clunking of their bells inspired a whole different kind of sentence."

She paused, as if for emphasis, but Hemingway was clearly impatient to hear more. Judging from the expression on his face, he truly believed that clinking and clunking were the muses of modern art. "Different?" he prompted. "How?"

"It was then that I realized that nouns are redundant and unnecessary. I began to write with verbs everywhere—verbs beginning, middling, and ending sentences. Tender verb paragraphs. Even you, Hemingway, will admit that nouns are hard."

He nodded, apparently impressed with the logic if not the logistics of Gertrude's pastoral linguistic experiments. Picasso, on the other hand, was doing all that he could to stifle his hilarity. I attributed this discrepancy to the difference between painters and writers. When it came to the rhythms of everyday sounds, Picasso was out of his element. He could recognize their visual patterns, but only Stein could hear the silent words whispered by everyday objects.

"That was how I invented the continuous present. You see, it's all about fluidity, and no museum could ever house the present. Which is fluid."

Hemingway looked puzzled. "So you write in pastures. And in the bathtub."

"And in Godiva, our automobile. I wrote *The Birthplace of Bonnes* and *American Biography* using the rhythm of the street and the purr of the motor like tuning forks, or a metronome. But *Mildred's Thoughts* is by far my best car piece."

"And where do you write, Hemingway?" I asked.

"He writes in museums," Gertrude Stein interjected, but fondly, like a coach trying to coax the best performance out of her athlete.

"No, I write in the bullfighting ring. The bulls whiz by and I finesse them. Simply. Cleanly."

"I let them gore me," Picasso said, suddenly serious. "I can never paint unless I'm bleeding all over the place."

"Which is, of course, just another example of autobiography," Gertrude said. "My ambition is to write *Everybody's Autobiography.*"

"My ambition is to distill the autobiographical imperfections out of my writing," Hemingway said.

"My ambition is to render reality, which is itself a form of autobiography, with unwavering precision," Picasso said.

"How can you say that when your work is often so abstract?" Hemingway asked.

Picasso immediately took offense. "Abstract? Never!"

"But what about your theory about camouflage?" Hemingway insisted. "How the camouflage of each country is different, and how the subtle differences are the signatures of each nationality? And that camouflage itself proves the organic inevitability of modern abstraction? Gertrude Stein told me you once said that it was you— the Cubists—who actually inspired camouflage."

"That's not abstraction," insisted Picasso, still very much annoyed. "That's self-preservation. What could be more autobiographical than self-preservation?"

Gertrude Stein looked equally scandalized. "Hemingway, the minute painting gets abstract it gets pornographic."

Hemingway looked sheepish. "But isn't that what modern art is all about?"

"Pornography?"

"Abstraction?"

Just as Gertrude Stein was filling her great lungs to launch into another aesthetic diatribe, Lily the Duchesse de Clermont-Tonnerre barged into the room with Djuna Barnes in tow. Djuna Barnes was no less than my professional hero, the famous American journalist who had submitted herself to force-feeding to generate an article documenting the hunger strikes of suffragettes protesting the Great War. She had also rushed into a burning building to experience—and write about—being rescued by the New York Fire Department's Emergency Squad. I aspired to the kind of hands-on journalism she had been acclaimed for in the States before her expatriation.

Professional admiration aside, she was a knockout, exquisite in her tight leopard pillbox, with her upturned, patrician nose. When they first arrived at the salon that night, Djuna was even more striking than Lily, though she was on the verge of being upstaged.

I had learned from Gertrude Stein that Lily, or "the Duchesse" as they all called her, was one of Natalie Barney's two main lovers, the other being the controversial portrait painter Romaine Brooks. The Duchesse had apparently given up her husband and a vast inheritance, including a seventeenth-century mansion in the Faubourg Saint-Germain, to be a sapphist. Not everyone was as lucky as Bryher, whose only real sacrifice to the cause of her sexuality was her given name, Winifred Ellerman. Ironically, that was all Lily had left; she was a duchess in name only.

With a flourish, the Duchesse de Clermont-Tonnerre removed her English bowler hat and everyone gasped. I mean they gasped really loudly, the way people do when a racehorse's bone snaps or a nun's habit blows off.

The Duchesse's hair was cropped short, above her ears even. She might as well have been bald. None of us had ever seen bristles on a woman's neck before, or knew that women, no different than men, have little sideburns and graying temple hair. The Duchesse was not an overly beautiful woman, certainly not one to turn heads. Until now. Now she was stunning.

At least Gertrude Stein was stunned, mesmerized so utterly that only the words "Fátima" and "Lourdes" can conjure up the way her gaze registered a beatific vision.

Hemingway headed straight for the eau-de-vie, looking very nervous.

Hadley, his wife, giggled and blushed.

Picasso whinnied his laugh, delighted by any breach of conventional propriety, especially among the nobility.

In the corner, Alice's wives burst into applause.

I noticed a spot the barber had missed just behind Lily's left ear lobe.

The Duchesse said to Gertrude Stein, "What do you think of it?"

"It suits your head," she stammered.

"This is what you will have to come to," Lily said prophetically.

"What on earth possessed you?" Bryher asked. Her own hair was cut rather short in a chic French coif, but she looked like Rapunzel next to the Duchesse.

"I've grown tired of being typecast. Now that I've shed my family legacy and my husband and even my long luxurious locks, maybe I can let my hair down without raising eyebrows or being written up in 'The Town Tattle' as some kind of prodigal aristocrat."

"I think we can safely say that you'll be disowned *tout de suite,*" Gertrude said. "It's a stroke of genius."

During this exchange I noticed that Hadley, who had moved well beyond the blushing stage, was slowly making her way across the room as if drawn like a magnet to Lily's coif. Hemingway had noticed it too.

When she came within striking distance of the Duchesse, Hadley said, "Can I touch it?"

"By all means, help yourself." A tall woman, Lily accommodated Hadley's desire by bending over slightly and bowing her head. Everybody, including the Duchesse herself, thought this a perfectly natural request. I know I longed to stroke the first bristles I had ever seen on a woman. There was, admittedly, a kind of orgiastic Dionysian look in Hadley's eyes, but every woman in the place was transfixed, and we thought nothing of it.

Hemingway, on the other hand, went raving mad. Just as Hadley was about to brush her fingers across the short hairs on the Duchesse's neck, he flew across the room and intercepted her caress.

"Hadley," he said with terrible politeness between clenched teeth, "we must go." I believe that even I would have obeyed the threat in his voice.

It was a very quiet and very terrifying scene, so dramatic we couldn't pretend it wasn't happening, but too intimate to know how to respond. As he dragged Hadley out of the salon, I was reminded of cartoons depicting cavemen dragging their women around by the hair.

We all stood dazed in their wake. The guest of honor had stormed out of his own party.

"What happened?" Lily finally said.

"You can't tell me Hemingway just noticed that Hadley was getting all hot and bothered with all the sapphists around," I said. "She practically mauled Bryher before you got here."

"I didn't even know that was Hadley Hemingway," Lily said. "I thought it was just another one of us."

Then I remembered what Hadley had said about Hemingway wanting them to have matching haircuts, and the brouhaha about dildos and bedroom role-playing. Suddenly it all fell into place.

"My God," I gasped. A momentary compunction seized me as I wondered if I should incriminate the Hemingways. But had they not incriminated themselves?

"What is it?" Gertrude Stein asked.

"Hemingway has been trying to get Hadley to cut her hair short. Like Lily's."

Everyone still looked baffled except Djuna Barnes, who had more experience with men than the rest of us. "Sure," she said. "It's OK for Hemingway to make his wife into a little boy. In the privacy of their bedroom she can be as masculine as she pleases—a regular rough rider. But God forbid she should want a woman. Then she's crossed the line."

"Come on," Picasso said. "Even Hemingway can't be that repressed. I barely know him, and even I know he's a sucker for sapphists. Heaven knows he's attracted enough to Gertrude."

Alice made an obscene gesture and a dirty noise.

"He hasn't admitted it to himself," Gertrude said.

"That he's a homosexual?"

"No. That he's got a fetish for homosexuals of the opposite sex."

Picasso squealed with glee. "Hemingway, the great white hunter of sapphists. I came tonight only as a favor to you, Gertrude. I never dreamed it would be so fun. But now you will excuse me. I have an irresistible urge to follow Hemingway's example. Let me go find Olga and show her who is boss, as you Americans say. Besides, I am the only man left here, and I am afraid of earning my own reputation as a connoisseur of masculine women."

Escorting him to the door, Gertrude and Alice assured him that all of Paris already knew about his sexual fetishes. The last thing I heard him say as he left was that in that case he would take up boxing like Hemingway so that he could beef up his image.

All the guests had gone home now and only the daughters of Sappho were left. We sat down on the overstuffed couches to gossip and rave periodically about Lily's daring coiffure. Alice made a delicious, very spicy herb tea, and everyone really relaxed until the inevitable question was raised.

"Where's Natalie?" the Duchesse asked. "I had hoped to debut my haircut with all of my best friends present."

Gertrude suddenly looked a little befuddled, and Alice appeared by her side within seconds to explain. "Natalie bowed out at the last minute. There's been a misunderstanding."

"A misunderstanding?"

"An unfortunate mistake."

"Aw, come on, Alice," said Gertrude. "Let's face it. Sometimes I have an enormous mouth."

"Nonsense, Gertrude. It was my fault." Alice looked Lily square in the face, as if admonishing her with her honesty. "I'm only telling you this so that you won't follow Natalie's cue and cut us off. Virgil Thomson was over the other night and we were gossiping about everybody American in Paris, as we often do. And he asked me, if Natalie was such a Casanova, who does she do it with, and where does she get them? And then I made a little joke."

"A not very funny joke, it turns out," Gertrude admitted.

"But a joke nevertheless. I said I thought Natalie shopped around in the toilets of the Louvre Department Store."

"Well, I guess I really didn't think it was a joke," Gertrude said, picking up the story. "It got me thinking. Who *did* Natalie sleep with? I had heard of *les grandes affaires,* like Renée Vivien and Romaine, of course, and, well, you, Lily. But what about all those other nights, what with Natalie's voracious appetite and all? I got to wondering if it were always literary ladies or actresses or whether she ever indulged in any kind of rough trade."

Gertrude paused to let us savor this deliciously raunchy detail.

"And then I saw Gwen in front of the Café des Deux-Magots and I really stuck my foot in it. She had been a house guest at Natalie's for quite some time, and I started asking her about Natalie's escapades. I guess my voice sort of carried and Natalie heard about my indiscreet questions not only from Gwen but from a few of her other friends who had been drinking *infusions* at the Deux-Magots."

Lily was shaking her head, wagging her finger at Gertrude Stein like a mother with her naughty child. Apparently, Stein had a reputation for outrageous faux pas.

"Gertrude," Lily said, "not everyone can be as married as you and Alice are."

The Duchesse immediately cut through all of the sloppy, gossipy details to the cold hard truth. Sapphic freedoms clearly galled Gertrude Stein. Where Natalie Barney was a confirmed libertine, Gertrude Stein was as loyal as a bloodhound. It was their one perennial bone of contention.

Personally, I had no idea where I stood in this debate. I certainly respected Gertrude Stein's devotion to Alice B. Toklas. But I also knew I couldn't wait to explore Natalie's Temple of Love at 20 rue Jacob.

Lily must have noticed my wistful availability. As the evening progressed, she made a point of sitting conspicuously close to me on a small love seat in the corner, despite the fact that there were any number of available chairs and settees throughout the room. We drank our spiced tea and chatted with the abrupt intimacy of strangers sharing a love seat.

The Duchesse Lily de Clermont-Tonnerre and Djuna Barnes were the first two women I had met from Natalie Barney's salon, and I was frankly bowled over. My awe was so transparent that Gertrude

Stein finally descended again from her Tuscan throne, signaling me to follow her to the back atelier where she closed the door behind us.

"What do you think you're doing?" Gertrude Stein demanded.

"What do you mean?"

"Are you flirting with the Duchesse, or am I losing my mind? I hope for your sake it's the latter."

"She's flirting with *me*," I said defensively.

"Yes," Gertrude Stein agreed. "Just like the Big Bad Wolf flirted with Little Red Riding Hood. It's your job to rebuff her advances, Henri. She's Natalie Barney's girlfriend, remember? Some things are sacred, even to Natalie."

"That's not what I heard." If only Gertrude Stein could have realized how ridiculous this all sounded to me—traveling halfway around the world to find a sapphic paradise, and then being told to look, not touch.

"You heard wrong," she said flatly.

"I thought Natalie Barney preached free love and sapphic promiscuity and all that."

"It's a myth, Henri," Gertrude Stein said adamantly. "It's just Natalie's way of feathering her own bed."

"That's precisely my point," I said, but Gertrude Stein clearly had a different understanding of the expression. Where I envisioned a harem of happy sapphists in well-feathered beds, she must have pictured a long line of jilted and angry women tapping their toes impatiently outside of Natalie Barney's bedroom. If I've said it once I've said it a thousand times—one sapphist's paradise is another's dread inferno.

I stared forlornly at Gertrude Stein, hoping against hope that sapphic promiscuity wasn't just a myth. By the time we rejoined the others, Lily and Djuna had put on their coats. They were off to 20 rue Jacob to show off Lily's new coif.

The Duchesse seemed to have utterly forgotten about her earlier advances. I didn't mind, really, since I imagined they all flirted mercilessly with one another simply as a matter of course. My only real regret was that they were leaving before I'd managed to get myself invited to Natalie Barney's salon.

Bidding us all an extravagant farewell, the Duchesse and Djuna seemed to take what was left of the night's festivities along with them. I felt like the gawky little sister stuck at home with Mom and Dad.

Miss Henrietta Adams
Hôtel Résidence les Cèdres
12 rue des Dames
17th Arrondissement
Paris, France

September 15, 1925

Dear Miss Adams:

We are very pleased with your most recent submission on
Matisse. The Board has approved it with minor revisions for
the November issue of En Vogue. I think you will see from
the enclosed final copy that the changes and deletions were
incidental, so I am assuming there is no need to wait for
you to sign off on them. Thus far, your editorials have been
so strong you've got us awaiting your next submission with
our rubber stamp of approval in hand.

Let me comment on a few of the most effective
segments of your portrait of Matisse. I will enumerate them
individually to give you a clear idea of exactly what the
members of the Board (and our subscribers) are looking for.
In effect, as was the case with your excellent piece on
Picasso, you are generating your own models and guidelines
for future biographical articles.

The tone you adopted throughout the piece is
extremely entertaining, especially the hyperbolic epic
quality of your prose. The idea that great historical
cataclysms coincided to advance Matisse's career is very
clever. Did changes in French law (such as the government's
ruling to separate church and state) actually enable Matisse
to buy the convent school he transformed into his atelier?
One way or the other, it's a very humorous story.

Furthermore, your description of the problem of hiring disinterested nudes is delightfully burlesque; at the same time it provides a realistic glimpse of the drama of the artist's studio. (Did the Italian model really paint a tattoo of a different woman's name on his buttocks every time he posed?) And I must report that the Board laughed out loud at your almost slapstick account of the impoverished Hungarian who quieted the rumblings of his empty belly by eating the bread cubes left sitting on the students' painting boards for the purpose of rubbing out crayon drawings. It is no less than hilarious. The tone of these descriptions is not unlike the American tourist scene in your Kahnweiler article, but they work much better here because Americans are not the butt of your subtle satire. Although not all of your articles need be (or even should be) so manifestly humorous, this light treatment of Matisse serves as an excellent counterpoint to your more serious pieces.

I send you greetings from the Board, especially Larry Strachey, who enjoys bragging about how he was responsible for hiring you in the first place. I think he wants to take credit for you as his protégée (which I suppose he thinks is a compliment!). Your new photographer seems to be working out very well, yet another example of your fine work. Full steam ahead!

Sincerely,

Irving P. Dickey
Senior Editor

cc: Board of Editors
En Vogue

CHAPTER SIX

The Paris Underground

Enough was enough. In the States, celibacy had never been my strong suit. In Paris, it was a crime against nature—a mortal sin. I could no longer wait passively for an invitation to Natalie Barney's sapphic salon. So I decided to seize the day.

The next night after a lively domestic dinner with Gertrude and Alice, I descended into the Paris underground without telling a soul. If the rumors I had heard were true, I was destined to find love, or at least lust, among the habitués of the night.

Desperation was not my only motivation. Looking back, I also think I needed the anonymity that nightclubs can provide—the anonymity we all need to act out our darkest and most exquisitely self-destructive impulses, the shadow of our desires. Like it or not, this shadowy alter-ego seems particularly well developed in homosexuals, who indulge it with flamboyant decadence.

The Byronic sapphists of the 1920s—captured so brilliantly in the dark, seductive portraits of Romaine Brooks—did their brooding not in the salons but in the clubs, the underworld of irresistible and sublime damnation. I had heard that women like the famous poet Anna Wickham frequented the Paris underground, maintaining a double life that shocked even Natalie Barney. Djuna Barnes was also well on her way to establishing a reputation as a tragic genius, partly due to her supposedly magnificent and alcoholic lover, Thelma Wood, an elusive legend few salonnières had actually ever met. Expatriate writers were notorious for their dedication to Bacchus. Prohibition in the States had made them chronically thirsty. If they drank for inspiration, their muses had hollow legs. Having progressed too far down the road of genius to tip a mere convivial glass, alcohol for them had become the sacred communion of fallen angels. Cloaked in the velvet night, a gorgeous Lucifer in drag beckoned me.

First I went to Les Lèvres, which had the reputation of being an elegant ladies' club. Women wearing makeup got in free and spent the night vying for drinks bought by the so-called mannish women.

As I said before, I had never thought I cut a particularly masculine figure. I had, after all, shaved my armpits until my arrival in Paris. And I seldom, if ever, wore vests. Next to Gertrude Stein, I was a frilly *femme,* but then who wasn't?

But I had heard there was no straddling of fences in the Paris underground, and my choice was clear. If you wanted an elegant lady—and I wanted one so badly I could taste her—you had to dress the part. So I really played it up, gleaming gold cuff links and all. I even had a red flower in my lapel. Red meant "go" in Paris.

I was surprised when the woman checking coats at Les Lèvres referred to me as *mon frère.* Still a little self-conscious about my newly acquired masculine attire, I took her comment personally, as if she were ridiculing me. Before long, I realized that virtually everybody at Les Lèvres referred to one another as *ma soeur* or *mon frère,* speaking a language that was as foreign to me as French itself had once been—a sapphic tongue whose tone and meaning I did not understand for quite some time.

But the education of Henri Adams was proceeding apace. I found that the sight of all those *soeurs* at Les Lèvres enabled me at least to play the part of the *frère.* And this boded well for a *malheureuse* expatriate in search of a cure for chronic virginity.

An unofficial record had been set among *les soeurs* by Sophie Léon, who had her own stool at the corner of the bar. Capable of snagging a mannish woman with a single bat of one heavily mascaraed eye, she had not found it necessary to buy a drink in over three years. Rumor had it she did not even need her own apartment.

I hadn't heard these rumors. I didn't even know about the stool, which had not yet been designated off limits by the needlepoint cushion emblazoned with the initials "SL," painstakingly stitched by one of Sophie's desperate, cast-off masculine squires. I think of that *frère* with her sewing needle—all thumbs and nowhere near enough thimbles—when I start to lose my temper and need a dose of the ridiculous to cleanse the palate of my warped perspective.

Sophie's famous stool looked like any other stool. I actually sat on it and signaled to the bartender. I had heard that Paris had just discovered the martini, so I ordered one.

A stunning, white-blonde bartender with a crew cut and chiseled cheekbones addressed me with consummate yet understated disdain. At first I didn't know whom she was talking to because she spoke without looking at me, the way real, inveterate mannish women do, staring off into space even when they're flirting with you. *"Cette place est occupée."*

I recount her words in French because the tone and intent were so clear they needed no translation. Everyone in the bar, whether they spoke French or not, knew exactly what the bartender had said. I would have to overcome my faux pas with all the nonchalance I could muster.

Selecting a new seat at the bar, embarrassed but not defeated, I momentarily second-guessed my decision to show up in masculine attire. Had I chosen to play the damsel, I could have just acted silly and flustered and waited for a more chivalrous woman to rescue me from my distress. The bartender never would have treated me with such contempt. But then I saw a pair of eyes staring surreptitiously at me from beneath softly feathered lashes, and I remembered my preference for actively courting ladies-in-waiting rather than passively playing the part myself.

I finally got my martini, though in a flute rather than in the proper conical glass. Then I set out to deflect my previous embarrassment into a performance for the French *femme* who was discreetly watching me from the other side of the bar.

I could tell by the way she was ignoring my smoke rings that I had a chance. So I turned my back to her with deliberate apathy to let her know I was surveying the range of her competition.

I was not disappointed in the decor. More sumptuous than sleazy, it was still reminiscent of a bordello—a touch of honesty rather than class. Languishing ladies were draped everywhere—on sofas, divans, and love seats—immobile except for the movement of arms conducting cigarettes to limpid lips. They would have looked ridiculous in their studied languor if they had not been so beautiful.

The women in neckties or ascots stood or straddled stools. I carefully avoided the myriad mirrors placed strategically in the parlor, to spare myself the vision of my own predatory demeanor. Let the *soeurs* do the looking.

The bartenders were stunning in their tuxedos with blood-red cummerbunds. Tending bar in a club is as provocative as stripping in a tease joint, and I imagined these bartenders had about as much need of their own apartments as Sophie Léon.

Within minutes at Les Lèvres, I had reached a fever pitch of anticipation. My heart beat persistently in my crotch.

By the time I turned back around to check the status of my *soeur*—like a baker checking the rise of her buns—she had finished her cigarette and decided to use the occasion of my attention to stamp it out emphatically.

In New York, such a deliberate snuffing out of a fag might have signified a demand that I terminate my unwonted attentions. But her eyes seemed to belie this interpretation, suggesting an even more figurative meaning. Assuming that she was announcing her impatience with the mere oral gratification of her cigarette, I left my stool and sauntered across the room to assure her that I could provide more substantial satisfactions.

"Hi. I'm Alec. Can I buy you a drink?" The stage name popped out of my mouth quite unexpectedly.

"Vous êtes américaine," she remarked.

"Oui. But I'd still like to buy you a drink."

"OK," she enunciated in clipped French syllables that made even this American expression sound foreign and provocative.

Although she was sitting on a fairly spacious divan, *ma femme* didn't offer to scoot over when I returned with our drinks. Nor did she volunteer her name. To ask would have broken the code of coquettish aloofness.

"Cigarette?"

"Non, merci." We stared in opposite directions for a very long time, but I noticed, with satisfaction, that she stole occasional looks at me. I had already made up my mind that I would pursue her until she either snubbed or embraced me. She was incredibly petite, wearing the kind of skirt only French girls can wear—so tight and tiny they look like dolls turned human.

"What are you doing in Paris?" she finally asked.

"Escaping my Puritan roots."

"You've come to the right place," she informed me. "In France we ostracize Puritans until they emigrate to England."

"Yet another one of your superior French customs. In America we elect them to office."

"Frightening." She paused, and then drew in her breath

emphatically between pursed lips. "Yet I suppose there is something sexy about all that repression and public humiliation. Stocks and pillories and...." She paused suggestively. "And bondage in general."

"Sure. If you're a disciple of the Marquis de Sade," I said ironically.

She looked me straight in the eyes for the first time. *"Mais oui. Et vous?"*

The question, coming as it did out of nowhere, shocked me, not so much because I was dead set against sadism but because I'd simply never been propositioned by someone who was dead set in favor of it. Like every other wide-eyed freshman, I had surreptitiously pored over *The Philosophy of the Bedroom* and *Justine,* hidden in the stacks of the Radcliffe library. But it had never occurred to me that I would meet people who indulged in real acts of erotic domination. (Or was it degradation?)

I tried to hide my sudden confusion. But it must have seeped through my impassive facade because my beloved's interest, which had been growing as steadily as my own, suddenly vanished. I was, after all, only an amateur in drag. A less exacting woman might have found my ingenuous bewilderment endearing, but this *soeur* obviously wanted a masterful *frère.* Within minutes, another suitor arrived with a second drink, summoned so discreetly I hadn't detected the exchange. I was dismissed without even learning her name.

Just then a commotion broke out at the door. A huge bouncer of indeterminate gender appeared from nowhere, quelling the disturbance as quickly as it had threatened. An apparition emerged from the nervous knot of women at the door, a magnificent personage who towered over everyone else in the room not only in height but in sexual mystique. At first I thought the scuffle at the door might have been caused because she was a man trying to crash a sapphic party. But the audacious curve of her unbridled breasts dispelled this explanation, as did every other curve beneath her shadow-gray suit.

She strode arrogantly though a little unsteadily into the center of the room. It seemed to take her a minute to get her bearings until I realized she was slowly staring everyone down, each in their turn, until the entire room returned their attention to their own circles of conversation. I, too, had looked down. Yet she chose to walk straight up to me.

"I love martinis," she said in a very deep but very feminine voice—feminine, that is, if you think of cats as feminine, for she sounded like a wild animal, simultaneously growling and purring as lions do when they feed.

"Let's drink a million of them," she continued as if she were challenging me to a hedonistic duel.

Without hesitation, I nodded, accepting the challenge. Yet I was shocked. Never before had I been attracted to a mannish woman. It felt as if my whole world was being turned upside down. Hulking continents clinging to the rigid bedrock of repression, and phobic hemispheres, were falling off the face of the map, leaving vast oceans of fluid sexuality.

I felt I might drown. For once in my life I didn't care. Abandoning all protocol, I committed my second major faux pas of the evening by coupling *frère* with *frère*. I wanted so much to get lost that night, and she had so clearly been lost for a long, long time.

I figured out later, when I also learned her name, that she chose me because she knew full well that none of the frilly *femmes* in the room could have handled her volatile seductions. I was also one of the few people there who didn't recognize her. We both advanced to the bar. Although the bartender resisted serving her, I managed to order two martinis. She drank hers with great relish and then finished mine when I wouldn't keep up, intimating that we were in a hurry. She didn't speak to me, but she let me know full well that I was hers for the night. Even if I had known what I know now, I couldn't have eluded the temptation of her eyes. She mesmerized me. It was nothing short of possession, and I knew I had found my guide to the delights only devils can offer.

She grabbed my hand and stomped back out into the middle of the room. She bowed elaborately and roared, "Goodnight, sweet ladies, good night." Given her ironic posture, there was no doubt in my mind that she knew she was quoting both Shakespeare's Ophelia and Eliot's *The Waste Land.* Her erudition tightened the screws on the rack to which she had bound me, an eager and grateful victim.

"Fear not," she continued. Virtually everyone in the bar was watching us. "I will leave all virgins intact this one night, to return on the morrow."

Then we exited with a flourish, leaving a stunned and no doubt relieved group of *frères* and more than a few wistful *soeurs* at Les Lèvres, with enough food for conversation to last them till dawn. On the street she became, if possible, even more dramatic, hailing and installing us in a cab with the authority of an imperious viscount.

In the cab, my escort acted as if she were on stage. Yet her behavior was not forced or artificial in any way. She produced a silver flask with the most intricate design I had ever seen etched on metal and offered me a drink.

"This is unbelievably beautiful. Where on earth did you get it?" I asked, accepting the flask, which was filled with a sluggish, infernally good brandy.

"I did it."

"You *did* it? What do you mean?"

"I'm an artist. I etch silver, a dying art I hope to resuscitate as the self-appointed savior of our endangered cultural aristocracy."

"It's absolutely exquisite. Where did you learn to do it?"

"Certainly not in Buffalo."

"You're from Buffalo? I'm from Utah. It's a wonder we ever made it to Paris at all."

"Not really. I'm a rebel. If I'd been born Oscar Wilde's child, I'd have married young, gotten fat, and had thirteen middle-class children just to be different. From him, I mean."

"I know what you mean." I couldn't stop staring at the way she carried herself, sprawled out like a man with lanky and disheveled indifference. Men virtually never inspired lust in me. For all their bluster, they were all as good as neutered as far as I was concerned. So why were these masculine mannerisms in a woman so seductive all of a sudden? Then I saw the answer in her thighs, and especially in her eyes. Power.

"I'd like to see more of your...work," I said blankly. My mind was racing too quickly to attach actual meaning to words. I seldom fantasize, so I was shocked by the lewd content of my accelerated thoughts.

She looked at me with a mixture of amusement and almost vicious aggression. There was never just one emotion on her face, or even in the gentle violence of our first kiss.

I tasted the earth in her mouth—dark, musky, subterranean peat and mosses, the dank fertility of death. Her mouth entombed me, yet when she released me I ached for more. I started to pull her back down on top of me, but she held a finger up and tilted the silver flask back again. A black cloud fell, lifted, and fell across her face. The instantaneous changes mesmerized me, and I suddenly knew the answer to the recently posed question about sadistic pleasures. *Mais oui.*

"You know, I've seen you around before," she said. "What's your name?"

"Alec."

"Alec," she repeated, rolling the name across her tongue as if to try to place me. Then her face lit up and she laughed abruptly. "I'm Lizzie," she said archly. "But my friends call me Manfred."

I believed her because I wanted to. It is so clear to me now that my pseudonym had given her the license to lie about who she really was. I had set my own trap.

Suddenly the cab lurched to a stop.

"We're here, Alec."

We entered another bar where the strict rules of *frère/soeur* etiquette, or indeed courtship rituals of any kind, were absent. Apparently, everyone skipped superfluous preliminaries altogether and went straight to the source of their desires.

Manfred pulled me along to the bar and ordered brandy. They handed her a bottle. Walking across the room, we slipped through a door in the far corner. I saw nothing. It was very dark and my eyes had not adjusted. I could only smell what must have been hashish smoke. With a wild animal's night vision, Manfred seemed to have no trouble seeing at all.

Manfred led me through a series of doors, maintaining a firm grip on my hand. No woman had ever treated me that way. I didn't necessarily relish being manhandled, but it fascinated me. I suppose my Radcliffe-bred devotion to the inalienable rights of women balked at the whole notion of domination, yet I must admit I respected her for being able to pull it off with such offhand authority. Besides, reservations seemed ridiculous, given the setting I had sought out with such unconscious diligence.

My eyes still shrouded in darkness, I followed Manfred with unwonted yet titillated passivity. But then the tables turned abruptly and completely. Throwing us down on a large divan whose billowy pillows immediately enveloped us, Manfred transformed at a touch into an amorous maiden whose submissive intentions were clear. Within seconds I was making love to her. Within minutes she had come, with a gentle desperation that almost moved me to tears. I wanted to hold her gently, to cradle the tenderness of her exquisite vulnerability, but she turned back into the manly Manfred as if nothing had happened.

I will never forget the way she kissed my ear with soft, defenseless passion just before metamorphosing back into the defiant viscount.

By now my eyes were accustomed to the darkness. I noticed what I thought were several other couples in the room, but as I looked more closely it became apparent that larger groups dominated the massive, crushed-velvet couches. One pile of five or six girls was particularly conspicuous; someone somewhere in the stack cried out in what sounded like stifled agony. Each muffled scream caused a ripple of throaty gasps. Finally the entire mound quaked with violent spasms and then shivered into an inert silence.

Another group of three, sprawled all over each other, had become too preoccupied with voyeurism to consummate their own desires. They reminded me of intertwined eels whose intimacy is both grotesque and random.

Passion seemed like a narcotic in that room—irresistibly seductive but ultimately never enough. I know, because several groups turned toward us the minute Manfred gasped her last orgiastic breath. Hunger lurked in everyone's eyes.

Where at the previous bar Manfred had been shunned, here she clearly enjoyed an exalted status. She held court for a few minutes, greeting old friends who mumbled their salutations from various contorted positions without so much as sitting up or even unwedging their heads or extracting their appendages.

Not once did Manfred make a move to introduce me to these admirers. My first real nibble of the anonymity I craved left a strange aftertaste.

Manfred suddenly seemed to tire of her entourage. Standing and zipping up her trousers with a single impatient gesture, she grabbed my hand once again and descended a staircase I had not noticed in a far corner of the sultry room.

The next chamber was even darker and more dense with smoke. As we walked in, another group accosted Manfred with drenched delight, almost inarticulate in their sedated euphoria.

One woman seemed to mistake Manfred for someone named Thelma, but quickly apologized with a sudden profusion of energy that immediately subsided into the gently rolling waves of inertia Manfred herself floated upon with amphibious ease.

Once again, no one really seemed to notice me, and I assumed that their distance was yet another manifestation of the clique mentality that makes sapphic circles so difficult to break into. But as I look back on that night, I suspect I was at the center of a potential explosion that barely escaped detonation. They all knew something I so clearly didn't know. No doubt that's why Manfred found me so appealing. An emotional pyromaniac, she was titillated only by danger.

A profusion of beautiful pipes and hookahs lay scattered around the room—mostly Turkish, with long, beaded mouthpieces like exotic musical instruments. One water pipe's tubes were so extensive they had been attached to the ceiling and dangled down like party streamers. One particularly fragile hookah could have been a sacred Limoges chalice, covered with intricately tooled blue and scarlet porcelain squares and studded with semiprecious stones. Rough brown chunks of hashish smoldered in an ornate filter the size of a finger bowl.

When we sat down, five arms extended in our direction, offering oblivion. Manfred declined, surprising me. Out of nowhere she produced two snifters and poured out the brandy. All through the night, amidst chambers of disheveled women, hash, marijuana, barbiturates, and even heroin, she stuck to alcohol and to me. Halfway through our brandy, Manfred looked at me urgently. All evening she acted as if she were in a hurry, as if the next drink or the next club held the secret to the pressing yet inarticulate question that seemed to haunt her. We rushed out into the night in search of the answers.

When we got to Le Masque I realized that Manfred had been working up to this final *mise-en-scène*, testing me with progressively taboo scenarios to make sure I was game. I was very pleased with myself for having passed each test. Unlike the other bars, Le Masque was not divided into separate dens of iniquity; one huge room housed contraptions ranging from pincers the size of tiny tweezers to racks and a pulley system stretching all the way to the ceiling, which was some three stories tall. It was fantastic.

Until that night I had no idea that I had gothic proclivities. Or even a predilection.

My response shocked me. In fact, I felt a real jolt not only in my sensibility but in my body—a kind of lightning bolt of recognition as if wandering aimlessly through a drama of assumed roles, I had suddenly stumbled on the script of my own life.

Although Manfred often seemed distracted, she acknowledged my shock of recognition by taking my hand, very gently this time, leading me into our secret mechanical garden.

At the mouth of Le Masque, she slipped a bill through some bars to a woman in a suspended cage, tattooed almost everywhere except her erect nipples, naked except for a panoramic scene of the African veld, complete with crouching animals and perched birds. The woman growled as we walked by, which sounds absurd as I reminisce about it now. At the time it seemed both natural and sexy. I remember feeling the urge to pet her.

"Looking good, as always," Manfred told her. Then Manfred whispered under her breath, "You'll stay on the lookout for me, won't you, Zelda?" The cat woman nodded, knowingly.

Manfred knew everyone, which made me feel safe. Rather than questioning why a lookout was necessary at all, I felt grateful for the protection.

I have since learned that this feeling of safety is what transforms imminent violence into eroticism. Sadistic masters stop just short of actually carrying out their insidious designs on enraptured slaves. The whole appeal is the threat, the tease, the promise of pleasure so intense it hurts.

What shocked me most was the bizarre familiarity of it all. I had certainly never made any moral judgments against the cults of de Sade and Sacher-Masoch. As a homosexual I steered clear of moral judgments, just in case I was living in a glass house. On the other hand, sadism and masochism had never aroused me either. Like Transylvanian castles and Persian minarets, they seemed too distant and hopelessly Romantic to be real. But when I walked into Le Masque, I instantaneously knew that I had been keeping a sinister secret from myself. It was like coming home, a cozy dungeon all my own strewn with the accoutrements of dark desires.

I was reminded once again of our Marquis de Sade phase at Radcliffe—cut all too short when Colleen Braithwaite announced that he was too misogynistic to be entertaining. I finally realized the full significance of one particularly evocative tale in which the savvy heroine was courting a new beau, conducting a kind of experiment whose outcome she knew full well. As they sipped their aperitif, she said, "Look around. There's someone in this room who loves it, but doesn't know it." The "it" was obviously the attendant penchants and passions of whips and chains.

"How do you know?" the innocent man asked.

"I can always tell," she claimed.

As he looked around, puzzling at the expressions on everyone's face, he caught his own eye in the mirror. Her fingernails suddenly dug into his arm, his countenance registered an epiphany, and page after page of blinding eroticism ensued.

I was that man. And, like the sexy de Sadean heroine, Manfred could read exactly what I was feeling on my face. She snickered.

Every wall at Le Masque was studded with rings, most of which were occupied by women strapped in with their hands above their heads, many of them alone and watching the scene serenely like wallflowers at a prom. A few were actively engaging their partners in the rings, teasing them mercilessly or roughing them up a little. Mouth gags abounded. Some masters had their slaves fastened onto racks, where everything from humping to tattooing was going on. One very young girl, who looked as if she should have been at home doing her homework, was asleep on a rack, her arms strapped down but her legs tucked up in a comfy fetal position.

In one far corner a gorgeous woman was stretched out in the splayed position of Leonardo da Vinci's famous Renaissance man, her hair coiling out like Medusa's snakes as she was spun around on one of a series of wheels. At one point she caught Manfred's eye, seemed to recognize her, and smiled out complacently at my friend as she went round and round. Lots of derrières were in the air, supported by padded contraptions designed to put butts on display in various vulnerable positions. I need not mention that most of the women straddling these derrières had dildos strapped to their groins. This whole scene really bothered or should I say bored me, smacking of the tedium of the phallus.

A woman fastened flat on her back screamed periodically. A masked, completely androgynous, handsome beauty was apparently whispering threats in her ear. A tight crowd had gathered around her, listening intently to the whispered litany of the things that would happen to her if she did not submit willingly, even eagerly. Or so I imagined.

The simple use of fantasy as a tool of torture appealed to me. But when I suggested listening in, Manfred said, "Lightweights."

There was another group in the center of the room that particularly appealed to my weakness for sexy villains, damsels, and delicious distress. Two striking voluptuaries were seated on either side of a muscular woman on an elevated table. She was not fettered, except by desire. One of the pair would attach or remove a clasp or a pincer as if anticipating the prone woman's every whim. Then the other would respond, clamping a different device to bring another part of her writhing flesh into focus. They played chess with her body, matching carefully considered moves, with every player at least pretending psychic connection. Each move was discreet and precise, and everyone was apparently poised on penultimate pleasure.

All that was missing was a shackled woman screaming, as a huge swinging bladed pendulum whisked inches away from her naked belly. Then I remembered reading Edgar Allan Poe as a child and identified for the first time the erotic thrill that had inspired me to devour his complete works at the age of twelve.

In the center of the room a hub of activity surrounded an enormous tower with several caged-in platforms, one shrouded with a thick black velvet curtain. Although it was presently in use by no fewer than five women, I could not figure out how it worked or what they were doing. I almost asked Manfred if we could take a closer look, but suddenly she grabbed my arm and twisted it around my back.

"You're going to need a password," she said. "To use if something goes wrong and you really need someone to stop doing something."

"How about 'uncle'?" I suggested, but was immediately embarrassed. I was so conventional, even my password was a cliché. Manfred thought it was funny.

"'Uncle' it is. If you say 'stop,' I *won't* stop. In fact, the word 'stop' around here means you want more of the same." She tightened her grip on my arm and led me to a contraption in a far corner.

"Stop," I whispered, and my eyes fairly sizzled with anticipation.

There, extending almost to the lofty ceiling of the three-story chamber, was an imposing mechanical wheel. It looked vaguely like a runner for rodents the size of human beings, except that straps and buckles and clips and belts were hanging everywhere.

Someone was already strapped into this huge wheel, but she was alone and had the air of just killing time. In fact, the machine was designed for use by two, and she cheerfully relinquished her place. Her polite generosity contrasted ironically with the territorial snobbery I had encountered at Les Lèvres. As she climbed out of the lower section of the apparatus, she asked eagerly, "Need help?"

"Maybe later," Manfred said. "You're Fontaine, aren't you? I saw you with Ligeia last week at La Marquise."

Fontaine brightened like an debutante at a coming-out ball. It seemed clear that she too knew and idolized Manfred.

"Maybe later," Manfred repeated, patting Fontaine's buttocks as she gently shoved her off.

"Cute kid," I said as Manfred turned to me.

"Actually she's wild. Maybe even a little dangerous. I'm not sure she really understands the meaning of 'uncle.'"

Manfred then gestured upward dramatically. "This is the Wheel," she announced.

With a broad sweep of her arm, she activated the whole contraption, which revolved with sheer, mechanistic elegance. It spun effortlessly as if each ball bearing had been individually oiled by tiny doting elves. There is nothing like the clack and glide of well-oiled metal on metal, unless it is the squeak of well-oiled leather or the perfume of well-oiled hair. I was getting well-oiled just listening to the Wheel. It was a day of firsts. I had certainly never been lubricated by a machine before. Suddenly precision had become erotic.

When the Wheel slowed down and stopped, Manfred maneuvered me into the lower section of the apparatus, clipping and snapping and strapping and fastening me into place. I had never felt safer in my life, with "uncle" so close at hand. She kissed me on the top of the head.

Then she turned on me. Instantaneously, her character splintered before my very eyes. Manfred Jekyll had turned into Manfred Hyde. Not a trace of "uncle" seemed to survive the transformation, though I had complete faith that it could be conjured up in a pinch.

She said nothing as she continued to pull straps and levers and pulleys. The noise that each movement caused—especially the click of metal and the squeaking, creaking of leather—seemed orchestrated for seduction. When I recall them even now, everything gets wet.

Suspended there, I felt like an integral organ in the huge, living machine—a machine with a heartbeat even louder than the pounding in my ears and in my groin. If Manfred gestured one way, I moved another. Freed of volition, my body ran wild with desire. She kept pulling and then releasing, staring into my eyes, deeper and deeper, without blinking. Once when I winced she smiled.

Before she even climbed into the machine, I was dripping. Before she climbed out of her pants and ripped off her shirt, all the while penetrating me with her eyes, I was so aroused it hurt. I had underestimated her body. Lean and hard and firm. She had the hips of an adolescent girl and the breasts of a prepubescent tomboy and the knowing looks of an androgynous god of ancient passions. I wondered if I would be attracted to elegant ladies ever again.

"Fontaine," she finally said, motioning to her understudy in the wings. "Lace me up."

Reverentially, Fontaine started suiting Manfred up, fitting her into the intricate apparatus of the Wheel. When she finished, Fontaine took a couple of clips out of her pocket.

"Want these?"

"What do you think?"

Fontaine opened the clips one by one and let them close slowly on Manfred's breasts, just outside her nipples, which immediately got very hard.

Then she tied the strings of a classic black silky mask around the back of Manfred's head. I know now why the dominatrix wears a mask. This superficial anonymity ensures profound intimacy. Like a priest confined in his confessional, these barriers guarantee the naked honesty that is only possible through the screen separating the priest from the penitent.

The ritual dance began.

Slowly Manfred moved her right arm in a circular motion, activating a lever-and-pulley system that pulled my left leg toward her, then away from her, back and forth within inches of her face. Her movements controlled my body completely. Once she jerked her arm very hard, and abruptly my foot actually brushed her lips. When she kissed my arch, I thought I had come, except that I was still too poised for more to call it an actual orgasm. I think she did this just to let me know that she could touch me if she chose to. But she never did again, not even once during our long, slow turn on the Wheel.

Suddenly, Manfred obliterated the fleeting tenderness of that isolated moment, executing a kind of half-somersault that landed me hanging on my back with all four extremities stretched straight out, as if ready to be quartered. Manfred was now suspended over me like a giant, smiling spider. When she bent down as if to kiss me, my own head followed suit, dipping just out of her reach.

She knew exactly how to move her body so that mine moved in tandem, straining toward her but barred from actual contact by an electrified corridor of air. A charged current jumped across this space, jolting me with orgiastic spasms.

I had been moaning and emitting clipped screams—more like barks—for God knows how long before I noticed that I was adding to the ghoulish din of Le Masque. I had never been one to make noises during sex. But then, I'd also never been hanging spread-eagled with my neck collared and my teeth bared like a dog growling for more.

The word "uncle" never even crossed my mind.

I became frightened, but not of Manfred or the Wheel. I feared I might never again be able to enjoy the kind of sex people have in bed, in the flesh.

Manfred teased me with minute motions—a jerk of a hand here, a slow sweep of a leg there—for what seemed liked tantalizing hours, until I thought I'd die of suspense. Her eyes bored holes into one part of my body and then another; I could feel them palpably entering my every pore. Everything had the intensity of a violation, as if her desire was so profound that only this kind of relentless penetration could approximate its virulence.

I had never before even fantasized about the eroticism of aggression, but from that day forward I longed to be violated. After Manfred, all subsequent lovers have been at a terrible disadvantage with me, handicapped in proportion to their relative mastery. Thankfully, some of them have played beyond their handicaps.

It's not that my sex life was forever ruined. But I became wary of the repression that transforms sex into a parlor game. Repress the beast and it will bite you. The new kick, in those days, was to listen to the noble promptings of your inner woman. Mine wore leather and liked to be spanked.

I wondered if Manfred's unflinching erotic power hadn't also provided me with a model of female self-determination. But I never told anyone this.

Before Manfred finished with me, we spun around countless times, moving all the way up and down the contraption like a gothic Ferris wheel. Quite suddenly, on one of my revolutions to the top of the Wheel, I felt myself abandoned, and a dire pulse of loneliness pierced through the erotic fog I had been suspended in for God knows how long. In fact, I had simply been disconnected. Manfred had disengaged herself from her berth with precipitous speed; the clamps had been popped open and the strings and belts hung down, empty. The cat woman, sprung from her cage, stood next to her, gesticulating toward the door.

Still too dazed to make much sense of the proceedings, I noticed that Manfred gestured in my direction as she quickly stepped into her clothes. She gave me one last look that I will never forget. The masterful Manfred had already departed, and a vulnerable, even frightened, girl peeked up at me with regret. Then she scurried off toward the back of Le Masque.

Zelda gave the Wheel a spin, bringing me to the floor, and freed me. I staggered as I tried to stand up and was so wobbly and dizzy I had to be supported. I tried to ask what was going on, but Zelda held a finger to her lips.

As she hurried me out a discreet exit, I heard shouts somewhere near the front door and craned my neck to try to catch a glimpse of who or what had caused the disturbance. But Zelda prevented me from identifying individual members of the crowd of yelling and gesticulating women. In the back of my mind, I think I assumed it was *les flics* performing their bimonthly raid on the sapphic clubs.

Once outside in a seedy alley whose dinginess was like a slap in the face after the plush decadence within, Zelda turned to me. "I think you'd better call it a night," she said, and then darted back inside.

I would forever call it *the* night.

Manfred was nowhere in sight. I realized I had no way to get in touch with her—no last name, no address, no telephone number.

I felt faint, yet I did not want the night to end. So I wandered in the direction of the Seine and sat on its banks until dawn silenced all the secret voices Manfred had awakened; like voluptuous vampires, they returned to their beds.

Miss Henrietta Adams
Hôtel Résidence les Cèdres
12 rue des Dames
17th Arrondissement
Paris, France

November 21, 1925

Dear Miss Adams:

Your most recent article on the almost unbelievable talent gathered at Gertrude Stein's salon was a big hit. The Board has approved it with minor revisions (more on that later) for the January issue of En Vogue. Once again, you have served up your aesthetic criticism on a most appealing platter, seasoning your serious analysis with exciting personal portraits of Picasso, Matisse, Braque, Gris, and Hemingway. We feel as though we are sitting down to eat Hélène's omelettes with them, as it were, in the privacy of Gertrude Stein's dining room. I cannot overestimate the entertainment value of your anecdotal descriptions of the artists' everyday personalities, which are intimate without lapsing into gossip. This is the kind of material our subscribers really relish.

Now about those revisions. Your article arrived rather late--not until November 14, in fact--so we should reconsider your submission deadline. Let's make it the 5th of the month rather than the 10th to ensure plenty of time for revisions, even if the mail gets held up. This means postmarking your submissions well before the end of the previous month. I hope this sudden change will not pose too great a problem for your February editorial. But I'm

assuming you can once again make use of your fabulous
connections to rummage up an expeditious topic.

Back to the revisions. Owing to time constraints,
we were forced to edit the piece ourselves, which in this
case proved more substantial than merely deleting
material, as we did with the American tourist section of
your Kahnweiler article. The main thrust of our revisions
was as follows:

Rather than focusing on the relationship between
the expatriate patrons (Gertrude Stein, and Etta and
Claribel Cone) and the artists, we have shifted the focus
to the factionalism within the salon itself, especially
the rivalry between Matisse and the Cubists. (The fact
that Matisse actually introduced Negro sculpture to
Picasso and therefore indirectly inaugurated Cubism's
preoccupation with primitivism was certainly news to us.)
Since this is clearly the second-most prominent topic in
your original piece, we trust you do not think this an
unwarranted editorial liberty. Let me reiterate that we
did not (and will not) add new material; rather, we have
simply shifted the focus. In fact, this shift seems
perfectly natural because it has the virtue of being a
more dramatic and therefore more vivid focal point for the
whole editorial. Like it or not, controversy sells
magazines!

For the sake of this new focus, we deleted the
sections on Marie Laurencin and Romaine Brooks, who seemed
to be peripheral to the Matisse/Cubist rivalry.

With the exception of the humorous description of
the fiasco of Hélène's omelette dinner (we especially
loved your description of Stein's strategy of catering to
each painter's ego by seating them opposite one of their

own paintings), we have deleted most of the domestic details of the Stein/Toklas ménage. Again, they seemed extraneous to the actual dynamics of the salon itself.

I apologize in advance for implementing these changes without your approval, but I would also remind you that your contract clearly states that the Board has complete editorial authority; in fact, this is standard procedure, especially when the correspondent is overseas. Nevertheless, we wish to honor your editorial prerogative as much as possible, and the new deadline schedule should ensure your more active involvement in the revision process.

Enclosed is the final copy of your January column. On this end, we are extremely pleased with this revised version and hope you will still find it a fair representation of the dynamics of Gertrude Stein's celebrated salon. I must say I envy the incredible social life you must be enduring as part of your "research."

Sincerely,

Irving P. Dickey

Irving P. Dickey
Senior Editor

cc: Board of Editors
En Vogue

CHAPTER SEVEN

The Genius and the Felon

Gertrude Stein was a big walker. She walked the way a steam engine chugs, a little labored but with tremendous energy. I took advantage of her penchant for walking in the Bois de Boulogne to get her away from 27 rue de Fleurus where we could talk out of Alice's earshot. Alice B. Toklas considered walking tedious. It was probably the only activity she let Gertrude engage in without her supervision.

Although Gertrude and Alice were practically joined at the hip, the intrigue surrounding Juan Gris's stolen painting seemed a little messy for Alice B. Toklas's meticulous, white-gloved sensibilities. Gertrude Stein, on the other hand, had always struck me as someone who wasn't afraid to get her hands dirty, if that's what it took to get what she wanted.

Even winter in Paris looks like a painting. Gaslights glow in the dusk, reflecting sparkling prisms on hushed beds of snow. But I was too preoccupied to savor the Impressionistic perfection of the Bois.

"Gertrude, do you mind if I ask you something?"

"Fire away."

"You know I never really talked to you about that hullabaloo at the police station. That whole Kahnweiler mess."

"Poor old Kahnweiler," Gertrude Stein replied. "He really should learn to stay out of trouble. It's such a waste of energy."

Gertrude Stein paused thoughtfully, though her brisk pace didn't slacken a bit. "I suppose it's because he's German. Nobody trusts Germans anymore."

"But should they?" I asked. "What I mean is, is he guilty of anything?"

"He's guilty of being German!" Gertrude Stein exclaimed. She said it with a kind of finality that made it very clear she felt we had exhausted all there was to say about Kahnweiler.

Ordinarily, I deferred to Gertrude Stein's almost dictatorial insistence on dominating conversations, but I was too desperate to back off. The whole Kahnweiler fiasco was seriously compromising my ability to enjoy myself in Paris. My debut in the charmed circle of Gertrude Stein's salon was being ruined by this pesky intrigue.

During the past few weeks, Lieutenant Dupin—or worse yet, one of his dopey cronies—had stopped by my hôtel at least twice a week. They took turns badgering me for clues I might have discovered in my journalistic rounds through the ateliers of avant-garde artists. It got so that I was afraid to return home at night for fear of seeing a uniform lurking in the lobby. They hovered like vultures waiting patiently for me to betray my new friends, but I stubbornly refused to play the role of stool pigeon. As days turned into weeks and weeks threatened to stretch out into months, I began to fear that they might wear me down.

I kept thinking of Braque as an accomplice rather than an artist. Juan Gris's swagger seemed more suited to a gangster than a painter. Even Picasso had two faces: the genius and the felon. I just couldn't stand it anymore. One way or the other, I needed to know what was really going on. And although I resisted playing the stoolie for the police, the journalist in me was taking copious notes, egged on by the idea of exposing an art scam of this magnitude.

Earlier that afternoon, I had barged into Picasso's studio on the pretense of asking him to let me write another feature article about him for *En Vogue*. Picasso disliked unexpected visitors, yet he welcomed me with open arms, which made me feel even more guilty. His wife, Olga, was somewhat less cordial. She knew I could advance her husband's career with publicity, which suited her rapacious appetite for fame and fortune, but she could not see beyond my sexual proclivities. Dripping with furs, she made a magnificently rude exit to spend the afternoon with Paris's most ornamental social butterflies.

Olga Picasso made no secret of the fact that she thought sapphists were an insult to femininity. She said she could understand male homosexuals—they had harsh mothers—but female inverts revolted her. A Russian soignée ballerina before her marriage to Picasso, she had a rigid, easily scandalized sense of propriety. She had even forbidden Gertrude and Alice to attend her wedding to Pablo, resulting in the longest of Stein and Picasso's perennial estrangements. And there I was, violating my own blossoming friendship with Picasso, not to mention my loyalty to Gertrude Stein, spying on genius itself just to sleuth the mystery of the stolen paintings.

Picasso ushered me into his studio, and again, I was struck by its magnificent squalor. Nothing could have been more diametrically opposed to the lavish respectability of their adjoining living quarters, his wife's domain. Despite Olga's efforts to domesticate Pablo, a menagerie of stray cats and a dog of uncertain lineage lounged on the jumble of cast-off furniture he had insisted on bringing from the Bateau Lavoir, his old bachelor's studio on Montmartre. Although Olga did find some solace in the fact that Picasso no longer owned a monkey, she didn't realize this was a Pyrrhic victory. The only real reason was that Picasso's beloved chimpanzee, Nono, had died recently, and his chums in the circus had not yet found a suitable replacement.

A chronic collector of vases and receptacles of any kind, Picasso had long since run out of shelves to house them. Flasks of every conceivable shape and size overflowed onto rickety tables. Chipped smoky-glass bottles were shoved indiscriminately against pure-cut crystal. Two or three bowls of rotting fruit filled the air with a faintly putrid perfume—unpainted still lifes waiting in patient disarray for their day of glory.

On this cold day, Picasso had stoked up an ancient potbellied stove. He had only grudgingly given up his old studio to try his hand at marriage and respectability, two sinking ships he was on the verge of abandoning. As Olga steadily climbed the social ladder of the glittering Parisian world, Pablo descended into the depths of his studio, clinging to his bohemian indigence like an aesthetic life preserver.

Picasso and I stood warming our hands over his stove's little blaze, while I surveyed the profusion of paintings, drawings, and stretched canvases that filled each and every corner of his atelier. I spotted both *Man with a Guitar* and *Calligraphic Still Life,* two of the works on Lieutenant Dupin's list. My memory had not deceived me. Picasso had apparently stolen his own paintings from Kahnweiler's gallery, presumably splitting the insurance money with the dealer himself. I wondered how many hats Olga had been able to buy with the proceeds.

As Gertrude Stein and I traversed the tree-lined esplanades of the Bois de Boulogne, I found myself impervious to the quaint charms of the several miniature parks we passed, each with its own statue of an obscure poet or forgotten composer. "Gertrude," I ventured, "I think I've seen some of the stolen paintings around... around several of the ateliers."

I had decided not to mention the fact that I was almost sure I had seen Juan Gris's *Dish of Pears* in her own studio. I thought she would be more apt to be frank if I didn't accuse her directly.

I expected Gertrude Stein to ask where I had seen the stolen paintings. And I secretly hoped she would deny outright the truth of what I had said. But she just walked on, oblivious, staring straight ahead at the frigid mauve sunset through the columns of stately elms lining the esplanade.

"What a beautiful night, Henri. Aren't you glad we all invented Paris to while away the twilights of our days?"

Given the fact that Gertrude Stein almost never waxed poetic, I suspected she was telling me to shut up and count my blessings. So for a while we walked silently, both pretending not to have the slightest idea what the other was talking about. But I could not leave well enough alone.

"One at Braque's. And two at Picasso's atelier—*Calligraphic Still Life* and *Man with a Guitar*. There's no question in my mind that those three paintings are registered as stolen at the police station. Meanwhile the artists themselves have them in their possession. What the hell is going on, Gertrude?"

"Don't ask, Henri," Gertrude Stein said, a little angrily.

I couldn't believe my ears. I had expected her to explain, to deny, to justify—anything but this. This was like telling a ravenous gourmand not to dig for truffles.

"Do the words 'insurance fraud' mean anything to you?" I insisted.

"Do the words 'butt out' mean anything to you?" she countered.

"No."

"Then we're even."

Gertrude Stein picked up her pace, as if she were trying to give me the slip. We were already practically running through the Bois de Boulogne, and I still can't believe anyone her size could move that quickly. Finally, I broke into a run to get in front of her, prepared to be mowed down if she didn't stop and answer my questions. She stopped just short of flattening me like a spare bowling pin.

"I'm sorry, Gertrude," I said, trying to catch my breath. "I respect your privacy, and God knows I respect your judgment as a patron. But I'm at a loss. I've got the police breathing down my back in Paris, and my editors breathing down my back in New York, and I've got to figure out what to tell them."

"Your editors?" Gertrude asked, suddenly alarmed.

"Yes. My editors. I made the mistake of telling them I might follow up my article on art theft with a sequel on a full-blown crime ring. That was before I really believed there was anything to report. I guess I was trying to impress them, to keep my job."

"Never try to impress people, Henri," Gertrude Stein warned. "You'll just end up making a fool of yourself."

"I could call my editors off simply by pretending I came up short. But what about the police? Lieutenant Dupin isn't going to let me put him off forever."

"And why not?" Gertrude Stein asked. "You know you're transparent, Henri. Remember that you're American, and Americans can't lie to save their lives. Tell the damned truth. You just don't approve. The Puritan in you is scandalized by the mere idea of foul play."

"Then you admit something is going on!"

"I admit nothing. Now stop this nonsense and let's start walking before you make me mad."

I had only heard Gertrude Stein use this tone of voice once before, when she caught a workman making fun of Alice's mustache. The big burly lout was called in to fix a broken pane of glass in the back atelier at 27 rue de Fleurus. But he never finished the job and barely escaped Gertrude Stein's fury. I'm sure I was as scared as he had been, but I had nowhere to run. I couldn't butt out; I just had to know.

I could see from Gertrude Stein's hostility that it had been a mistake trying to corral her. So we resumed our walk at breakneck speed. As with the bulls Hemingway loved so much in Pamplona, the best thing to do was to run along with her, to dodge the hooves and horns of her tremendous momentum until her wrath was spent. Sure enough, her anger waned as we raced along, and I resumed my interrogation. I jogged a step ahead of her so that I could see her face as we talked. I figured if she wouldn't tell me anything outright, at least her physiognomy might give me a clue as to whether or not she were guilty. Gertrude Stein may have grown up in Europe, but she too had been born American and should therefore be partially transparent, at least according to her own theory of national types.

"Look, Gertrude. I'm not trying to cause trouble. But now that I've inadvertently stumbled into this mess, I've got to figure out how to get out. If you expect me to lie—to the police, for example—I've got to know what I'm lying about."

Gertrude Stein raised her eyebrows. This idea seemed to intrigue her. "I wonder if that's true—that you can't really lie in ignorance." She clapped her hands together the way Picasso always did when he got excited—the gesture of geniuses applauding their own thought processes. "You know, you're quite right, Henri. Knowledge itself is the source of dishonesty. Yet another testament to the terrible dangers of knowledge," she concluded deliberately, as if warning me.

"Dangerous but necessary."

"Sad but true."

"So tell me," I insisted.

"I can't."

"Why not?"

"Because it is mere conjecture and I am devoted to the truth."

"Baloney. You're devoted to art."

"Exactly. And art is truth."

"Art may be a truth. Someone's truth. But it's not *the* truth. Please, Gertrude. You're treating me like a fool. Level with me."

"Art is my truth. And that's the truth."

"And you'd do anything for the sake of art?"

"I would."

I was beginning to figure out that as long as we communicated indirectly—using the kind of encoded meaning that made Gertrude Stein's writing so difficult to read until you found the key—she'd probably tell me what I needed to know. So I proceeded obliquely, hiding incriminating questions behind innocuous generalities.

"Even if the art itself promoted some dangerous cause, or was supported by one?"

I was thinking of Kahnweiler's notorious reputation during the war, allegedly trafficking with the Germans in his lawless efforts to champion Cubism.

"Causes bore me, Henri," Gertrude Stein replied. "You know that." Judging from her expression and the fact that she didn't skip a beat, I assumed she knew exactly what I was talking about. Finally, we were speaking her language, and her reticence dissolved. "They've always bored me, especially when they get in the way of art."

"Are you suggesting that politics and aesthetics are mutually exclusive?"

"No. Just separate. Completely separate. That's why our art is so superior. That's why even you, Henri, have made your pilgrimage here to worship at the altar of the avant-garde. Even you, Henri, can see that the result is genius."

So that's how Gertrude Stein defines the avant-garde, I thought. She actually believes they create masterpieces by separating aesthetics and politics, and divorcing art from life. Some, of course, took exception to this rule, all the more noteworthy for being so few and far between. Gertrude Stein was so weary of what she called Bryher's "obsession with other people's business" that she was on the brink of expelling her from the salon at 27 rue de Fleurus. One more peep about pogroms or the Progressive Party and she'd be a goner. And though Janet Flanner was already writing about Soviet Communism and Italy's National Fascist Party in her "Letter from Paris" in *The New Yorker*, even she refrained from mentioning Stalin or Mussolini in front of Natalie Barney or Gertrude Stein. Gertrude's manifesto of aesthetic purity made me uneasy, to say the least.

"But Gertrude, don't artists have a responsibility to the people? I thought you said art was democratic."

"It is. It should be accessible to everyone. Just like Paris is. Anyone and everyone can enjoy the beauty of Paris," she said, flourishing her hand as if offering the Bois de Boulogne to the masses, "but they didn't *make* Paris. We did."

"Now you sound like my Classics professor at Radcliffe—the boob who said slavery in Greece was justified because it helped build the Parthenon." Mocking Professor Mendelssohn's elitism, I raised my voice in a parody of intellectual pomp and circumstance. "Which everyone—from the lowliest slave to the most exalted patrician—could look to as an ideal of democracy and justice."

"Leave history out of this, Henri. We're talking about the new, the modern."

"And?"

"And that's how we created the salons—by liberating art from politics. The salons are a haven from everything and everyone that tries to compromise and even kill art. Pure art."

My back bristled whenever I heard the word "pure." It must be the Catholic in me. Heir to centuries of atrocities committed in the name of a perfect Father, I despised even the concept of purity, which I held responsible for sins far greater than the sum of mere human frailties. "You're making me nervous, Gertrude."

"Why?"

"Because art is a powerful force *in* the world, not apart from it."

"Of course. But I don't think you understand where it comes from. Be careful you don't inadvertently destroy the Genesis of art."

"Don't tell me you're comparing the salons to the Garden of Eden," I said, laughing apprehensively.

"Not exactly. But they *are* the source of creative inspiration. And if you want to stay here—in Eden, or whatever you call it—you've got to follow the rules."

"Is that a threat?"

"Do you want to remain in the salon?"

"Yes."

"Then yes."

"Yes what?"

"Yes, we have no bananas," she said, quoting a popular song. Her patience with my annoying ethics and politics was obviously reaching a breaking point.

"But why, Gertrude? I'm still lost. What's the point of stealing paintings? What's that got to do with pure art?"

Gertrude Stein gave me a sharp look.

"I'm sorry. Forget I mentioned anything about stolen paintings or crime rings or insurance fraud or anything else."

"Henri!" Gertrude Stein shouted.

Turning to her, I made a gesture of buttoning my lip. "But *if* all this were happening, which I'm not saying it is, you'd turn a blind eye to it?"

"They need money, don't they?" Gertrude Stein asked emphatically. "You would deny a man his medicine, just because he's an artist?"

Then it was true. My worst suspicions were confirmed. I had heard, for one thing, that Juan Gris was seriously ill and needed money to cover medical expenses. When geniuses desperately needed money, they were apparently above the law.

Having recently witnessed the source of Picasso's financial woes, I also knew that poor Pablo went through money almost as quickly as F. Scott Fitzgerald did, their wives Olga and Zelda trying to buy their way into the most exalted echelons of high society. Even Gertrude Stein called Olga Picasso a golden cow. And the less politic Dadaist Tristan Tzara, renowned throughout Paris for his charming vulgarity, even warned Pablo that Olga was so extravagant she would one day force him to goldplate her cunt.

Braque's presumed motives for participating in the crime ring were less dramatic, but equally compelling. He was just plain impoverished, the son of a cobbler in Villeneuve-lès-Avignon, a town with one too many cobblers.

"If a mother stole a loaf of bread to feed her starving child, would you throw her in jail?" Gertrude Stein asked me accusingly.

"Do you really think that's a fair analogy?"

"If anything were really going on, it would be. But since there isn't, it isn't."

I had no idea what I really thought of all this now that I understood the humane motivation behind what I had assumed was cold-blooded theft. Gertrude Stein tried to make it sound like just another form of patronage. But benevolent designs don't justify criminal activities. On the other hand, I cringed at the idea that I was reverting back to the middle-American holier-than-thou-ism I had so desperately tried to escape. God knows that's what kind of stock I came from. The last thing Paris needed was an expatriate tattletale.

And then there was the other, less altruistic side of my dilemma. As a journalist, I needed a powerful incentive to convince me not to report this groundbreaking story—something as immutable as my loyalty to Gertrude Stein. I had uncovered a story that would shock and delight the American public. *En Vogue* would have to double its run of that month's issue, and I felt sure I could sell the story to the

New York Times. This piece could clinch my career as a foreign correspondent. How could I resist the temptation of a feature article in the *Times?* Never in my wildest professional dreams had I imagined that such a golden opportunity would present itself. And never in a million years could I have conceived of not seizing it.

I felt like Eve in the Garden of Eden. Loyalty to God himself hadn't stopped *her.*

Cashing in on tens of thousands of illegal insurance dollars looked a lot more like greed than charity to me, despite Gertrude Stein's cryptic rhetoric. Was she an accomplice or just an innocent bystander? Without knowing this, how could I possibly decide what to do with the forbidden fruit dangling in front of me?

Just as I was about to broach this last, most delicate aspect of the case, the sound of galloping hooves caused us to whirl around and freeze in our tracks. I cringed, but Gertrude Stein held her ground with unfaltering courage as a larger-than-life horse and rider bore down on us, thundering to a halt just a few feet away. I suddenly realized it was Natalie Barney.

Never before had I seen a more statuesque woman, nor one who wore her sexuality more triumphantly. I suspected that her stature had very little to do with the fact that she was astraddle a huge white horse; she was, it turned out, equally splendid in a drawing room.

The flagrancy with which she immediately flirted with me made me weak in the knees, momentarily competing with my obsessive memory of Manfred. She was magnificent, even heroic, bearing her sapphism like a coat of arms and waving her sensuality like a royal banner.

No one with a vagina was safe from the Amazon.

I knew immediately why she was Gertrude Stein's only real rival as the most famous salonnière in Paris. And I noticed as I glanced at my companion that she too was ruffling herself up to her full, broad stature to repel the challenge of Natalie's aggressive personality. They preened. They strutted. They flexed their charismatic muscles like two gladiators preparing for combat, with all of Paris as their prize.

The sheer breadth of Natalie's toothy smile marked her as an American. And when she opened her mouth, she spoke with a very broad American accent that somehow clashed with her classical nobility and grace.

"Hello, Gertrude. Who's this?" Natalie asked, nodding seductively at me. "Do you mean to tell me there's a new American in town and I haven't had the chance to..." Natalie paused suggestively "...to welcome her to Paris?"

"I've been deliberately hiding her from you," Gertrude Stein said in the kind of joking tone of voice people use to disguise unpleasant truths. "To protect her."

"It's no use," Natalie insisted. "All roads lead to..." she paused again "...my salon."

I felt like a shy little girl for the first time in decades, except that this time it felt very sexy.

"Aren't you going to introduce us?" Natalie demanded.

"I'm afraid to," Gertrude Stein answered. "It would be like introducing the spider to the fly."

"Oh come now, Gertrude. I'm ever so much nicer than a hairy little spider."

True enough. Yet Gertrude Stein had a point. Natalie looked at me like tomorrow morning's breakfast.

"But equally dangerous." Despite her reservations, Gertrude Stein finally presented me with a flourish. "Natalie, this is Henri."

"Henri Adams," I said bashfully. To this day I am embarrassed to report that my voice actually cracked. Natalie had me exactly where she wanted me.

"Charmed," Natalie said. Then she leaned down from her elaborately tooled leather saddle, reaching out as if to shake my hand. But when I extended my arm, she took my hand and kissed it, leaving the dewy imprint of lips far more full and feminine than I had expected from an Amazon warrior. Instantaneously, I was all riled up and so flustered I felt almost relieved when Gertrude Stein came to my rescue.

"Go easy, Natalie. Henri's not used to your extravagant, sapphic liberties. She's a dear friend, and I expect you to treat her like a gentleman."

Natalie laughed, a beautiful trilling light-hearted innocent laugh that utterly contradicted the smoldering expression of her eyes. "Oh, I will. Don't you worry about that. But you'll let her out of your sight long enough to come to my salon next Friday night, won't you, Gertrude? Surely you don't mean to keep Henri locked up in your salon forever!"

"Henri is free to move about as she pleases," Gertrude Stein said. "But I'm not kidding, Natalie. No monkey business, OK?"

"Cross my heart," Natalie said ambiguously, saluting Gertrude Stein with mock deference. Then, turning to me, she shot a final seductive arrow in my direction. Purposely missing my heart, it stabbed my groin. "A bientôt," she said in a voice so gentle it clashed with the swagger of her bearing. She was both princess and prince, a gallant girl and lovely lad all rolled into one.

Elaborate entrances and dramatic departures are the bread and butter of truly captivating women. Having cast her spell on me, Natalie knew better than to linger long enough for the fairy dust to settle. She wheeled her bright white steed around with a graceful violence that reminded me of Manfred and galloped off into the gathering dusk.

Gertrude Stein stood with her arms folded across her chest, shaking her head with a mixture of amusement and annoyance as we watched the Amazon's blond mane disappear into the distance. "She's a mouthful, isn't she?"

I only wished I knew.

Then Gertrude Stein began walking even more briskly than before, evidently concerned about making it back to 27 rue de Fleurus in time for dinner. Still a little weak in the knees, I stumbled repeatedly and lagged behind. My companion looked back over her shoulder, trying to spur me on. "I don't mean to rush you, Henri," she said apologetically. Even she was slightly winded. "But supper's at eight o'clock."

If there was one thing Alice B. Toklas couldn't tolerate, it was a delayed meal. Any number of catastrophes could befall the cuisine in the space of a mere minute or two—fallen omelettes, crystallized meringues, even scorched tarts—and Gertrude Stein wasn't about to risk the consequences of such serious domestic disasters.

Alice B. Toklas loved her food piping hot. Gertrude Stein, on the other hand, preferred hers cold and always tried to engage in conversation when Hélène served their meals, thus posing a constant threat to the temperature of Alice's food. But after twenty-two years of marriage, they had reached a kind of compromise. Gertrude would monologue while Alice ate, and then Toklas would return the favor as Stein consumed her dinner, even though by then, Alice insisted, the food was hardly worth eating.

I was still too stunned by my encounter with Natalie Barney to really keep up with Gertrude Stein's relentless pace. I kept bumping into the protruding baguettes husbands were carrying home to their wives for dinner. Gertrude was quick to pinpoint the source of my continued distraction.

"Henri," she said firmly, "I meant what I said about Natalie. I wouldn't take her advances too seriously. She flirts with anything fuzzy, even peaches."

Gertrude Stein had a way of saying things that didn't literally make sense, but nevertheless captured the real essence of the situation at hand. I found myself wishing I were a peach.

"Be careful," Stein warned me. "She can be dangerous. Especially to someone like you."

Someone like me. What did that mean? Why did I always feel I was being treated like a gullible, defenseless child in the presence of consenting adults? Was I really still just a country bumpkin, an American hick incapable of appreciating the erotic sophistication of Paris's sexual avant-garde? And so what if I was? Natalie Barney didn't seem to mind. With a pang, I remembered that Manfred had also apparently singled me out in spite of—or perhaps even because of—my ingenuous desire.

I was willing to take my chances. What, after all, had I come to Paris for in the first place, if not to have my heart broken, or at least toyed with? Natalie had every reason to reprimand Gertrude Stein for locking me up in her salon, expecting me to sit tight until I met a suitable, devoted wife like Alice B. Toklas. Although I did envy the emotional depth of her marriage, I definitely had a more adventurous, not to say promiscuous, side. It was high time I tried my luck in Natalie's more libertine sapphic salon.

My encounter with Natalie Barney had changed my center of gravity. I couldn't bring myself to resume my interrogation of Gertrude's possible involvement in the Kahnweiler case. My overzealous ethics and professional ambitions were suddenly taking a back seat to my romantic aspirations. I realized that I had been so off balance, obsessing over the Kahnweiler scandal, partially because I had lost sight of my original motive as an expatriate—to sow my wild amorous oats. My primary goal in Paris was to come of age as a sapphist, not as a journalist. Determined to let my emotional dreams take precedence over my professional nightmares, I decided to plunge back into the dark decadence of the Paris underground. So for the first time since my arrival in Paris, I declined Gertrude Stein's last-minute offer to join her and Alice for dinner, pretending I was racing the clock to meet an editorial deadline.

I returned to my hôtel to transform myself into Alec. More than anything else in the world, I longed to lose myself in the silky folds of Manfred's cape, and the even softer, more voluptuous folds she hid beneath her trousers.

I wandered all night through the secret chambers of prone oblivion and masked women at Le Petit Bouton, Le Masque, and even Les Lèvres, but Manfred was nowhere to be found. I began to fear I might never see her again. Then it occurred to me that if all sapphic roads really did lead to Natalie Barney's salon, I might find Manfred there.

I spent the intervening week searching for a second, even more elegant black silk suit for my debut at 20 rue Jacob. Ironically, it took the mannish woman in me to finally activate my vanity. I had never been much of a shopper, but Alec was a regular clotheshorse.

Miss Henrietta Adams
Hôtel Résidence les Cèdres
12 rue des Dames
17th Arrondissement
Paris, France

January 19, 1926

Dear Miss Adams:

First of all, let me congratulate you on the response to
your last editorial on Gertrude Stein's celebrated salon.
The number of cards and letters we received raving about
your column exceeded even those in response to the feature
article we ran on the influence of flappers on the fashion
industry. Needless to say, our readers just love
celebrities--even Hollywood can't produce them fast enough
to satisfy the insatiable appetite of the American public
for stardom. And you have succeeded in providing them with a
glimpse into a whole new constellation of stars. This also
speaks very well of our editorial collaboration, since the
Board edited your original piece quite substantially. We're
all very pleased with the result.

The Board's reaction to your most recent submission
on the volatile relationship between avant-garde aesthetics
and politics was somewhat more ambivalent. Given my interest
in the intersection between art and life, I quite liked the
piece. So did Larry Strachey (who continues, by the way, to
be your biggest fan). But I must tell you that a few other
members of the Board, especially Egbert Hoover, found it a
little too polemical or, as he himself put it, "dangerously
controversial." As the designated liaison between you and

the Board, I feel it is my duty to inform you that the general feeling at En Vogue is that art should remain unsullied by politics. Although we seek to instruct as we entertain, the magazine should never engage in anything that might inflame the public mind. I'm quite sure, given your keen journalistic eye, that you understand all of the ramifications of this ticklish subject. Enough said.

Fortunately, your submission ran on the long side, so Larry and I were able to edit out the more volatile segments and still piece together a very compelling historical sketch of the French government's confiscation of Kahnweiler's collection in the wake of the War. Since history is intrinsically more neutral than contemporary events, one can usually disguise current affairs in the guise of backward glances. If I may venture to pass on the wisdom that was bestowed upon me as a young journalist, I suggest you bear this in mind if you wish to continue to explore controversial topics--one of many tricks of the trade I learned from my mentor, Frances Langley of Saturday Evening Post fame. I half suspect, given the length of your original submission--almost twice as long as any of your previous editorials--that you anticipated the Board's reaction and the subsequent need to delete the more strident references to the politics of art. As you can see from the enclosed revised manuscript, we maintained the original focus of your piece--namely, the inflated value of Cubist art in general, and Kahnweiler's collection in particular, thanks to the public notoriety of the case as well as the temporary scarcity of available Picassos, Matisses, and Braques in the European art marketplace. Larry and I hope you will agree that the ironic edge of your original editorial remains intact, despite our deletions.

Without intending to belabor the topic of audience appeal, I remind you that your most popular columns to date have been portraits of celebrities. Now might be the perfect time to put together another of your wonderful interviews (those with Picasso and Matisse were huge hits) or, better yet, an even more dramatic piece in the vein of September's art theft article. What ever happened to the possible sequel you promised to write? Were you able to follow up, as you had hoped, with more information about the police investigation of a possible Cubist crime ring? I sincerely hope your hunches are panning out, because a story like this would be more than sensational. This is the kind of story that gets people nominated for national journalist awards, and it's high time we all won one!

Despite the fact that this letter seems top-heavy with editorial concerns, rest assured that they are minor in comparison with the overall quality of your work as a whole. Unforeseen problems are bound to crop up, especially in the beginning as authors adjust to the editorial criteria of the magazine. We remain, as always, very pleased with the success of your column thus far and equally confident that it will enjoy an even more prodigious future once we have worked out some of these incidental kinks.

Sincerely,

Irving P. Dickey
Senior Editor

cc: Board of Editors
En Vogue

CHAPTER EIGHT

20 rue Jacob

I was disappointed that Gertrude Stein wouldn't escort me to my first salon at 20 rue Jacob. But she said she couldn't bring herself to attend another of Natalie Barney's soirées. All their cant about Greek sorority, Bacchic revelry, and free love made her skin crawl. She preferred fidelity and the security of a good, home-cooked meal.

Women who cherish our rich sapphic legacy will not be surprised when I say that my heart was in my throat as I entered the heavy wooden double doors at 20 rue Jacob and traversed the stone courtyard to Natalie Barney's two-storied *pavillon*, a quaint house standing alone in a garden which grew with the natural disorder of wild and enchanted Romanticism.

In the corner of the garden, I spied the Doric Temple à l'Amitié, the site of Natalie's countless conquests. Rumor had it that Adrienne Lecouvreur, the most notorious lover of eighteenth-century Paris, had been poisoned by a jealous rival in this secret temple of love, inaugurating years of illicit trysts and delicious scandals.

The staid interior of the pavillon and its bohemian guests struck an unlikely balance between respectability and exoticism. The ceiling arched into an impressive oval dome, flanked by murals depicting cavorting nymphs. Of the portraits lining the walls, one in particular intrigued me: the single male presence in the room. I assumed it was

the likeness of Rémy de Gourmont, the reclusive pornographer and
literary critic of the Symbolist school of poetry whom Natalie, with her
unparalleled charm, had somehow coaxed out of hiding. Their
platonic courtship had given rise to de Gourmont's famous memoir,
Lettres à l'Amazone, the source of her nickname.

Berthe, Natalie's housekeeper and social secretary, stood at the
entrance to the drawing room. I introduced myself, and she clapped
her hands together and exclaimed, "Gertrude's new sapphist! I'll let
Natalie know you've finally arrived."

Natalie's manner was even more elegant than her gown, suggesting that the rough-hewn equestrienne in the Bois had been stabled
along with her stallion. Despite my newfound infatuation with the
masculine charms of Manfred, I preferred this feminine, drawing-
room version of Natalie Barney. Natalie wafted toward me, extending
her arms with theatrical yet genuine warmth. She greeted me in the
most impeccable French I had yet to hear among the expatriates in
Paris. In the Bois with Gertrude Stein, Natalie Barney had spoken
English like a midwesterner, but in the refined environs of her salon,
French was the official language.

"Welcome to my salon, Henri. We're delighted you've finally
come," she said, taking my hand in both of hers. An undercurrent of
innuendo flowed just beneath the surface of virtually everything she
said. "It was uncharacteristically generous of Gertrude Stein to lend
you to us for the evening."

I knew instantly that her jest contained absolutely no malice and
that the rivalry between Stein and Barney was just another part of the
rich lore of bohemian Paris, a delicious condiment spicing up the
moveable feast of the expatriate salons.

It was also immediately apparent why Gertrude Stein had chosen
to stay at home. The idea of Stein blending into this gaggle of
sapphists—for I had already decided that nobody in the room, except

perhaps Berthe, was heterosexual—was preposterous. A veritable sun, Gertrude Stein never placed herself in a position to be categorized as simply one of many stars, no matter how bright.

As I met one woman after another milling around a sumptuously appointed hors d'oeuvres table, I had to remind myself to close my gaping mouth, which flapped open in astonishment after each mind-boggling sighting: Colette, Romaine Brooks, Anna Wickham, Janet Flanner, Djuna Barnes, and Una, Lady Troubridge on the arm of Radclyffe Hall.

Natalie must have noticed my awe. "You know, Proust wanted to come to our Fridays—the ones reserved exclusively for the daughters of Sappho. But I reminded him that, though he had the sensibilities of a sapphist, he had the genitalia of a chorus boy. I say that with all due respect, of course."

I grinned obligingly, having heard the rumors of Proust's flamboyant quest to achieve what he called complete androgyny.

"Of course, you've heard of the scandal Rilke caused when he dressed up as a woman and crashed one of our meetings of the Académie des Femmes last June. He's lucky he escaped intact. I know there was some talk of obliging his desire to be one of the girls by removing that which stands between him and the angels—"

"In England we call that castration," said a woman with one of the most striking, though far from pleasing, countenances I had ever encountered. She looked vaguely familiar, with her cut, walrus-like buck teeth and her horsy face. "I'm sorry to have eavesdropped," she continued in a high, nervous, trilling voice, "but I can't resist Natalie's gossip."

"Dolly Wilde, this is Henri Adams from America. Gertrude Stein's been hoarding her over at the rue de Fleurus."

The resemblance was immediately apparent. She was Oscar Wilde's niece and so like him that reincarnation seemed the only possible explanation. Except that where Oscar was the epitome of flamboyance, Dolly Wilde was even more dowdy than the Cone sisters.

Presumably the accoutrements of Dolly's position in British society were more difficult to transcend than for the rest of us. Miss Dolly Wilde had to contend with the legacy of generations of frumpy matriarchs, their closets brimming with atrociously tasteful hats, and she was clearly losing the battle.

I had heard that Dolly and Natalie had an on-again-off-again affair. But though Dolly flirted openly and vigorously, Natalie was expressly noncommittal.

"Delighted, I'm sure," said Dolly, barely even looking at me. "Say, Natalie, where's Mata Hari?"

"She sent word she has a cold."

"Poor dear," Dolly said archly. "No doubt she caught it riding naked in the wilds of someone's salon last week. I understand it can get very drafty perched up on a horse's ass." Dolly turned to me. "We're so sorry you missed Mata Hari as Lady Godiva, here in this very room. I doubt very much that today's theatrical will be able to match the drama of that historic moment."

Natalie ignored Dolly's sarcasm. "What you don't know, Dolly, is that Mata Hari had planned on making her entrance on an elephant. No, really. But I vetoed the idea, fearing for the china tea cups."

"Natalie," Dolly laughed, "don't tell me you're getting conservative in your old age. Mata Hari as Hannibal! Now that would have been a treat."

"Not conservative, Dolly, just practical. Besides, the attraction had nothing to do with whatever animal was between Mata Hari's naked legs. Who cares about smelly old elephants anyway? Admit that Mata Hari made a fabulous Lady Godiva."

"Frankly, I'd rather see you, fully clothed, riding through the Bois de Boulogne," Dolly retorted. Then she turned to me again, as if

I were her straight man. "You know, of course, that this is Natalie's morning ritual, riding like an Amazon through the Bois, terrorizing innocent young girls with the sight of rampant, galloping sapphism. Scandalizing the neighborhood."

"Hence her nickname," I said obligingly.

"Precisely."

"Scandal is in the eyes of the beholder, Dolly," insisted Natalie. "Actually, I'm the picture of respectability, except, of course, that I don't ride sidesaddle." She winked at me, which really miffed Dolly. "Now if you'll excuse me, I must attend to my guests. Henri, I leave you with Dolly, though I shouldn't. I've no doubt that half of the rumors circulating in Paris start with her. And Henri," Natalie continued in a more intimate tone, "there's someone special I want to introduce you to before the theatrical begins, so don't stray too far."

"More special than me?" Dolly called after her.

It was immediately apparent that Dolly Wilde didn't give a rip about me, so I took advantage of her obvious indifference to circulate on my own.

"If you'll excuse me for a second, I'm ravenous," I said, moving toward the cucumber sandwiches.

"Aren't we all?" Dolly said offhandedly, completely devoid of the animation she had aimed at Natalie Barney.

Both Bryher and Djuna Barnes nodded hello to me as I poured myself a glass of champagne. Next to Djuna, wearing an elegant top hat, I recognized Romaine Brooks, whose scandalous paintings of Paris's expatriate sapphists revolutionized portraiture. She looked suitably discerning and distinguished, and not a little bored.

I also picked out Radclyffe Hall without benefit of an introduction. She was, sad but true, the most morose woman in the room. Alice B. Toklas, who knew everything about everybody, recently bemoaned the fact that Hall was becoming obsessed with Havelock

Ellis's theory of inversion, and all that garbage about male souls trapped in female bodies. In fact, Hall was allegedly at work on some fictional magnum opus about inversion, though she refused to show it to anyone in the salons for fear they'd recognize themselves in the novel's characters. Her companion, Una, Lady Troubridge, was glued to her side with a similarly grim countenance.

I kept an eye out for Manfred among the suits and ties of the more mannish guests. But she was nowhere to be found. It suddenly occurred to me that Manfred inhabited another world where even the aesthetics of beauty had been forged on a much fiercer fire. Seeing Manfred at Natalie Barney's salon was about as likely as seeing Vulcan on Olympus.

Most of the women in the room were decked out as if attending a toga party. The curves of their bodies caused undulations in the long vertical lines of their robes, pastel and very sheer. Some even had laurel wreaths in their hair. There were elegant women everywhere. I had begun to sorely miss them, for they were all but banished from Gertrude Stein's salon, at least this frilly kind that made me feel so tongue-tied and self-conscious.

But they, of course, did not approach me. The debonair Bryher did—with a business proposition, no less. I felt I was being wrenched away from my sapphic fantasies back into a mundane world. Bryher was a woman of few words, but her silence was more a function of economy of language than reticence. The more I got to know her, the more I realized that she was shrewd rather than shy, formidable despite her diminutive stature. I liked Bryher from the moment I had met her at Gertrude Stein's salon, but I was hardly in the mood for her tactical maneuvers.

"Say, I wanted to run something by you, old sport," she said in a confidential tone.

"What's that?" I asked, still a little preoccupied with *les femmes*.

"For the past couple of years I've been trying to start up a publishing house in New York City. Something like the Contact Editions that McAlmon and I run out of Paris. Or Alice's Plain Edition, but on a much larger scale. But I can't find a suitable senior editor. It occurred to me after meeting you at Gertrude's that you'd be perfect."

I was startled and a little befuddled by her proposition. I don't think well on my feet, which is why I always preferred writing editorials rather than news columns.

"But I'm a journalist," I protested.

"You're smart and you understand the American public. That's all I need. Besides, I want someone who's not afraid to stir up a little trouble. Nobody can beat a journalist at that game. You guys thrive on trouble. You sniff it out like dogs."

While of course she was right, I didn't appreciate Bryher's canine comparisons, especially since I was still feeling guilty about sniffing around Picasso's studio like a bloodhound on the trail of stolen paintings. I didn't need Bryher's reminding me of my mercenary violations of the simplest rules of friendship and loyalty.

She must have taken my silence for acquiescence. "You're not afraid of politics, are you," she added. It was a statement rather than a question.

For a fleeting moment, Bryher actually wrenched my attention away from *les femmes* surrounding the champagne punch bowl. It was almost uncanny, given my ethical frustrations with the Kahnweiler case, to say nothing of Irving P. Dickey's mounting displeasure with the controversial nature of my *En Vogue* columns, that Bryher suddenly approached me with the idea of editing expressly political publications. I wondered if Gertrude Stein had reported our argument to her, though I couldn't think why she would have bothered.

One thing was clear. Bryher was as much a bulldog about politics as I was.

"No, why?" I finally answered, dragging my heels to resist getting involved in a serious conversation that might scare the poodles away.

"Because I'm tired of all this nonsense about art for art's sake," Bryher complained. "Even McAlmon won't let me publish H. L. Mencken's stuff because he thinks it's too political, whatever that means."

"It means they've all got their heads in the sand."

"Exactly. Or somewhere a little less picturesque, if you know what I mean."

Of course I did. And no doubt I would have welcomed Bryher's worldliness and candor if I had been in a less Romantic frame of mind. But how, in the midst of all that sapphic pleasure, could anyone talk about business? Either Bryher was jaded after one too many infidelities on the part of stunning sapphic artists, like H. D., who let her romance them in exchange for patronage, or she was a eunuch. I, on the other hand, was more like a dog in heat.

"But I just got here," I said, realizing immediately that I sounded a little like a child whose toy is being taken away.

"What do you mean?"

"I've been trying to get to Paris for years, and now you want me to leave? I'm flattered, Bryher, I really am. But you couldn't pull me away from here with a tractor."

She smiled. "Listen to you. Anyone who uses homespun American analogies like that is bound to end up back in the States. Keep it in mind. Just in case. OK?"

"OK." Frankly, the whole idea scared me.

"Hear no evil, see no evil, speak no evil," Bryher said enigmatically. As she spoke, she covered her ears, eyes, and mouth, emulating the dutiful oblivion of that famous trio of monkeys.

A rowdy peal of laughter and scandalized gasps caught our attention. Several salonnières had retired to a corner and were passing around some apparently outrageous photographs. Anxious to replace business with pleasure, I suggested that we join this group. A very striking woman in a pale peach robe was acting as emcee, narrating the supposed events surrounding the photographs. She was so perfectly sensual—discreet, yet with the sexual promise of a cloistered madame—that I was not surprised to learn that she was Colette herself. As she narrated the official history of each picture, a peanut gallery of tittering spectators exposed the underbelly of the famous summer Natalie Barney spent with the poet Renée Vivien on the Isle of Lesbos.

Holding up a stylized photograph of Natalie feeding Renée grapes in a garden bower, Colette conjured up a sapphic sacrament. "Natalie Barney transubstantiates the grape, turning it from the banal food of Bacchus into the sacred nectar of love. Now a priceless photograph, it's known the world 'round as *Sappho's Communion.*"

"Subtitled *Renée Vivien's Last Meal*" was someone's sacrilegious version of the same picture.

Even Radclyffe Hall cracked a smile amidst everyone else's hilarity. This reference to Vivien's fatal anorexia nervosa apparently appealed to Hall's chronic morbidity.

Colette called the next picture, a shot of Renée half naked in the ocean, *Sapphic Baptism.*

Dolly Wilde, whose hostility was clearly related to her progressive interest in the quality of the champagne, provided a somewhat less lofty version of the motivation behind Renée Vivien's expression of abandon as she entered the rising waves. "Renée's response to Natalie's latest infidelity. Saved from a watery death only by the Amazon's timely arrival and the promise of love eternal."

"—not to be confused with fidelity which is a sentiment suitable only to dogs—"

"—and stale heterosexual marriages—"

Everyone burst out laughing, then tried to curb their merriment as Natalie herself approached the group, suspecting her role as the butt of their satire. With the magnanimous flourish I have come to admire, she didn't seem to mind at all and just joined in on the fun. "Poor old Renée," she said. "She always took everything so seriously. Especially love. God knows what she saw in me."

"Exquisite torture," said Djuna Barnes with a knowing smile. Her own gorgeous suffering at the hands of her alcoholic lover Thelma Wood was well-known throughout Paris. "What could be sexier?"

"Almost anything," said Natalie. "Spare me the reminder of that ghastly summer. Trust Renée to turn Lesbos into a prison. But then, I shouldn't defame the dead. Where are those other pictures? They're much more fun—just good clean sapphic pornography."

The next set of photographs was, if possible, even more self-consciously Hellenic, featuring Natalie and others indulging in exotic and, more often than not, erotic poses. I had never seen anything like these photographs. Oscar Wilde himself, and the whole clan of turn-of-the-century Decadents and Pre-Raphaelite pornographers, would have blushed at the shot of Natalie's vagina, spread not in an attitude of crass exploitation but with the simple purity of nature itself, as if the very folds of her lips had budded into a flowery bush whose half-open petals were but lightly touched with dew. Using some kind of filter, the photographer had blurred the edges of her prone body so that it blended imperceptibly into a lush bed of ferns on a forest floor. The inevitable shock of seeing a vagina at all—something I had certainly never seen in print, and seldom even in the light of day—was dispelled by its utterly natural surroundings.

"And of course this is Natalie's twat, not to put too fine a point on it," said Dolly Wilde.

"Which launched a thousand ships," I said, surprising myself by speaking up in such prodigious company. Natalie had a magnificent physique. And she was voluptuous with or without the costumes of femininity.

Dolly answered me with a dry look, obviously annoyed that I had waxed so poetic about Natalie's bodily parts.

In the next photograph, Natalie and a group of six other naked women cavorted amidst dappled stumps in the Bois de Fontainebleau, dancing in a pattern that recalled Botticelli's *The Three Graces.* In another, *The Nymph and the Shepherdess,* Natalie danced with a rustic female goatherd, barefoot and clad in a sheepskin tunic that barely covered a telltale bosom. In a third, Natalie and the same woman were locked in a passionate embrace, the first time I had ever seen a representation in any medium of two women kissing on the mouth.

"Where on earth did you get those outfits? And that woman?" Djuna Barnes exclaimed. It took a lot to impress Djuna.

"I commissioned an ancient Montmartre crone to make the costumes," Natalie explained. "She used to be a costume designer for the Paris Opéra, before her eyes failed her. But she still sees well enough to suit my purposes. Rustic outfits don't require straight seams. And I hired a discreet photographer. I refuse to divulge the name of the mystery woman; let's just say she sailed in from Lesbos to add local color. God knows I couldn't have used one of you." She looked right at Dolly Wilde. "Even *I* am sometimes aware of the jealousy factor, especially when it gets in the way of making good art."

Dolly snickered. "So now you're calling your promiscuity art?"

"Yes," Natalie said lightly. "Sapphic art. The heterosexuals have the ninety-nine positions at Pompeii, and I don't intend to stop until we've got a complete representation of our sexuality. In fact, I think it's high time we codified an entire sapphic aesthetic. Not a manifesto necessarily, but a body of work—our own tradition."

After almost a year in Paris, I felt that I had finally arrived. I was beginning to understand that the function of the salons was to pretend every Friday evening, from five to eight o'clock, that the world was not crass and cramped. Shutting out the conventional prejudices of the rabble, the salonnières engendered art and eroticism, free of the chains of propriety and the morality of procreation.

Later I was to wonder whether there was also something censorious about this privacy, no matter how high-minded. The salons not only shut out the banal world but kept us cloistered like so many promiscuous nuns in erotic Temples of Love. That first night, however, I was utterly taken. The caviar tasted of the wild liberty of the sea and the salty nether regions of the amphibious mermaids afloat in Natalie's drawing room.

"That concludes our tour of the pastoral haunts of the timeless woods of Fontainebleau," said Natalie with a vocal flourish. "But the main attraction of the day is yet to come—a performance of my very own *Douces Rivalités*. Let the players ready themselves, while the rest of us make gluttons of ourselves."

Clearly used to taking such cues, everyone dispersed, replenishing their glasses and pretending to squabble over the most delectable cakes.

Natalie appeared at my side. "Henri, you haven't had a chance to take a peek at the Temple à l'Amitié."

"I'd love to," I replied.

"I know. Everyone does," she said, embracing my eyes with hers. But then she continued much more nonchalantly. "Unfortunately, I've got too many guests to give you the grand tour myself, but why don't you tootle on over there and show yourself around."

"Thanks, I will," I said, unsuspectingly. I've learned since that nothing Natalie does is ever spontaneous or innocent.

At first glance, the Temple reminded me of the lavish dollhouses built by Marie Antoinette for her royal children. Yet its solid stone construction and Doric design dispelled any such thoughts of childish frivolity. The exterior had the ambiance of a classical scholar's library, or of a *temple de l'amour* whose very dignity elevated homosexual love to the exalted level of wisdom it enjoys in Plato's *Symposium*.

I felt as though I should remove my shoes as I climbed the steps and stood between the pillars, the cool of the interior wafting out with the faint aroma of incense.

Inside, there was one small but magnificent oval room with a towering domed ceiling and massive mirrors built into the walls, giving it the illusion of ballroom grandiosity. Candles burned in sconce chandeliers, placed on either side of the mirrors to heighten the effect of space through the play of light in seemingly endless prisms.

A bust of a woman, probably Aphrodite, graced the mantle of a mottled, pink-marble fireplace. And, to my surprise, there was a real woman reclining on the divan, though she could have been a specter from another era, looking very much like part of the decor with her sandled feet and long white robe gathered at the waist by a golden rope. She set aside the book she had been reading, *Idylle saphique,* and smiled. She was dark and exotic like Alice B. Toklas, with ebony tresses so long they overflowed her shoulders and cascaded onto the couch.

I was just about to excuse myself for disturbing her when she said, "You've come at last."

"At last?"

"I've been expecting you," she said as she sat up and patted the cushion next to her. I didn't obey her summons right away, but then it slowly dawned on me that this was a setup.

"I'm Simone."

"I'm Henri."

"I know."

I have often fantasized about the dark, exotic charms of Delilah and Salomé. Their sensuality was like a magical spell—deadly if resisted and, if indulged in, capable of engulfing the senses as completely as the whale did Jonah. All thoughts of the salon and the celebrities and the cucumber sandwiches vanished as I was transported into the belly of the whale with one kiss.

Where sex with Manfred had been dark and hard and thrillingly sinister, everything with Simone had an almost religious intensity to it—as if we were consummating some sacred, mysterious rite that would either save or destroy the world, depending on the strength of our faith. Talk about preaching to the converted! A part of me, a tiny black blemish on my soul, still hoped that Manfred would show up at the salon that night. But the rest of me was resplendent, already redeemed by Simone's embrace.

Just when I thought I had died and gone to the Isle of Lesbos, Simone stopped. "We must go now," she whispered. "I promised Natalie I'd bring you back for the theatrical."

She stood up, tugging gently on my outstretched hand. I tried to follow suit, but my legs wobbled a little and I plopped back down on the divan. This kind of heightened sensuality may have become the daily bread of the habitués of Natalie Barney's salon, but to me it was still the communion of the goddesses. I was too intoxicated to even stand up, let alone walk.

Simone smiled. Perhaps she even found it endearing, a quaint reminder of her own early days as a débutante salonnière. "Don't worry," she said, brushing my hair away from my forehead with a sweet, maternal touch. The temptress had transformed into the Madonna. "We've got all night."

As we walked back to the salon, I slowly emerged from my sensual stupor. Outside of the fairy-tale realm of the Temple, Simone's libertine availability seemed all the more fantastic.

"Are you so devoted to Natalie that you agreed to wait for me in the Temple?" I asked as we paused before reentering the drawing room. "What if I had been a monster?"

"I must admit that I'm pretty damned devoted. And Natalie knows what she's doing. She's famous for her delectable matches. Besides, I just love Americans."

"Why?"

"You're all so hopelessly sincere, so earnest. And there's nothing sexier than sincerity in bed."

There I was fantasizing about the redemptive seductions of Old Testament whores, and she was attracted to my sincerity.

Just call me Ernest.

Simone led me through the garden to where the salonnières had seated themselves beneath a stage complete with royal red curtains. Natalie was distributing programs that had been printed at some expense on very rough, elegant gray paper. On the front, a heart was superimposed on a triangle. Inside, the title read *Douces Rivalités*—Tender Rivals. According to the program, Colette, Eva Palmer, and Penelope Sikelianos had been cast as the drama's three inextricably entwined lovers.

I had, of course, heard of Eva Palmer. Rumor had it she had been Natalie's first lover, and that the Amazon still kept a strand of her flaming auburn hair in her lingerie drawer. Penelope, it turns out, was Isadora Duncan's sister-in-law. And Colette needed no introduction at all. The mere fact of her name listed in the cast of characters nudged half of the audience to the edge of their seats.

Darkness had descended upon the courtyard, and when two spots illuminated the stage, a hush fell over the audience. One by one the actors walked through the rich velvet curtain and stood for a moment in highly stylized Greek postures reminiscent of the statues we had all seen in the antiquities section of the Louvre. The overall effect was magical, as if the players onstage, the Temple in the garden, and the ambiance of that enchanting evening had conspired to transport us back in time to Sappho's court of love. After a breathtaking interval of silence, Colette began expounding the virtues of promiscuity. It didn't take long to realize that she was a thinly disguised Hellenic version of Natalie Barney herself. Love triangles, she proclaimed, were like aphrodisiacs. Though paradoxical, her logic was classically sapphic, based on the premise that romantic rivalries fan the fires of passion.

I cannot begin to describe the vision of Colette's voluptuous curves scarcely covered by a flesh-colored robe so silky smooth it caressed each contour, each crevasse. Barely backlit in blue, a spot illuminated a soft halo around her freely flowing hair. Her voice alone embodied complete and utter desirability, quite apart from these stunning theatrical effects. Never before had the wayward virtues of Sappho's inconstant constancy sounded so sublime.

At the conclusion of Act I, Simone temporarily let go of my hand to applaud the play's promiscuous ethic. As I looked around, I observed that the reaction of the audience was mixed. Radclyffe Hall and Una, Lady Troubridge clapped begrudgingly, staring with hostile expressions in opposite directions. Dolly Wilde had a smirk on her face, but she looked more angry than amused. Romaine Brooks had her head in her hands.

Though even Natalie herself admitted that her true love was Romaine Brooks, there was no stopping the Amazon's wanderlust. Briefing me for my debut at Natalie's salon, Gertrude Stein had informed me that, next to herself (and of course Alice B. Toklas), Romaine was Paris's most adamant opponent of sapphic libertinism. But unlike Gertrude Stein, who blamed Natalie's promiscuity on the loose ethics of the cult of sapphism, Romaine considered it an unfortunate eruption of masculine sensibility. Natalie pretended to emulate Sappho, but Romaine knew better.

Brooks had finally succeeded in forcing Natalie to be discreet in her indiscretions, which is why Dolly Wilde had been stricken from her sexual dance card. The rule was, if Romaine was expected to fraternize with a given sapphist at the salon, Natalie was expected to keep her hands off said sapphist. Natalie cheated, of course. But Romaine managed to turn a blind eye to the revolving door of the Temple of Love, so long as she was treated with the consummate respect befitting the queen of the harem. The exception was Lily, the Duchesse de Clermont-Tonnerre. A French noblewoman, she claimed discretion was beneath her. The Duchesse's on-again-off-again affair with the Amazon was like a proverbial elephant in Romaine and Natalie's bedroom. They both expended a great deal of energy pretending not to see her.

I tried to locate Natalie to gauge her response to the drama in the audience. She was nowhere to be seen, though I guessed she was situated where she could observe both the formal spectacle onstage and its impromptu offstage counterpart.

During this brief intermission, I heard the crush of footsteps on the stone courtyard and an expectant rustle in the audience. I turned around just in time to see a woman seating herself furtively, dressed in a blinding white ascot and black silk suit whose elegance exceeded even that of Una, Lady Troubridge's debonair attire. It was, of course, the Duchesse de Clermont-Tonnerre, sporting her new spectacular haircut.

I had admired her from the instant I met her at Gertrude Stein's salon. Yet I noticed that my thrill at Lily's arrival was not shared by the audience, and even I felt a ripple of apprehension.

Then, just as the actors returned to the stage for Act II, someone groaned in the back row. When I peeked over my shoulder, I saw Romaine Brooks stand up. With dignified fury, she abandoned her seat and was striding ferociously across the courtyard toward the gate on the rue Jacob. Ignoring this dramatic exit, the players recited their lines with admirable professional concentration, lamenting the agonies and extolling the ecstasies of triangular desire.

Simone giggled and nudged my side. "Life imitates art," she whispered. But I could not share her amusement. Though I was reaping the benefits of Natalie's free-spirited Hellenism, sitting there with one of her most devoted and available protégés, I found myself siding with Romaine, who was clearly infuriated by the arrival of her rival, the Duchesse.

Moments later, Natalie emerged from her hiding place behind the stage and gave chase to Romaine. This development amused Lily de Tonnerre, who smirked and said, "Here we go again."

Her flippant comment apparently pushed Dolly over the edge. She took this cue to stand up and announce, "That's all very easy for you to say, Lily, since you've got Natalie wrapped around your little finger!" And then Dolly disappeared in the opposite direction.

A chain reaction of indignation ensued, and it was all the actors could do to finish the play as the rest of us sat stunned and gaping, trying to salvage what was left of the bedraggled fourth wall separating the audience from the drama onstage. Finally, they retreated with apparent relief behind the curtain.

Thus abandoned by the actors, by our hostess, and even by numerous members of our own audience, we all burst out laughing to relieve the tension. Simone, whose enjoyment of the fiasco never skipped a beat, turned to Lily and said, "Your entrance was certainly a show stopper!" Then Natalie reappeared, sauntering through the front gate. Romaine, who had only agreed to attend the salon that Friday because Lily had made a fickle promise to stay away, was nowhere to be found.

"You're late," Natalie said playfully to Lily as she beckoned to us all. "Shall we reconvene in the salon?" We all followed our stage manager, and within minutes everyone was pretending nothing had happened.

When the smoke cleared, Lily's flippancy had clearly won the day. Simone and I excused ourselves to pick up where we had left off in the Temple a l'Amitié, as Lily braided Natalie's hair and the entire group discussed the merits of Colette's performance in the theatrical, which they all agreed had been a great success.

Miss Henrietta Adams
Hôtel Résidence les Cèdres
12 rue des Dames
17th Arrondissement
Paris, France

March 15, 1926

Dear Miss Adams:

I applaud your decision to make Man Ray the focus of this
month's editorial. Covering a photographer at all
(especially a portraitist) makes a bold statement about
the status of photography as an essential art form in the
avant-garde. The fact that Ray's subjects are primarily
the artists themselves adds another dimension to this
multilayered treatment, which is both sophisticated and
entertaining. In some ways this is one of your most
original and provocative editorials thus far, and for this
I congratulate you.

There are, however, some real problems with your
submission that will require more than the incidental
changes performed on your previous pieces. I don't know
how to put this delicately, so I'll just put it plainly.
Thankfully, you are a very straightforward person
yourself--a real straight shooter--so I know you will
appreciate my candor. Although Paris may have adopted a
rather lenient (if not indulgent!) approach to the
phenomenon of homosexuality among the avant-garde, our
readers are not so liberal in their views. Therefore, the
Board feels that the primary thesis of your editorial--
that sexual innovation and the dislocation of standard

gender roles are the touchstones of the avant-garde--is inappropriate (even if partially true), at least as far as En Vogue's audience is concerned.

I don't know exactly where you stand on the ticklish issues of inversion in particular and deviance in general--nor do I need to know--but I do know that it is not necessary for you to reflect Paris's avant-garde morality, as it were, in order to capture its avant-garde aesthetics. I suggest turning a blind eye to the whole phenomenon insofar as it exists at all, and devising a new perspective or lens through which to critique Man Ray's significance both as an innovator and as what you call the pictorial biographer of modern art. For one thing, the whole notion of the "candid camera," which you allude to several times, obviously reflects the avant-garde's revolutionary approach to realism itself, which has become a psychological as opposed to physical or material entity. Obviously you will know best which of these implicit parallels to make explicit as the new thesis of your article.

Don't despair. This sort of substantial revision is actually standard procedure. The wonder is that you haven't been asked to thoroughly revamp any of your previous submissions. Your track record remains excellent. Let me remind you that in order to meet the deadline for the May issue of En Vogue you must postmark your revision by March 26. This should give you almost a full week, which, of course, is considered a luxurious expanse of time in our business!

One final note of advice: although your subject is the avant-garde and is therefore destined to broach topics that, though not necessarily racy, are nevertheless

liminal and bohemian, don't forget the old ladies with
blue hair in your home state of Utah. They're not your
primary audience, but they have been known to pick up
En Vogue in the beauty parlor, and we want them to feel as
if our magazine has something to offer them too. On behalf
of the Board, let me assure you we look forward to
receiving your revision with complete confidence in your
sensitivity to these matters.

Sincerely,

Irving P. Dickey
Senior Editor

cc: Board of Editors
En Vogue

CHAPTER NINE

The Atelier

About a week after Natalie's salon, I received a card from her, thanking me for coming and wondering if I would join her for lunch the following Tuesday. She had something very special she wanted to show me, a surprise she was sure I would just love. Given her reputation and my native cynicism, I immediately thought of the Fontainebleau photographs and wondered if the surprise looked anything like a flower.

I was shocked that Natalie would spend her time escorting me around Paris, especially since she knew I already had a social patron in Gertrude Stein. Then I remembered the perennial rivalry between them, a salonnière game of chess in which I, among others, was a pawn.

Although they pretended not to care, all salonnières worth their salt took attendance, which is why they held their salons on different days. Natalie Barney had dibs on Fridays, Gertrude Stein monopolized Saturdays, and Edith Wharton was forced to catch-as-catch-can any other day, forever upstaged by the weekend girls. Absences could mark the beginning of defection, in which case they orchestrated particularly delectable, star-studded extravaganzas to lure back prodigal habitués. Despite claims to higher aesthetic purposes, the salon system relied on recruitment, and Natalie had obviously set her sights on me.

No doubt all my neighbors watched from behind their shutters when she picked me up, at one o'clock sharp, in front of the Hôtel Résidence les Cèdres. We were not accustomed to chauffeurs, or even cars, on the rue des Dames.

"Henri, how delightful to have you all to myself." Natalie greeted me with the genuine warmth she always exuded—and something more.

"The pleasure is all mine," I said, trying to respond to the layers of her magnanimity.

Natalie looked completely different than she had on the occasions of our two previous encounters. Outside of her salon and her equestrian jaunts in the Bois, the statuesque Amazon looked more like someone's Presbyterian great-aunt. Her incredible long blond mane had been tamed into an unflattering bun, knotted tightly at the back rather than loosely on top of her head. Yet there was still something outrageously sexy about her, despite the knotted hair and sensible pumps—the kind of appeal spinster librarians hide behind their spectacles, barely camouflaging the nascent butterfly in the bookworm.

I once heard a dilettante expatriate comment on the discrepancy between Natalie's flamboyance at home and her conservative demeanor on the street, suggesting that the Amazon was still partially self-conscious of her sapphism, despite the notoriety of her salon. This, of course, was poppycock. Natalie was equally bold in her frumpy, gray skirts, charming unsuspecting women in broad daylight on the streets of Paris until they either indignantly rebuffed her advances or accepted her invitation to tea. I always suspected Natalie's dumpy alter-ego was nothing more than a Faubourg Saint-Germain mannerism, the same kind of aristocratic indifference to fashion that enabled her neighbor the Duchesse de Polignac to dress like a scullery maid without jeopardizing her blue-blooded dignity. I noticed a similar phenomenon in Virginia Woolf, whose uncompromising feminism was somehow housed in the mannerisms of a British schoolmarm. Profoundly radical in the very marrow of their bones, they didn't have to worry so much if they looked the part.

"Don't you just love surprises?" Natalie asked as we sped off in her sedan.

Actually I don't. But then I remembered that Simone had been one of Natalie's surprises.

"Love them. *Live* for them," I lied.

When we seated ourselves in a quirky little neighborhood restaurant near l'Arc de Triomphe, where the garçons knew her by name, Natalie asked me about my affiliation with *En Vogue*. At first, I was a little taken aback by her interest in journalism. Except for Bryher's inopportune business proposition, I had noticed that in Paris no one ever talked about work at all, which, of course, Americans do incessantly. I found myself excited to discuss my profession with Natalie. Then I remembered that she and I had actually broached the subject fleetingly the previous week as we stood chatting at her salon. I had let slip a comment about my suspicions concerning the art theft crime ring. She had given me a queer look, and then laughed outright.

"That's old news, Henri," she had said glibly. "I could tell you stories that would make your hair curl. For all Gertrude Stein's moral posturing, she's involved in some pretty shady deals, if you ask me. Gertrude thinks morality extends only to sexuality. Whereas of course I think it covers everything *except* sexuality. That, and a few pounds of flesh, is what makes Gertrude Gertrude and me me." When Simone had returned with another round of champagne, we had dropped business in favor of pleasure.

As if the incriminating conversation in the Bois with Gertrude Stein weren't enough, I kept amassing more and more evidence that key members of the avant-garde, under the cagey leadership of

Kahnweiler, were in fact systematically stealing their own paintings. They were undoubtedly making a bundle on insurance fraud.

I tried to pretend that as an innocent bystander it was none of my business. But just as persistently, Lieutenant Dupin kept hounding me. He had a smoking gun on his hands but couldn't for the life of him figure out who had fired it. Given the insularity of the salons, he must have figured I was by far his best bet. Truth be told, his hunch about me wasn't far off the mark. But eventually I managed to give him the slip by quelling my own ethical qualms.

I kept reminding myself that the cardinal rule of expatriation was to shed national characteristics that perpetuate the kind of foreignness Parisians so disdain. And though I couldn't instantaneously exorcise my Puritan moral fastidiousness, I knew I'd sooner be damned than blow the whistle on my friends just to appease Lieutenant Dupin. So, taking Gertrude Stein's cue, I justified my silence as patronage rather than perjury. And, like Natalie Barney, I immersed myself in the pleasures of the flesh. If America was essentially pragmatic and prudish, France was aesthetic and hedonistic. So imagine my surprise when Natalie actually proposed over lunch that we mix business with pleasure, something almost unheard of in Paris.

"Part of the surprise is related to your work," Natalie said, as we sipped our apéritifs. She gazed at me even more provocatively than usual.

Her innuendo piqued my romantic curiosity. But then the waiter served our lunch and Natalie clammed up, refusing to divulge anything further until the actual unveiling she had scheduled later that afternoon.

Natalie had oysters on the half shell, and I had duck à l'orange. The meal was a model of poetic justice, though I was initially oblivious to what would have been painfully obvious to a more seasoned sapphic palate. With classic Hellenistic hyperbole, Natalie always claimed she ate oysters in honor of Aphrodite. I can never think of that meal today without picturing the salty aphrodisiacs on her plate having lunch with the sitting duck on mine.

After lunch Natalie ditched the gray car and chauffeur, a probably completely unnecessary precaution designed to heighten the mystery of our mission, and we walked further into the increasingly shoddy depths of the nondescript neighborhood around *l'Etoile*. Finally Natalie stopped at a shabby *pension*, whose steps were littered with cigarette butts and empty wine bottles, and led me inside to a lobby that reeked of cats. As the elevator ascended it creaked and shrieked so menacingly I almost suggested taking the stairs. It was one of those heavy, elaborate ironwork elevators from which beautiful women always fall to their deaths in Sherlock Holmes novels. Advancing to a battered door at the end of the hall, Natalie dipped her hand into her big old grandmothery gray leather purse and extracted a monstrous key. After a good deal of jimmying, the lock sprang open and I prepared to follow her in, but she detained me with her hand on my arm. Her touch was electrifying, and I jumped a little, realizing that, for all her suggestive glances and verbal innuendo, this was the first time she had actually laid hands on me that afternoon.

I suppose her hand rested on my arm no more than five or six seconds, yet I started shaking the way I had in the limousine with Manfred—the way virgins quake and quiver on the brink of the inevitable. Fortunately, the semidarkness concealed my agitation. "Wait here," she whispered. "It's very dark inside, and I've got to pull back the curtains to let the light in."

"Isn't there a light switch?" I whispered back.

"No. That's why it's on the top floor—for the light."

I waited impatiently for what seemed like ten minutes before Natalie finally returned and led me into a gargantuan loft-studio, brilliant light now streaming through the huge, high windows that lined all three of the distant adjacent walls. Beneath the windows on the walls, and scattered around the room on freestanding easels, were what seemed like hundreds of paintings, shrouded with black cloth. They were everywhere, each with a pull-cord on the side of its frame.

Before I could say anything—I was absolutely stunned—Natalie approached one of the frames and pulled its cord so that the curtain folded back, revealing a jarring portrait of none other than herself.

"Guess who?" she asked playfully.

"I know *who* it is, but whose is it?" I asked.

A hint of disappointment registered on Natalie's face, and then it dawned on me. I knew exactly where we were and why we had come so surreptitiously.

"My God," I gasped. "It's Romaine's atelier. You've brought me to Romaine Brooks's studio."

Then Natalie looked triumphant. Romaine was notorious for her privacy, which was one of the reasons why she kept her studio in such an obscure part of the city, far removed from prying eyes. It occurred to me that Natalie must have heard me begging Romaine to let me write an article about her work for *En Vogue.*

"You sly devil," I said gleefully.

"Just a very good friend. Romaine's work deserves more recognition, especially outside of Paris. And this way no one will be the wiser about how you gathered your information, at least until the article is safely in print."

"How much time have we got?" I asked, imagining Romaine walking in on us.

"At least until five o'clock. I roped Gertrude into it, and she agreed to have Romaine to lunch. She promised to keep her occupied through at least three courses, and Romaine is a very slow eater."

I had heard a great deal about Romaine's paintings but seen very little. Ever since her famous exhibition at the Galeries Durand-Ruel in

1910, she had been reticent to show her work. Actually the exhibition had been a great success, but showing her work felt like baring her soul, and she didn't need to sell paintings like so many of the others, thanks to the legacy of her fabulously mad and fortunately dead mother. Besides, when she chose to, she received outrageously extravagant commissions for her portraits. Everybody who was anybody in Paris wanted to be a Brooks original. Romaine Brooks's portraits chronicled and often lampooned the hidden foibles of the aristocracy. But like Man Ray, she also energized her art with the vitality of bohemia. After all, the salons consisted of both extremes, and it was this mixture of the avant-garde and the anachronistic—two polar and highly stylized opposites—that allowed them to thrive side by side for so many decades, oblivious to the real world of real people that surrounded them.

Unlike Picasso's studio, where there was paint everywhere—on the floor and on chairs (and even on his bald head)—Romaine's atelier was spotless. In the center of the room stood a small table lined with tubes of paint, each carefully rolled up like toothpaste in the medicine chests of finicky brushes. The colors were arranged from left to right in accordance with their place on the spectrum. There were many more darker hues, with only those pastels necessary to produce skin tones.

Clean brushes, which looked practically new, hung like marionettes on clips suspended from the ceiling on what could have been fishing line, one brush per clip. An assortment of stretched canvases was stored in the only cabinet in the whole studio. The rest of the room was bare and starkly beautiful—bright white walls and a gorgeous parquet floor stained deep mahogany, surprisingly ornate for such a seedy building.

"I assume she had the floor installed," I said, thinking aloud about how I might frame my article.

"Yes," Natalie said. "Her one concession to the beautiful. Romaine always says that she works better when surrounded by squalor. It leaves her free to concentrate everything exquisite onto the canvas."

"Gertrude Stein says the same thing about writing English sentences in France," I replied. "She says there's something pure about the complete contrast, like the French air isn't all cluttered up with English words as if to confuse her."

Natalie laughed. "Meanwhile, it's probably all about cheap rent. Expatriates always come up with such idealistic reasons for slumming in Paris."

In the middle of the room, on the only unshrouded easel, stood a half-finished painting. While it looked like a man, I assumed it was a sapphic *frère* except that she seemed too effeminate. Her hands caressed a piano draped with a fantastic piece of sheet music that flowed off the keys and into the sky like a glorious musical ribbon held on high by a chorus of what looked like angels, though they were still silhouetted in pencil and not yet painted in.

Describing this painting now, it sounds absurd, almost as sappy as a holiday greeting card. Yet it was magnificent. Romaine had a way of rendering the corny into the sublime that reminded me of Djuna Barnes's drawings. "Who is that woman?" I asked.

"Actually, it's not a woman, believe it or not. Sometimes Romaine deigns to paint particularly outrageous sissies and nancies, usually to reward them for their infamy. And, of course, their effeminacy. That's Reynaldo Hahn, the noted pianist and personage of the 1880s and '90s. He was a great friend of Proust. One of his ancient amours is having his seventieth birthday next month. That's Romaine's gift."

"Does he show up in *Remembrance of Things Past?*"

"Of course. We all do. In fact, Lily was the model for the Duchesse de Guermantes, one of my favorite characters in the novel. Robert de Montesquoi should also be here somewhere. He's Proust's

Baron de Charklus and has the dubious distinction of being the most notorious homosexual in Paris."

"I thought *you* were."

Natalie laughed. "No, I'm not notorious at all, though de Montesquoi and I were great friends. On the contrary, I'm the most respectable homosexual in town. Ask anyone."

"Even all your ex-lovers?" I asked playfully.

"Oh, everyone turns a blind eye to all that. That's why Paris is so marvelous—one's sex life is one's own. How else could I be so respectable and so promiscuous at the same time?"

Everyone except Renée and Romaine, I thought.

"Look, Henri," Natalie continued. "Let me give you a lesson in Parisian etiquette. As long as you don't flaunt it, you can do whatever you want, short of murder. Which is exactly what separated Montesquoi from me. It's one thing to be a bit of a dandy and a libertine in your own salon, but Robert flaunted it. And since a good deal of the bluest blood in Paris flowed in his veins, when he flaunted he did it on a grand scale. I actually owe much of my initial success in Paris to Robert, who was kind enough to introduce me to the most brilliant figures in his rather exalted caste. There was no more discriminating patron of writers and artists than he was, I assure you."

This fact, though complimentary, seemed to dismay Natalie. She paused as if to try to collect herself, but then continued with mounting vehemence. "But he let his eccentricity get the best of him, and he alienated virtually everyone before he died. Why, he used to fondle his young chorus boys—and I mean *too* young—in his box at the Paris Opéra, right there in front of God *and* the Princesse de Polignac. But I loved him so very much. That's his Persian tapestry hanging on the wall of my drawing room. I'm sure you saw it. He willed it to me with a note saying now he'd be a permanent member of my salon."

Natalie's eyes were swimming in these memories.

"Now I ask you. Is it necessary to parade your genitals around for all of Paris to see?"

She wiped one eye, looking suddenly but only momentarily helpless. Never had I seen her look less like an Amazon, all weepy in that dowdy, gray skirt.

Overwhelmed by the intrigue and nostalgia of unveiling Romaine Brooks's private collection, I sensed that Natalie's oysters had apparently, if only temporarily, forgotten their amorous designs on my duck. As *En Vogue*'s avant-garde art correspondent, I was relieved. I've never been very good at doing two things at once, and I had my hands full with all those paintings. But as a sapphist whose arm still buzzed with the electrifying aftershock of Natalie's touch, I felt disappointed.

"What am I doing dwelling on the past?" Natalie asked. "We've got so much to look at, and Hélène could very well be serving the second course already at Gertrude's. The point is he should have kept his penis in his pants," she said with finality, assuming a much more determined expression. "I'm going to have to watch myself or I'll rhapsodize for hours in front of every painting. Each portrait tells a thousand and one tales, most of them flamboyant and wonderful. This gallery is nothing less than the most complete archive of homosexual culture in all of Paris, perhaps in all the world."

"And you're the curator," I said, more than a little awed.

"Yes," Natalie said with modest pleasure. "I am."

We started making our way around the room. As Natalie did the honors, pulling the cords and revealing the most famous sapphists in Europe, she couldn't resist providing detailed genealogies of their liaisons and achievements, usually scandalous. Never before and probably never again will there be such a complete gallery of the Who's Who of the sapphic universe. Romaine's larger-than-life canvases read like a catalogue of epic heroes. And I felt, for the first time in my life, that I too was a part of history.

Here was Violet Trefusis, Virginia Woolf's on-again-off-again romantic interest, whose ugliness Romaine Brooks had elevated to the level of monstrous magnificence. Here was Mata Hari, looking her usual exotic and vaguely ridiculous self, a touch of the simian in her temptress pout.

Renée Vivien's portrait could not have been more fragile or more unlike that of Radclyffe Hall, nearby in a sleek hunting outfit, complete with a jaunty, animal-skin hat.

Romaine had painted Paris's two distinguished booksellers Sylvia Beach and Adrienne Monnier, who had lived with each other almost as long as Gertrude and Alice, looking straight ahead with chastised expressions, hands clasped on their laps as if they had been caught cheating. In another portrait Lady Anglesy and Princess Edmond de Polignac looked very very rich and even more vapid.

Marie Lenéru looked exactly like the word "fop" sounds.

Janet Flanner could have been the dashing Prince Charming our mothers all dreamed we would marry. Dr. Faustus was there in the portrait of the English poet Anna Wickham, whose likeness suggested she was even more masculine yet more beautiful than she had actually looked at Natalie's salon. And that was saying a lot about Romaine's ability to paint sheer, androgynous beauty.

Eva Palmer was there too, fingering the famous lock of hair she had given to Natalie in 1894.

The portrait of Vita Sackville-West seemed to beckon to me personally, inviting me for a tryst in one of the thousand and four rooms of her castle at Knole. She was so firmly holding her riding crop, yet there were, tellingly, no horses in sight. Let the world call Natalie Barney what they will, Sackville-West was the true Amazon of modern Europe. I, for one, would gladly have submitted to the discipline of her switch.

Then there was Lily, Elisabeth de Gramont, Duchesse de Clermont-Tonnerre, looking extremely dignified, with a rare aura of class and discernment, almost as if she had been knighted by Romaine's esteem. Given the scene involving this particular love triangle at Natalie's salon, I was surprised by the dignity of Lily's portrait. My reaction did not escape Natalie.

"Grand, isn't it? Here you can see the generous and expansive side of Romaine's work. She can transcend petty feuds and personal grudges when the subject deserves her respect."

"Especially if the subject is a sapphist," I remarked.

"Quite so. For all her crusty disparagement of the cult of Sappho, Romaine has done more to promote our cause than anyone else."

"Except, of course, you and Gertrude Stein," I added.

"There are the obvious exceptions," Natalie admitted with very becoming pride.

Needless to say, Natalie was a brilliant oral historian in every sense of the term. She took particular delight in pointing out a quirky painting of Liane de Pougy, one of the most accomplished courtesans of La Belle Epoque, whom Natalie had somehow lured away from her customary entourage of noble gentlemen for a highly publicized dalliance. Both were so pleased with the controversy their affair stirred up that they published choice autobiographical tidbits, Natalie in her *Souvenirs indiscrets* and Liane de Pougy in her only novel, *Idylle saphique*. Remarkably, de Pougy crowned her career by marrying Prince Ghika, becoming a perfectly respectable member of the society she had sexually infiltrated for the two decades surrounding the turn of the century. World renowned in *l'art de l'amour*, Liane had been Natalie's first and some say greatest conquest in Paris. Quite a feat for a greenhorn expatriate.

A fabulous novella lay nascent in all those portraits hidden away in Romaine's atelier—the definitive pictorial history of the most flamboyant and influential group of homosexuals ever to conquer a city. My favorite was one of Romaine's self-portraits. Reserved and debonair in her characteristic formal black suit and gloves, with bright cuffs and a stiff white collar, Romaine redefines elegance. Let alone gender. But her face. The pasty white pallor and blood-red lips of a vampire, and the very dark eyes shaded seductively by the brim of her elegant top hat. I could only think of a cult of blood—not the messy and deadly blood of war but cups and cups of blood brought to the lips of the grateful vampire, sensual, life-giving blood.

Her eyes mesmerized me. I must say that I had never before thought about blood cults of any kind, except perhaps those depicted in the Christian rituals of Medieval art. Looking at Romaine's self-portrait, I had an awakening, a very morbid and disturbingly sexual awakening. Already, I was beginning to worry about the direction my *En Vogue* article might take. Paris was notoriously decadent. And I didn't think that my American readers were ready for the seductions of sapphic vampires.

Of course there were several portraits of Natalie herself. The most magnificent of them, showing Natalie sitting behind a black ceramic horse that seems to be galloping off into a wooded background, suggests that she was prone to riding off rather too frequently, despite her otherwise conventional appearance, the fur coat, the brooch at her throat, the moderately bored aristocratic expression.

There was something vaguely nasty and certainly ironic about Romaine Brooks's constant use of animals in her paintings. In one, a *grande dame* whom Romaine obviously despises sits next to a small goat figurine, their expressions so alike they look like twins.

"Don't you just love it?" Natalie gushed. "That woman, who has a lot more money than brains, actually liked her portrait until it was exhibited at the Salon de la Société Nationale des Beaux Arts. Apparently she overheard some critic pointing out that she and the goat look like blood relatives."

Natalie clapped her hands. "I'll never forget it, Romaine and I laughed so hard. Elsie wanted the picture destroyed, and Romaine went so far as to pretend she had done the dirty deed. So you'd better not include this one in your article, though I know it's tempting." Natalie pulled the cord and *La Chèvre Blanche* disappeared behind black velvet.

Then she turned with a flourish to a much larger easel, one well worth the fanfare. Costumed in a tuxedo complete with cravat, Una, Lady Troubridge scowls at her audience, penetrating the object of her disdain all the more sharply through her monocle. She is the first woman in the history of painting to wear a monocle, and she does so with scornful authority.

Una's portrait seems to be telling us to bugger off, to leave her alone with her very long, very phallic dachshunds, one of which she has hooked around the collar with an especially long and curved thumb. Her hair is short and clipped and sort of snotty the way Little Lord Fauntleroy is snotty—a priggish homosexual, if you can imagine that.

"You know, of course, where she got those damned dogs," Natalie said, suddenly annoyed.

"Actually, I don't."

"From Radclyffe Hall. Two championship dachshunds. How romantic," Natalie said sarcastically. "I will never understand what Romaine saw in her."

"What do you mean? She's a great subject. This is the most interesting—not the most beautiful, mind you—but the most interesting portrait I've seen yet."

"The portrait is a stroke of genius, though I do think it's a little over the top, even for Romaine. But to actually sleep with that goon. It's disgusting."

"I didn't know that."

"Oh yes. Romaine got mad at me for spending so much time with Rémy de Gourmont, as if I could ever have designs on a man, let alone a man with lupus. So she ran off with Lady Troubridge for a few weeks just to punish me. I swear to you it put me off my food for a week. It's one thing for Radclyffe and Una to carry on—they're practically married, you know, except that they can't agree on what brand of mustache wax to keep in the medicine chest. But for Romaine to actually get involved with such a pinched-up old prude, even if it was for a good cause, is disgusting."

"A sapphic prude?"

"Sure, you know the type. A regular old spinster. God knows you spent enough time in New England to have met a few."

"Let alone Bliss, Utah. But what do you mean, 'for a good cause'?"

"Jealousy. Sometimes I just love Romaine's little flirtations. I pretend to hate them, of course, but they give me a little room to breathe, which I need. I have a very claustrophobic heart, you know."

"Don't make it sound like such a liability. Let's just say you're extremely gregarious." Although I meant this as a joke, I knew immediately from the change in Natalie's expression that I'd made a mistake. Far from forgotten, her saucy, romantic scenario had simply been simmering until the duck was done to a turn.

"So much so that Gertrude Stein made me promise to leave you alone," Natalie said, suddenly giving me a look that suggested she planned to do anything but leave me alone.

"What do you mean?"

"That's how I got Gertrude to baby-sit Romaine today. I promised I wouldn't try to get you into the Temple of Love, if you know what I mean."

Needless to say, I was flattered, but I didn't let on. Truth be told, my ambivalence was all but paralyzing me. On the one hand, the idea of turning down a tryst with the most accomplished lover in Paris—

perhaps even the world—seemed insane. On the other hand, I felt a certain loyalty to Lily, who had actually become quite a good friend in the six months since our initial introduction at Gertrude Stein's.

But even if Lily didn't mind—and there was a good chance she wouldn't, since she embraced promiscuity almost as passionately as Natalie herself—the image of Romaine Brooks storming out of Natalie Barney's salon still haunted me. I had empathized more with Romaine's indignation at the theatrical than with Lily's or Natalie's nonchalance. Perhaps I was more in Gertrude Stein's camp than I had previously thought—not exactly a wild fan of fidelity but at least sensitive to the natural instincts of emotional territorialism. The idea of succumbing to Natalie's coquetries right there in Romaine Brooks's own private atelier seemed too indecent to be sexy.

That day, my education took an unexpected turn when it dawned on me that, paradoxically, eroticism is actually contingent on propriety—that the most outrageously seductive scenarios are those that flirt with modesty rather than completely disregard it. That's why nuns and librarians and even Natalie herself in her staid, gray skirt are so provocative and tempting.

"Gertrude Stein is very protective of you, you know," Natalie said suggestively. She grabbed a buttonhole on my jacket, stuck her index finger through it, and pulled gently. "Why is that?"

"Gertrude has always been something of a mentor to me," I replied, still pretending to be oblivious, despite being literally buttonholed. "Almost like a mother, except she's not the mothering type. But as much like a sapphic mother as I've ever had. I was very backward when I arrived in Paris."

"Well, you're a very astute pupil, or daughter, or whatever. A very accomplished sapphist, at any rate." Natalie paused quite deliberately. "Of course, having promised, now I'm finding it almost impossible to resist seducing you. Forbidden fruit, you understand."

I felt objectified, but naturally I didn't mind that a bit. Her finger still hooked in my buttonhole, Natalie pulled me more firmly toward her, her eyes wide open and smiling. Her face was close to mine and our lips threatened to collide, hers full and wet and unspeakably inviting.

I wanted nothing more than to give into Natalie's chronic impulse to add to her long list of conquests, but there was too much at stake. I knew, for one thing, Gertrude Stein would read it as a breach of loyalty. Let alone Lily and Romaine. I also knew full well that Natalie would dismiss these reservations as profane impediments to the higher purpose of sacred sapphic love. Natalie Barney was perfectly capable of proving it would be sacrilegious *not* to indulge in sex with her. So I decided to turn the tables and blame myself by pretending my heart was already spoken for.

There was at least a modicum of truth behind this strategy, given my obsession with the memory of Manfred. Yet I hestitated to mention Manfred for fear that Natalie would trivialize my glorious paramour. I stumbled on my defense just as the proximity of Natalie's blue eyes started to blur beyond vision into deep pools of water much wetter than the sea.

"But what about Simone?" I asked frantically, jerking my head back.

Natalie laughed so hard her finger slipped out of my jacket. "Simone! What possessed you to think of Simone at a time like this? Don't you know that she was just an appetizer? I'm the entrée. The main dish. *La pièce de la résistance.*"

This was so obviously true, I immediately abandoned my fib, a little embarrassed by the inadequacy of my own defense. Then it occurred to me that all I really had to do was stall, which was easily accomplished, given the goal of our visit to Romaine's atelier.

"Then let's hold off till we can really savor it," I replied as sincerely as possible, which wasn't much of a stretch since I was actually swinging between loyalty and lust like a sapphic flying-trapeze artist. "Don't forget that Romaine herself is probably well on her way to consuming her own entrée at Gertrude Stein's, and we haven't got much time."

Far from spurring Natalie on to even more grandiose heights of seductive hyperbole, rejection seemed to bore her. "True enough," she said flatly. She turned her back on me and walked over to a corner crowded with shrouded easels.

"I guess we'll just have to admire each other from afar," I said, disappointed by her abrupt indifference. "It seems we're destined for romantic love—painful and unrequited."

"No thanks," she said, making a sour face. "Romantic love is for melancholiacs and masochists. I've always preferred Classical love— joyous and polygamous. You'll let me know if you ever see the light?"

Natalie Barney took me at my word. To this day, I still can't believe I rejected the Amazon's advances. Even sapphists can be too noble for their own good.

Yet my disappointment was short-lived. Natalie beckoned to me from the corner. "It's getting late," she said, "and if Romaine finds us here she'll cut me off for a year. There's one last painting you've simply got to see, and then we've got to scram."

There was no doubt as to why Natalie saved *Peter* for last. Very erect in a great big captain's coat with shiny gold buttons, one thumb hooked in her pocket in a classic sapphic pose, sat Peter. The boyish haircut, one lock astray across her forehead, did nothing to detract from the intensity of her gaze, almost stern yet innocent. Never had a chiseled profile rested so blithely on such a tender, exquisite neck. The sculpted nostril embodied that perfect, androgynous mixture of power and grace, slightly arched not with disdain but with a discernment impossible on such a hopelessly young and perpetually innocent face.

Peter was magnificent. Breathtaking. She was a sapphic Platonic form, an archetype, Greek god and goddess rolled into one, the ideal conclusion to every form of evolution ever conceived of by the universe.

If I had been given a choice that day, I would have foregone looking at all the preceding wonders and spent the whole afternoon with *Peter*.

At length I felt Natalie's hand on my shoulder. "And now we really do have to go," she whispered. She closed the little black curtain on *Peter*'s radiance.

Once out on the Parisian streets, which usually looked so beautiful to me, I felt catapulted back into a fallen world. I was dazed, and clearly suffering from the art lover's equivalent of postcoital depression.

Honoring my mood, and sharing my reverence for the artist, Natalie kept a respectful silence until we located the gray car and the gray chauffeur, who deposited me at the door of my hôtel. The Amazon made one last half-hearted attempt to entice me back to the Temple à l'Amitié. But finally we both accepted the fact that I was far too smitten with the aesthetic transcendence of Romaine's art to appreciate the profane beauty of Natalie's body.

Even so, she couldn't resist slipping me the tongue when she kissed me good-bye. "Don't forget. Mum's the word," she reminded me. Thanking her again, I promised to keep our pilgrimage a secret. I also assured her that though my article could never do full justice to Romaine's genius, I would write as I had never written before.

It is true that I experienced an unprecedented surge of inspiration. I felt compelled to write about the aesthetic ideal of androgyny and the sensuous vitality of sapphists and the tran-scendental nature of both. But my audience was the American public. Clearly, I had a problem.

I could have written an article from a more generic point of view. I could have said, as I have heard it said so often by critics blinded by their fear of homosexuals, that Romaine's paintings were a classic example of decadence taken to its most depressing extreme. But those who do not think inversion is sexy should stick to religious art and other subjects concentrating on human beings from the waist up.

The fact that Romaine's portraits depict her subjects from the waist up is deceptive. They invariably sit or stand in front of tables crowded with the black animals—horses, dogs, and cats—that represent their wild sexuality. Brooks's portraits actually resemble Hemingway's iceberg technique in which the most important aspects of the story are left out, looming beneath the surface and in the unconscious, the seat of latent desire. Of course I was perfectly capable of ignoring all this to cater to Irving P. Dickey's editorial sensibilities. After all, I had been raised in Utah where everyone was amputated from the waist down.

So I played it safe and wrote a whole article pretending that the aristocrats and bohemians and inverts shared the same melancholic loneliness and bitter beauty. I pretended they were all descendants of the Pre-Raphaelite aesthetic cult whose strange monastic expressions, exquisite yet sexless, emanated not from innocence but from sensuality purged of its fleshy encumbrances—the ultimate triumph of the spirit over the corruption of the flesh.

My article was garbage. A feedbag of trite lies to placate the masses. No doubt Irving P. Dickey and his Board would have been pleased with my efforts to repress the truth. But I felt like a prostitute.

I ripped up the crap I had written.

And then I knew I was in trouble, because there was no nice way to tell the readers of *En Vogue* that Romaine's androgynes had ascended to a higher spiritual plane.

How could I explain to Americans, who quote God incessantly but know nothing of spirituality, that Romaine Brooks's sapphists were the avant-garde expression of ancient mystical cults of androgyny; that they had successfully returned to the original Evadam—Eve and Adam joined in perfect gender wholism before the severance of the rib and the terrible fall into heterosexuality? *Peter*, of course, was the archetype: perfect gender intercourse within one androgynous body.

For five feverish days I wrote the best article I had ever written in my life, and I knew it would jeopardize my job. I called it "Romaine Brooks's Sapphic Eden in Paris." Having sealed my editorial, and probably my fate, in an overseas envelope, I ran to the post office to send it off before I lost my nerve.

Miss Henrietta Adams
Hôtel Résidence les Cèdres
12 rue des Dames
17th Arrondissement
Paris, France

April 10, 1926

Dear Miss Adams:

I must say I am mystified by your latest submission,
especially after our lengthy correspondence on the subject
of elderly ladies with blue hair. You will notice from the
date of this letter (which precedes our regularly
scheduled Board Approval Meeting) that I am taking the
liberty to write to you independently--to intervene, as it
were, to counsel you to write an entirely new editorial
and send it post haste. Frankly, it's not worth trying to
get your Romaine Brooks submission approved, even with
major revisions. I can assure you its subject matter is
best left behind closed doors. I cannot help but think
that since you submitted this month's editorial so early,
you anticipated a problem. Obviously we've got one.

I daresay Romaine Brooks herself is a worthy
subject. I share your assessment of her as the preeminent
portraitist of the avant-garde and think your idea of
presenting this editorial as a companion piece to that of
Man Ray--Paris's two pictorial biographers--is a worthy
strategy. But why, with so many handles and angles to
choose from, do you persist in pursuing the subject of
inversion? I thought I had made myself clear, but I will
say it once more even more baldly.

Sexuality has nothing to do with art, at least as far as our readers are concerned. Furthermore, homosexuality is a topic more suited to medical journals than to art magazines. It is safe to say that if a subject crops up on the psychoanalyst's couch, it does not belong in En Vogue. I must say I feel awkward reprimanding you in this way. You are a smart woman, Miss Adams, with a reputation for mature and appropriate journalism. This isn't really a question of ethics or even of taste--it's a matter of professionalism. Frankly, I would have thought all of this was self-evident. But I am certain, having made myself very clear now, that we have seen the last of this problem.

Since there are so many excellent tangents that you could develop into the focus of the Brooks piece, I hesitate to offer any suggestions. Yet I cannot help but tell you that I was particularly intrigued by the contrast between anachronistic aristocrats and avant-garde bohemians coexisting both in the salons and in Romaine Brooks's oeuvre. Needless to say, the description of Brooks's atelier itself, and the way you compare its spartan minimalism with the sublime chaos of Picasso's studio, is excellent. I have always found you to be particularly eloquent on the subject of the logistics of artistic production. Yet these topics might very well prove tangential. I still have every confidence in your judgment and defer to your discretion with regard to the new focus of your Brooks editorial.

I hope you will honor my discretion with a little of your own. When the Board meets next Monday, I will tell them that you stumbled on a brilliant story at the last minute and requested a brief extension. As long as your

new article is postmarked by the 20th, we should be able
to meet the press deadline (provided you steer clear of
the obvious taboos!). Remember, we've also got that
reserve editorial I asked you to write for emergencies
such as this--"Le Vernissage des Independents: A
Retrospective"--which provides a very compelling account
of the origins of Cubism and the apprenticeships of all
our favorite modern artists. I would rather keep this
piece in reserve, but I will pull it out at the end of the
month if necessary. I am, however, operating on the
premise that I will be receiving your new Brooks piece by
the 30th.

     As far as I'm concerned, your talents as a
journalist and art critic far outweigh these momentary
lapses of judgment. There are bound to be snags along the
way, especially with regard to getting to know the
sensibilities of your target audience. This problem is no
doubt exacerbated since, being overseas in a somewhat more
lax, not to say promiscuous, culture, you are so far
removed from your readers. But let us put all this behind
us and start anew. I assure you, barring future incident,
all is well.

Sincerely,

Irving P. Dickey
Senior Editor

CHAPTER TEN

Sappho's Temple

I felt like Prince Charming looking for Cinderella, except my princess was shrouded in gothic mystery rather than sprinkled with fairy dust. I suspected that Manfred's coach had turned into a coffin instead of a pumpkin, and her escorts into bats rather than mice. The glass slipper was more like a nipple clamp.

I was still convinced I couldn't approach Gertrude Stein for help in my search. I hadn't even planned on telling her about my journeys into the Parisian underworld, let alone the fact that I had fallen for a dominatrix. Besides, what were the chances of the thoroughly domestic Stein knowing Manfred? I underestimated Gertrude Stein's eclectic range of friends and acquaintances. As it turned out, she could have saved me considerable emotional trauma if I'd gone straight to her.

Instead, I finally caved in and decided to confide in Natalie Barney, but only after several more failed attempts to find Manfred on my own. A couple of times I thought I caught glimpses of her across nightclubs thick with cigarette smoke, but she vanished by the time I slithered my way through the crowd. I couldn't exorcise the memory of Manfred, the smoldering eyes and sleek hard thighs of the imperious viscount who had abducted my soul in the Paris underground.

Rather than fading with the passage of time, these visions of Manfred loomed larger every day until I could think of nothing else. Finally, I just couldn't stand it anymore. I decided to consult the sapphic Oracle of Paris, but I had to wait a full day, brimming with anticipation. It was Thursday and of course Natalie's salon was held on Friday evenings.

I tried to kill time by writing my response to Irving Dickey's ultimatum concerning my Romaine Brooks editorial. But I couldn't concentrate. Manfred stalked me. I imagined her laid out pallid and peaceful in a coffin in some dank vault, sleeping through the glaring daylight until the vampiric moon heralded the gorgeous eternal life of the night, the swishing of black, velvety capes and the cold shiver of steel against cool, quivering flesh.

I arrived at five o'clock, hoping to catch a moment with Natalie before the throngs arrived. Her drawing room was already filled with people anxiously anticipating an event I had not heard about. I knew immediately why I had been kept in the dark. James Joyce, whose *Ulysses* was being reissued in a limited reprint edition by Sylvia Beach at Shakespeare and Company, was following up a reading at her bookstore with one at Natalie's salon. Since Joyce was Gertrude Stein's nemesis, more despicable even than Ezra Pound (whom Gertrude called "the village idiot"), she had not bothered to mention this event.

I had never seen a more distinguished group of salonniers. The very shy Joyce with his thick lenses and magnified fish eyes was conversing in a corner with Pound, who always looked as if he had just been let loose on a day's furlough from some insane asylum. Joyce's wife, Nora, who, I had heard, was as vital to his career as Alice B. Toklas was to Gertrude Stein's, looked surprisingly sexy in an Irish, boorish way, which probably explained why she was being entertained by a highly attentive Colette.

Even Rémy de Gourmont was there for this auspicious occasion, lurking like the Phantom of the Opera in the shadows to hide the ravages of lupus. A recluse, he only emerged when Paris was entertaining literary royalty. And Joyce was the king.

Hemingway, who was as ungracious with rivals as Gertrude Stein, was conspicuously absent.

I finally located Natalie talking to Sylvia Beach, presumably about the logistics of the reading. "Henri! You made it. We didn't know if Gertrude would let you visit the enemy camp." Her greeting was friendly but distracted.

"Yes. Quite a gathering, Natalie. You've really outdone yourself."

Sylvia Beach concurred proudly.

"Listen, Natalie," I said in a confidential tone. "I know you're busy, but when you get a minute I need to ask you something. It's important."

Natalie raised her eyebrows. She could smell romance a billion miles away.

"OK. It's urgent," I admitted.

"Finally, Henri," Natalie said enthusiastically. "I was beginning to think we were going to lose you to a convent. I'll be all ears the minute I'm free. But right now I've got to tend to Joyce. He's a nervous wreck."

Satisfied that I had done what I could for the time being, I helped myself to some champagne and a couple of cucumber sandwiches, which I had grown to love in my new life as a salonnière, and I ensconced myself in a corner to await the beginning of the reading. I was in a solitary mood, too preoccupied with my fantasies to make small talk.

Unfortunately, I hadn't seen Bryher when I chose my corner. Don't get me wrong. I liked Bryher a lot. She was perhaps the shrewdest woman I'd met in Paris. But I was so absorbed in my fairy-tale romantic abstractions, I had absolutely no head for business or anything else that didn't advance my search for Manfred.

I remembered that Bryher had helped Sylvia Beach as the printing costs of *Ulysses* continued to mount unpredictably. Within a few moments she had disentangled herself from a conversation she was having with some man I didn't know (who turned out to be her "husband," McAlmon) and turned to me. Inevitably she steered our conversation toward her perennial business proposition—opening an avant-garde press in New York with me as the senior editor—which, I must say, both intrigued and flattered me more and more as each passing day soured my relations with *En Vogue*.

"So have you come around yet, Henri?" she asked.

"Not quite yet. But just for the sake of argument, have *you* come around to the idea of attaching a magazine to the press?"

"Actually, I have. It just takes me a while to get used to new ideas." She smiled. "Especially when they're not mine."

Manfred kept creeping into my mind, distracting me so that I knew I was in danger of being rude.

"After our last talk, I realized you were right," Bryher continued. "Over here everybody publishes their aesthetic manifestoes in Jane Heap and Margaret Anderson's *Little Review* or Harriet Monroe's *Poetry*. And of course we've got Harriet Weaver's *Egoist* and even Virginia Woolf's Hogarth Press. Over there they've got nothing—an aesthetic void. Besides, we could market our own publications. Built-in advertising."

"Precisely," I said, thinking of the sound Manfred's boots had made on the cobblestones outside Le Masque.

"But of course our press, and especially the magazine, would be much more political—much more volatile," Bryher explained with mounting excitement. "Just imagine, Henri. A chance to expose the naked truth at last in print!"

It was, without a doubt, the chance of a lifetime. But all I could think about was Manfred's naked body.

"Sounds divine," I said ambiguously. "But all this is hypothetical, you understand. At least for the time being."

"The offer stands, Henri. Why work *for* someone when you could be the boss?"

The word "boss" reverberated in my fantasies.

"Let me know when you're ready—"

Suddenly a hush fell over the room, catching Bryher's attention. She squeezed my arm and whispered "Let's talk some more later" before taking leave of me to rejoin McAlmon. As Joyce fumbled his way toward the podium, the salonniers shuffled and jockeyed for position in the crowded drawing room.

When James Joyce started reading from *Ulysses,* approximately one-half of the audience took on a reverential air, transformed by his voice into awed worshippers drinking in the eucharistic words of their highest priest. Rémy de Gourmont and Sylvia Beach actually closed their eyes as if in prayer, while the majority of the others assumed a glazed expression of unflinching piety, despite Joyce's squeaky voice and quivering hands.

The other half of the room looked like a choir loft filled with mischievous adolescents whose mouths held spitballs rather than communion wafers. Needless to say, this profane group was dominated by sapphists whose piety was undermined by various degrees of feminism.

I don't think anyone planned on or even anticipated being irreverent, but Joyce had made the mistake of reading from the last section of *Ulysses,* the part where Molly—who has defied her role as dutiful wife throughout the novel, preferring instead the more liberated life of a preconversion Magdalene—suddenly embraces the Victorian model of domesticity that her husband, Leopold Bloom, has been pining after for the preceding seven hundred and eighty-two pages.

I know that the literary world has dubbed Joyce their shining knight of the avant-garde. And certainly his profanity and perversion have perked up the ears of the censors. Yet Gertrude Stein was right. The odor of museums wafts from the pages of James Joyce's masterpiece. Although dressed in the style of modern stream of consciousness, Molly wears a whalebone corset under her negligee. Every sapphist in that room balked at the pinching suffocation that finally squeezed the life out of Molly's fleeting bloom of freedom.

In deference to the solemnity of the occasion, most of us tried to muffle our impulse to titter or even jeer at Joyce. But Djuna Barnes dared to openly express her contempt. It was she, after all, who depicted truly liberated women in her *Ladies Almanack*. The loose-tongued proclivities and freewheeling moral amnesia of her Evangeline Musset made Molly Bloom look more like a prostitute than a New Woman. I shared Barnes's disgust.

Molly's famous "yes" sounded suspiciously like every other male fantasy of female desire I'd ever read.

I returned Djuna Barnes's look of revulsion when she caught my eye. So when she got up and slipped discreetly to the back of the drawing room, I thought she was just fed up and wanted to hide her repugnance in the anonymity of the back row. I lost sight of her and had just resumed marveling at how my antipathy contrasted with the rapture of Joyce's admirers when I heard the name "Alec" near my left ear. At first I thought nothing of it, assuming someone next to me was being addressed.

Then I heard it again, this time whispered much closer to my ear. "Hello, Alec," the voice hissed with considerable hostility.

I turned around, and there was Djuna, staring at me with the same disgust I had thought she was aiming at Joyce. It took me a minute to understand—one of those minutes when you can almost physically feel the arduous turning of the brain's wheels like the cylinder of a lock.

The significance of the name "Alec" clicked into place.

Suddenly I knew who Manfred was. My clandestine dream date was no less than Thelma Wood, Djuna Barnes's outrageous lover, infamous for her debauched and wandering promiscuity in the Paris underground. Although she seldom if ever frequented the salons, dismissing them as naggingly conventional, her sensual charisma was as legendary as it was elusive. Salonnières steered clear of her for fear of being caught in her sticky web, which was guarded by the black widow of jealousy herself. Virtually everyone dreaded Djuna's wrath, even Natalie Barney, whose universal flirtations brooked one exception. Thelma Wood was strictly off limits.

Talk about getting the answer to my Cinderella riddle straight from the horse's mouth. I wondered if Djuna had found out from Thelma herself, which was unlikely, given her reputation for blackouts. Perhaps if I hadn't stalked Manfred night after night, not so discreetly asking after her in virtually every nightclub in the city, our brief fling would have slipped through the cracks. But no, I couldn't leave well enough alone. I remembered Bryher's comment that journalists were like dogs with overgrown noses for trouble. Apparently this professional characteristic had crossed over into my personal life.

As Djuna continued to glare mercilessly at me, I was struck by the full force of my terrible transgression. I was horrified not only because I had inadvertently betrayed Djuna Barnes but also because she was one of Natalie Barney's best friends. My life as a salonnière flashed before my eyes. Sapphists had been ostracized for much less serious offenses.

The reading progressed interminably. I realized that the intensity of Djuna's unabated visual attack served a double purpose.

Of course she was quite simply transmitting her antagonism, hoping no doubt that somehow the evil eye would do me in. But she was also marking me in front of all the others, branding me as an outcast to be spurned for having broken the only really serious taboo: cheating with the lover of a sapphist whose rank on the social ladder is higher than your own. It was perfectly apparent that every woman in that room knew about Thelma's escapade and Djuna's raw love wound. As they became aware, one by one, that I had caused that wound, the room began to buzz.

Joyce droned on and on about his phallic fantasies, forced into Molly's mouth, and I was stabbed over and over by one sapphic dagger after another as each salonnière took turns punishing me with her eyes. I understood the impulse. It took me back to an incident from my junior year at Radcliffe when I had finally landed a relationship that lasted more than a few weeks. A woman who claimed she was a friend of mine—a woman we all thought only dated men, no less—slept with my lover. I used to shoot her looks like this at the biology lab table, glaring over test tubes with homicidal eyes. How she survived the semester I shall never know. If I had had access to a voodoo doll, I would have pricked her to death the way I was being impaled by the merciless eyes of virtually every sapphist in the salon that Friday. But unlike that Radcliffe bisexual wolf in sheep's clothing, I was innocent. I wanted desperately for Joyce to finish so that I could explain to Djuna that I really had thought Thelma was Manfred. I couldn't believe I was being convicted without a trial.

Joyce went on and on. Once he had crawled into Molly's brain and seized her tongue, he couldn't stop playing Tereus to her Philomela. The words kept gushing out like an endless stream of semen.

Finally I couldn't take it anymore, and I turned around to confront Djuna on the spot. Reading or no reading, I had to establish my innocence. But having fingered me as the traitor, she had disappeared.

I could see that half the room was watching my every move by now. There wasn't an ounce of pity anywhere in anyone's eyes. I decided to make a quick escape. Just as I started slinking toward the side French doors leading out to the garden, Natalie's eyes caught mine. I almost sobbed with relief.

There was the sympathy I needed so desperately. Was it because she herself was a philanderer and empathized with the plight of the home-wrecker? Natalie steered us into the hallway adjoining the drawing room. She took both of my hands into hers and looked me straight in the eyes.

"Don't worry, I saw what was going on out there," she said hurriedly.

"Yes, but—"

"Did you do it?"

"Yes, but—"

Natalie groaned. "You, of all people. Here I thought you were such an innocent. All those jokes I made about you and the convent!" Natalie's concern gave way momentarily to guarded satisfaction, like a worried but proud mother. "I hope it was worth the trouble you've caused. Now we've got to try to nip this thing in the bud before Djuna gets her hands on you."

"But don't you see? I had no idea it was Thelma, or I would have steered clear. She said her name was Manfred."

Natalie burst out laughing, and then remembered the reading and clapped a hand over her mouth.

"For all her debauchery, Thelma is really a very funny woman. How could you have fallen for such a transparent disguise? It's like Lucifer using the name Lucy as a cover. Manfred. It's straight from the Marquis de Sade."

"Actually, it's Byron. But come on, Natalie, we were in the Paris underground. Everyone plays roles there, or at least I thought they did. I admit I'm new to all this, but God knows you don't frequent Le Masque to engage in a deep heart-to-heart." I hesitated, embarrassed. Then I figured it would all come out in the long run anyway. "I used a fake name, too...Alec."

Once again, Natalie couldn't contain her laughter. "But your name was so sweet and innocent. No wonder Manfred, as you call her, fell for you. Sister Mary Alec, it is your innocence that is so damned appealing. I thought everyone knew who Thelma was. She's got such a reputation. And the penalty for trespassing against Djuna is so great—"

"You forget, Natalie. I'm relatively new to all this. I've only been a member of your salon for six months now. Not even. And things are somewhat less complicated in Gertrude Stein's salon."

"Yes, I suppose you aren't used to being careful where you step."

Although the image of dog manure on Parisian cobblestones offended, it was an analogy well suited to my predicament. "Please, Natalie, when was the last time Thelma actually attended your salon, or even showed her face in the light of day?"

"Months. Maybe even years," Natalie admitted. "But what I can't figure out," she continued, "is whether or not Thelma knew it was you. Things between Djuna and Thelma have been particularly rocky lately. She might have been using you as bait."

"Bait?"

"To punish Djuna. To hook her where it hurts."

This suggestion devastated me. Despite all the deceit and role-playing, I had really fallen for Manfred.

"How drunk was she?" Natalie asked, still clearly trying to piece together Thelma's motivation. I was being cast as a mere pawn in her relationship with Djuna.

"Not really drunk at all. Drinking a lot—constantly, in fact. But as far as I could tell, not really drunk."

Suddenly I remembered the smirk Manfred had flashed me when I had told her my name was Alec. Then, and only then, had she manufactured her own disguise or code name for the night. I did not like the explanation that was taking shape in my mind's eye. Like everyone else, Manfred must have assumed that I knew what I was getting into and that "Alec" was throwing caution to the wind for the sake of one wild night.

"I think I see what you mean," I said reluctantly.

"Mean?"

"Now that I think about it, Manfred looked at me funny when I told her my name was Alec. As if we were conspirators. At the time I just thought she was having fun. It all seemed, well, not exactly innocent, but mutual. I thought she liked me as much as I liked her—" I was close to tears.

Natalie put her arm around me and pulled me toward her ample frame. I buried myself in her nurturing embrace and for one fleeting moment I felt safe and protected.

I will never forget that sensation. Let people say what they want about Natalie Barney's promiscuity and social snobbery. For me, in that single sororal instant, she became the big sister I never had.

"Don't worry," Natalie crooned. "I know you feel even more betrayed now. But this will all work out. If I can just convince Djuna that Thelma tricked you into this because she knew it would cause the biggest possible stir, then we can salvage this mess. Even Djuna Barnes is susceptible to flattery. Believe it or not, I think we can turn this whole thing around by making it look as if Thelma's infidelity was actually an act of misguided love. Are you following me?"

I nodded. It sounded vaguely like the convoluted logic in one of Natalie's sapphic dramas about how infidelity makes the heart grow fonder.

"I'm sorry that it makes you look like bait, but it's our only chance," she went on. "We'll never know for sure if Thelma was just using you. It's conceivable that she fell for you as hard as you did for her. But we've got to pretend the whole thing was just one big ploy to get a rise out of Djuna. Can you do that?"

"I've got no choice."

"Good. Now get back in there." Natalie motioned toward the ongoing reading. "Leaving now would be like admitting you're guilty, and you've got to keep pleading ignorance."

"But I *was* ignorant. I mean, I'm innocent."

"Good. Then you'll be that much more convincing. Go act ignorant and innocent. Tell Romaine to play the part of hostess for me temporarily if the reading finishes before I get back. I'm going to find Djuna. I'll smooth this thing over if it kills me."

"Thanks, Natalie," I said feebly.

As she disappeared down the hall, I heard her muttering, "I'm so goddamned tired of all this flap about something as trivial as infidelity—"

Taking several deep breaths, I returned to the salon. Joyce's violation of Molly's stream of consciousness continued with the persistence of a serial rapist. I was so preoccupied and mortified by the renewed onslaught of dirty looks from all of Djuna's friends in the audience, I even forgot to be horrified by *Ulysses*. I almost wished Joyce would never quit reading, or at least that he would read until Natalie returned to rescue me once again. But he stopped abruptly after Molly's climax of contrived affirmations, and the room burst into applause, wildly enthusiastic except for the sapphists' desultory and barely polite claps.

I managed to slip across the room to where Romaine stood feigning appreciation. "Natalie sent me to tell you to fill in for her till she gets back. She's talking to Djuna about...well, you know."

Romaine rolled her eyes. "Here we go again," she said wearily.

Without further comment, she made a beeline for Joyce, who was now fumbling blindly toward the champagne punch bowl.

Having recovered my wits sufficiently to strategize, I decided my best defense would be to attach myself to some unwitting man whose conversation would protect me from the onslaughts of Djuna Barnes's cronies.

I noticed Gertrude Stein's friend Man Ray nearby. Judging from his rapt expression, still basking in the afterglow of Joyce's reading, I assumed he was oblivious to my plight.

I approached him and after a few preliminary niceties regarding Joyce's literary ventriloquism, we settled into a conversation about the article I had written up for the May issue of *En Vogue* in which I had praised Man Ray's now-famous photographs of Paris's bohemians and expatriates. He was both pleased and grateful for my rave reviews, which, he told me, had already expanded the market for his work in the States. Acting thrilled to death over his good fortune did nothing to lessen my dread, but I thought at least I would be safe from attack.

I was wrong.

After a few minutes I felt a presence unnaturally close to my back. When I turned around, Una, Lady Troubridge's face loomed within inches of my own. She looked even more sour than usual.

"It's a big sea," she hissed cryptically with her characteristically affected diction. "Couldn't you have found your own damned fish?" Her stilted, patrician manner seemed ridiculous, given her petty message. As abruptly as she had appeared, she retired, and I turned back to Man Ray, who gave me a queer look. Following my cue, he chose to ignore this little conversational aside, and we resumed our discussion of the relative merits of the candid camera in favor of the posed portrait.

Less than a minute later, Mata Hari appeared by my side, mumbling an excuse for the interruption as she took me aside momentarily.

"I know how you feel," she said. "I always get blamed for it, too, as if their randy little girlfriends didn't ask for it." She squeezed my hand. "Don't let them get you down," she said, flitting off with all her bangles jangling.

This time when I turned back to my conversation with Man, I made a little joke about how scandalous gossip was "simply ruining the salons." He obviously wasn't at all fooled by my levity, but when I threw myself with renewed vigor into our conversation, he obliged me with his protective attention.

We didn't remain unmolested for long. Dolly Wilde wobbled by en route to the champagne punch bowl, one of many trips, judging from her comportment. "Been taking lessons from Natalie?" she asked accusingly. Almost immediately thereafter, a very young woman I didn't even know murmured discreetly as she passed, "Did you really think you'd get away with it, with half of Paris watching?" She withdrew to a clutch of sapphists close by, to join their en-masse glaring. She looked an awful lot like Fontaine, the little ingénue at Le Masque who had assisted Manfred, strapping her into the buckles and belts of the Wheel.

Finally, Man Ray could no longer ignore this sapphic circus. "What on earth is going on?" he asked with genuine concern. "Are you OK?"

"Not really," I said, on the verge of tears again. "I guess I'd better retreat." And I did. Seeking refuge in the hall, I tried to decide if there was any point in trying to face this thing down.

There was something almost prudish about the way everyone was scapegoating me, as if they were all so goddamned squeaky clean and morally upright. Having already suffered a crisis of faith in America, growing up an invert in Utah where the very idea inspired nausea and the actual practice constituted social suicide, I was weary of witch hunts. I had thought I could escape all this in Paris. Instead, there I was, suffering the agonizing dark night of my sapphic soul. Who would have thought it possible to lean dejectedly against the hallowed wall of Natalie Barney's world-renowned salon, weighing the merits of eternal celibacy against the torturous fires of wayward passions.

Before my fantasies progressed too far down this conventional path of maiden aunts and spinsters, Natalie Barney returned to save me from the horrors of chastity. She looked harried but hopeful.

"Listen," she said, putting her hands on my shoulders once again. "I'm not sure where we stand, but Djuna has agreed to talk to you. She's in the Temple à l'Amitié."

Even in my distress, the irony of our rendezvous in the Temple of Love did not escape me. I grimaced.

"I tried to convince her that you were an innocent pawn in Thelma's misguided scheme to make her jealous," Natalie continued.

"What did she say?"

"Nothing. But that's not necessarily bad. Let her mull it over for a minute or two, and then join her in the Temple. She's expecting you."

Natalie had a reputation for always doing and saying very memorable things, an impeccable dramatic sense of timing that secured for her a place in history as a personage, despite the fact that she never really achieved or produced anything commensurate with her fame.

Just then the towering Amazon leaned down and kissed me on the forehead, and something in the solemnity of her gesture awakened an almost chivalrous resolve in me. She said nothing, but I felt that she had dubbed me into some sacred knighthood and the whole terrible ordeal was my initiation into the secret society I had been longing to join my whole life.

As if I wasn't in enough trouble already, I fleetingly regretted rebuffing Natalie's advances at Romaine's studio. I understood now that Natalie Barney must have been a Titan in bed. A powerful electric current seemed to pass from her lips into my body. By the time Natalie straightened back up, I felt equipped to face Djuna.

"I've got to get back in there," Natalie said, and she started toward the drawing room but paused mid-stride.

"One more thing," she advised over her shoulder. "I wouldn't let Djuna know how you really feel about Manfred."

As I traversed the pebbled walkway through the garden to the Temple, Natalie's kiss of courage began to wear off, and images of Marie Antoinette's last walk to the guillotine flashed through my mind. The victorious knight and the doomed Antoinette vied for power as I crossed the threshold of the Temple.

Djuna Barnes stood defiantly next to a marble reproduction of Athena springing from Zeus's head.

"Hello, *Alec,*" she said again. Her tone this time was only slightly less snide, and equally hostile.

I felt shaky and wanted to sit down on the divan but didn't wish to appear disrespectful.

Djuna tried to look at me, but what must have been contempt whirled her around. She spoke with her back to me, gazing out into the falling Parisian night.

"You know that 'innocent pawn' drivel doesn't fool me a bit."

"I didn't think it would."

"So get it over with. What's your goddamned alibi?"

"I didn't know it was her."

"Yeah. And I don't know who Charlie Chaplin is. And Gertrude Stein isn't fat. Tell me another one."

"I didn't. Surely you don't think I'd be that stupid. To sleep with her if I knew."

Djuna spun around, making me jump. "You didn't sleep with her. Only I do that. When she passes out."

"Yes. I didn't mean—"

"So Radcliffe girls are too bloody smart to horn in on big-league bohemians?"

"Of course we are. You know it's true, Djuna. It would be social suicide. Or sapphic suicide. I may be dumb—and I admit I was stupid for not figuring out who Manfred was—but I'm not suicidal."

Contempt spun her around again. "Her name is not Manfred. Don't call her that. Don't call her anything."

Djuna brooded with her back to me. I think she wanted me to feel guilty so that she could scapegoat me and hate me and thus save what was left of her image of Thelma's devotion. But on some level she also knew that this was an irrational scenario. Someone as mild-mannered as me could never have successfully seduced Manfred. And no one, no matter how gutsy, could ever have gotten away with sleeping with Djuna Barnes's lover. It would be like having an affair with Alice B. Toklas or Romaine Brooks. It would be insane.

Djuna traversed the room, circling me like a prowling beast. Even though I rotated to face her as she paced, I felt cornered at every turn. Now and then she opened her mouth as if to speak. But we remained silent, measuring each other at a distance for a long, long time. With every turn, something seemed to dissipate, as though we were engaged in a soundless, ritual dance exorcising fury. Finally she spoke in a very sad, soft voice.

"How could you?"

She looked at me, not in anger anymore but with supplication, pleading for a way to make sense of the betrayal.

"How could you?" she repeated, and I could feel the depth of her love for Thelma. It was bottomless, tragic.

"I didn't know," I said, but by then I realized she wasn't pleading with me in particular or even listening to my words, which were peripheral to the perpetual saga of her grief.

"She's lost, you know. She's like a somnambulist. There's almost no real consciousness left. Maybe there never was any." Djuna spoke almost in a monotone, as if reciting a mantra or recounting a dream that haunted her every night. "She's like a primitive, terribly charismatic beast, wandering around looking for something she lost, some forgotten archetypal past that I half-remember when I am with her, and then I want it too."

"I know," I said quietly, taking a chance. I remembered what Natalie had said about not telling Djuna how I felt about Thelma. But somehow I guessed that the real reason Djuna seemed on the verge of forgiving me was that I had recognized Thelma's outrageous, mythic qualities, like a fallen angel whose tragic stature makes other women seem trivial and lifeless.

"You really fell for her, didn't you?" Djuna asked.

"Yes. But I know I can't have her. I know that she's yours."

"She may not be anyone's."

"Perhaps none of us are," I said, but I had barely gotten the words out before I started to cry, wrenching, uncontrollable sobs that surprised me and made me grab onto myself to keep from breaking apart.

And then Djuna was crying and before I knew it we were on the divan wailing in each other's arms, both completely abandoned to grief over everything we had ever lost, yet simultaneously comforting each other like the sisters neither of us ever had.

I have no idea how long we sat entwined in this cathartic communion. When Natalie finally came out to check on us, it was pitch black outside. Then, one after another, all of the sapphists defected from the celebration of Joyce's epic phallus to join us in the Temple à l'Amitié. Everyone acted a little sheepishly toward me until Natalie made a joke about the value of hazing in initiation rituals. Having been ostracized so viciously, I was now in like Flynn.

April 11, 1926

Dear Henrietta:

SOS! Why are you flirting with disaster? Irving waltzed
into my office yesterday and closed the door (and we all
know what that means). Imagine my surprise when it was
about you! Here I thought you were our golden girl, and
now this--trouble in Paradise. Why are you jeopardizing
what you've worked so hard for? You know me, Henrietta.
When I'm in trouble like you are, clichés--the cornier the
better--are my most reliable guiding light. Have you
forgotten the motto that has protected us for centuries:
"Don't mix business with pleasure"? Between you and me,
Henrietta, I think Paris has gone to your head.

So I'm going to give it to you straight, though I
know you may find that hard to believe. You're a good
friend and I have a sneaking suspicion you're
underestimating the gravity of the situation we've got
here. Either you play their game, or they're going to kick
you off the jungle-gym, my dear. And to give the Board
(Bored) credit (for the sake of argument--you see I'm
desperate!), they're not even quibbling with your choice
of topic, which I think is uncharacteristically liberal
given Romaine Brooks's relatively flamboyant oeuvre.
(Don't kick a gift horse in the mouth, Henrietta.) It's
more the tone of your editorial or, as Irving put it with
the delicacy of a man with ten thumbs--"we find a
remarkable absence of critical analysis concerning her
subject matter; though we are sure it was not her
intention, her editorial seems to accept inversion at face
value." I promised myself to keep this short so that the

message wouldn't get watered down. Don't let Dickey's formalities fool you. If you don't back off, they'll have your head. The Board is one step away from sending you a ticket on the next steamer home.

You're in Paris, Henrietta! Don't mess it up unless you want to end up back here in purgatory!

Love,

Larry

CHAPTER ELEVEN

The Gilded Closet

"And what fabulous masterpiece shall we create today?"

Only the monarchy and hairdressers use the royal "we." This one, who had been recommended by the Duchesse de Clermont-Tonnerre, was a queen.

"Take it off," I said dramatically.

"*Comment?* What do you mean?"

"Take it all off."

"Like a flapper?"

"No. I'm Lily's friend."

"Ah!" A naughty expression spread over my coiffeur's face as he swooped down to look at me in the mirror. "Like a man!"

I shook my head emphatically. "No. Quite the opposite. Like a woman who wants nothing to do with men."

"*Exactement!*" He giggled, and went to work.

It's funny, but I had never even contemplated getting my hair cropped until I was forced to consider leaving Paris. I had no one to blame but myself. Certainly not Larry, who had tried to warn me. Not even Irving P. Dickey, who was simply doing his job, desperately shielding the American public from the terrible truth that modern art defied more than just traditional aesthetics. The paintings they were importing in voluminous quantities second only to crates of Bordeaux were largely the production of reckless bohemians and homosexuals. I smiled in the barber's chair, thinking that the famous avant-garde movement known as Vorticism might as well be called Inverticism. With each clump of hair that hit the floor, I pictured myself floating further down the River of No Return. I had gotten letters before asking me to edit my work. And I had always obliged, revising just enough so that the editors at *En Vogue* would OK the piece for publication. This time, however, I knew I couldn't oblige.

In the coiffeur's mirror, I watched as my naked face emerged from beneath the curls. When Delilah cut Samson's hair, he lost his strength and virility. Times had changed. Where Samson's sexuality doomed him, I would wear mine like a badge of honor. Being shorn was his castration, but it was my battle cry. With each snip I steeled my resolve to defy the censorship of Irving P. Dickey and his Board.

My coiffeur was whistling a raucous, military march. A typical Frenchman, he was most passionate about his profession when it involved radical change. I would miss this rebellious spirit.

But not everyone could be an expatriate. Someone had to take this spirit home and cultivate bohemia on American soil. Somewhere deep in our Puritan roots, surely this seed longed to be sown.

"C'est fini," he announced, spinning me around in his barber's chair, and then pulling off the protective drape. *"Vous avez l'air très chic et très dangereuse."*

I couldn't believe it. I had never looked more feminine in my life, with every long line and curve exposed, and the delicate neck. If I had seen that neck on another woman I would have likened it to a swan. Why had I always associated long hair with femininity?

Something very strange had happened. I had expatriated to Paris to find romance, but the city had made an activist out of me, awakening a revolutionary zeal I never knew I had. I wanted to be the Susan B. Anthony of sapphic freedom, crusading for our embattled right to live boldly, in broad daylight, rather than cowering behind the editorial discretion of Irving P. Dickey. Or closeted behind the discreet anonymity of the salons.

A year ago, any comparison at all between Gertrude Stein and Irving Dickey would have struck me as ridiculous. My strangest epiphany of all was that I had discovered a parallel between the cloistered aestheticism of the salons and the provincial ethics of *En Vogue*'s Board of Editors. Every which way I turned, someone was telling me not to investigate this and not to report that. Stein insisted that I ignore insurance fraud, and Dickey forbade any mention of inversion. If anyone else asked me to turn a blind eye to the obvious, I'd have to invest in a guide dog.

I felt as if I were being forever silenced by the ideal of aesthetic purity, which had begun to look suspiciously like a glorified excuse for closed-mindedness. And it wasn't just me. After repeated warnings, Gertrude Stein had finally banished Bryher from 27 rue de Fleurus for daring to talk about Russian pogroms. And Natalie Barney had succeeded in silencing Janet Flanner, who kept her political opinions to herself at 20 rue Jacob. As a journalist, I felt that I no longer wanted to check my profession at the door.

There was something truly mysterious, almost magical, about the metamorphosis of my character during the past year. Suspended in the tranquil spots of time I discovered in Paris, especially in my favorite cafés, I often marveled at the protean influence of the city. But though I tried to retrace the incremental, subtle influences that had changed me so profoundly, they continued to elude me. I only knew that I hardly recognized in myself the bumpkin who had arrived in Paris a year before.

I liked what I saw each morning in the antique mirror of my room at the Hôtel les Cèdres. Since becoming a seasoned salonnière, I walked into Sylvia Beach's Shakespeare & Company to buy books rather than to stalk celebrities. I may not have been a living legend in Paris, like Colette and Romaine Brooks. But at the salons, no one bothered to introduce me anymore. They just called me Henri. On days when spring swung wide the glass panels at the Café des Deux-Magots, I no longer strained my neck when I saw Hemingway sitting at the next table reading American newspapers. He drank his pastis, and I my café crème, and then maybe Djuna Barnes wandered in and sat down to her Côtes du Rhône.

We might nod, but we might not. We'd all been there long enough to have sloughed off the hyperactive friendliness that grips Americans, compelling them to shout maniacally exuberant greetings and slap each other on the backs. When I saw American tourists I cringed, wondering if I too had exuded that ridiculous optimism when I first arrived in Paris. They grinned and gaped and gesticulated wildly, almost desperate to maintain a facade of perpetual happiness. In Paris, on the other hand, all pretense had been mellowed by centuries of charming skepticism.

Sliding Dickey's ultimatum into my pocket, I decided to take a long walk. My most important decisions have always been made while putting one foot in front of the other. It was bad enough contemplating leaving the Paris of the Champs-Elysées and les Tuileries, but when I got to the rue Jacob and passed by the gate to Natalie Barney's courtyard and garden, with its Temple and exotic salon, I made up my mind to sell out. If I had to censor my work to avoid returning to the streets of my homeland, then by God I would. I felt certain that I had made the right decision and veered into one of my favorite bistros, le Café de Flore, to treat myself to a café crème.

I sat on the terrace and ordered, feeling like I used to after confession, disburdened and light and free. The grumpy old waiter's crusty superiority complex reminded me of the pathologically polite waiters in the States who would be only too happy to kill me with contrived kindness if I made the fatal mistake of returning home.

Across the heads of the gesticulating café, I saw Djuna Barnes sitting alone. Sure that this was a sign, I rose to join her. But then I noticed her abstracted and troubled expression, which seemed to send out the stringent repellent of the recluse, an odor that would become more and more powerful as she grew older and more averse to human companionship.

Thinking immediately of Manfred/Thelma, I suddenly realized why Djuna loved her so desperately. For Thelma was scarcely human, more like a beast whose presence would do nothing to disrupt Barnes's isolation. In a flash I recognized my own reclusive tendencies. Never before had I acknowledged them. No wonder I had joined Djuna Barnes, worshipping at the feet of Thelma's disembodied spirit.

I sat back down. There was Djuna, sitting with a glass of wine as if she were waiting for something. Djuna Barnes, whom I had idolized back in the States as the hands-on journalist who was willing to risk her life for a story. Djuna Barnes, who now sat with her Côtes du Rhône (we all knew her vintage) and her dazed expression.

Her isolation and passivity frightened me, as if I were looking into the mirror of my future. The anonymity of the crowded cafés protected us from the world we were there to escape. No wonder I had fled to Paris. Here, I could be an island. And no one would ever notice.

It made sense, of course, especially for expatriate homosexuals. Gertrude and Alice locked themselves up in their own little sanctuary on the rue de Fleurus; Natalie and her salonnières were ensconced safely behind closed doors. Somehow, being in Paris—expatriation itself—was like being hidden in a closet. A huge, well-appointed closet filled with Paris's glittering elite, but a closet just the same. Watching Djuna Barnes, I realized we were little more than voyeurs.

I was being summoned home. *En Vogue* was tolling the curfew of my expatriation. By the time I had finished my café, I knew Gertrude Stein was wrong. You *can* go home again, and I was going to be the first to do exactly that. I would miss the splendor of Paris, but I was committed to returning to the States with the closet door flung wide open.

My biggest loss would be Gertrude Stein, of course. I headed straight for the rue de Fleurus to break the news.

When I walked into ıer atelier, Gertrude Stein looked taken aback, which puzzled me momentarily until I remembered my hair. Unbelievably, despite its outrageousness, I was already at home with my new coif.

"What happened to *you?*" Gertrude Stein asked.

"My God, it's an epidemic," said Alice B. Toklas.

"I've had an epiphany," I explained.

"Not another bout of sapphic sorority," groaned Stein, who had been suspicious of my induction into Natalie's salon.

"Yet another epidemic," said Toklas.

"No," I assured them. "This one is in spite of that one. I'm returning to the States."

Gertrude Stein's face fell and Alice B. Toklas left the room. "What on earth for?" Stein asked.

"To get on with my life."

Gertrude Stein raised her eyebrows.

"Look, Gertrude, *En Vogue* has pulled the plug unless I censor my article on Romaine's work. I've seen this coming for a long time. Every time I turn around, they want to expurgate my column, as if the avant-garde exists in a vacuum. As if it were a purely aesthetic movement divorced from politics and sexuality and everything else that makes Paris Paris and Pablo Pablo and you you."

In an effort to clarify my motives, I spoke what I thought was Gertrude Stein's language, fraught with repetitious diction and circular logic. Yet she seemed unimpressed.

"They want me to lie," I persisted.

"And?"

"And I won't."

"Congratulations. So quit and stay."

"I can't, Gertrude. I'm not rich. I'm not an artist. I'm not even a bohemian."

"What the hell are you, then?"

"I'm a voyeur. And I'm going home."

Gertrude Stein looked at me intently for a long time, apparently weighing my words. For all her posturing as an American in Paris, Gertrude Stein had grown up in Europe. She had seen so many Americans come and go, and knew that some should come and some should go. "You're sure, aren't you?"

I nodded.

"What will you do?"

"I'm going to take Bryher up on her offer to back an American version of McAlmon's Contact Press. Something like Alice's Plain Edition. A New York press that will publish all of us—all of you—over there. If she'll fund it, I'll run it. We'll call it Inverted Commas."

"Very funny," Stein said. "But you know how I hate commas. Besides, you're a journalist, not an editor."

"If McAlmon and Alice can do it, I can do it. Alice can give me pointers. She's already taught me everything there is to know about kitchens and eggs. Why not printing presses and books? And Bryher knows I'm only interested if there's a magazine attached to the press. She actually sounded excited about the magazine idea, the last time we spoke."

"You didn't tell me you'd been plotting this, Henri. And with Bryher, of all people," Gertrude Stein said accusingly. She was still very protective of me, maybe even a little jealous.

"I haven't been plotting anything, Gertrude. I just can't prostitute my work anymore."

Gertrude Stein drummed her fingers. I had never seen her fidget before, and it touched me.

"I'm tired of working for the likes of Irving P. Dickey. He's tried to bowdlerize me and my work one too many times."

I had decided not to tell Gertrude Stein that I had also grown impatient with the avant-garde's own impulse to pretend that their work existed in a vacuum, shut off from the real world, just as the sapphists caroused only behind the closed doors of the salons. In every possible way, I was ready to leap into the fray. The candor of America's wide-open spaces had beckoned me across the Atlantic. Surely it was too early to write off the States as an aesthetic wasteland. Although uncultivated, the land was rich and fertile and fallow— eminently ready for the seeds of the avant-garde.

"We've created a monster," Stein said through a melancholy smile.

"I'm ready for this, Gertrude. If Radcliffe was my college, Paris has been my graduate school. And of course you're my alma mater. Now I'm ready for my actual career. I'll start my own damned salon. A paupers' salon for American homebodies, as opposed to rich Parisian expatriates."

Gertrude Stein sat down on her heavy Tuscan throne, looking uncharacteristically sad. "Don't forget to write," she said softly.

Then she did something really weird, especially given her discomfort with physical contact. She patted her generous lap and motioned me over. I sat on her knee and she wrapped me in a bear hug for a very long time while the light slowly faded from the room in the late afternoon, obscuring one after another of the Picassos and Matisses and Braques on the walls. Once, Alice B. Toklas stuck her head in the crack of the door but retreated wordlessly.

I cried a little, entwined in loss. But the tears were more comforting than tragic, as though I had finally found myself in the powerful embrace of the mother of us all. I knew it was time to cut the umbilical cord—to be the hero of my own life rather than a mere member of the chorus. Admittedly, the salons boasted the most exalted chorus in the entire sapphic universe. Yet as Gertrude Stein herself would have said, excellent if you were a chorister, but if you were not, not.

I felt too complete and at peace in the fading light to truly mourn much, though I wondered fleetingly if my moment in the Parisian sun, with its sparkling salons and dazzling celebrities, would be the highlight of my life. I was almost thirty, which seemed to add to the threat of an anticlimactic future. How could I have known that Sappho herself had recently left Paris and expatriated to Greenwich Village?

ABOUT THE AUTHOR

Margaret Vandenburg is Associate Director of the Writing Program at Barnard College of Columbia University. She lives in New York.